I0726255

MASTER CHEF

GOLDEN ANGEL

Cover Photo Photographer - Golden Czermak

Cover Designer - Eris Adderly

Edited by Personal Touch Editing

Copyright © 2021 by Golden Angel

All rights reserved.

No part of this book may be reproduced in any form or by any electronic or mechanical means, including information storage and retrieval systems, without written permission from the author, except for the use of brief quotations in a book review.

PROLOGUE

NICK

As much as Nick loved his job, it wasn't nearly as much fun on nights when his sous chef, Avery, wasn't working, especially on the weekends. He couldn't stop thinking about what she might be doing instead.

Not going on a date, he was pretty sure, but all she'd said was she had 'plans' and needed tonight off. It made him grit his teeth, but he'd agreed... what else was he supposed to do?

Demand she tell him her plans?

As her boss, that wasn't allowed.

Despite a few hot kisses and a wild attraction, they weren't dating. Technically, that probably wasn't allowed as her boss, but as long as she was willing, he wasn't pushing her into anything she didn't want, and they didn't let it affect their work.

Still, he was in a worse mood than usual when he had to go upstairs to ask his brother's girlfriend, who was also the manager, about the wine that was supposed to have been delivered today to be the pairing for tonight's special. He had to do his best not to take his mood out on her because she was his brother's girlfriend, and his brother owned the place.

Yeah, Nick got his job through good old-fashioned nepotism. At least, that's how it sometimes felt, even though the other two owners had interviewed him and agreed to hire him. He didn't consider it a bad thing. It just made him that much more determined to make Marquis one of the top restaurants in the city and prove his place as executive chef was deserved.

Marquis worked a little differently than most restaurants because it was only a restaurant on the main floor. The second floor was a BDSM theater and hotel, which also provided dinner and room service, along with their other offerings.

It was the BDSM part that made Nick uncertain and uncomfortable, in large part because he knew his brother and his brother's girlfriend were participating in some of those activities.

The fact Luke was Olivia's submissive, rather than the other way round, made him even more conflicted. When he'd first learned Luke was interested in kink, he'd been horrified—men shouldn't hit women. Period. It turned out, Luke was the one getting spanked.

Which really fucked with Nick's head.

His big, strong, bossy brother being spanked—and other things he didn't like to think about—by a woman?

It didn't make sense, although meeting Olivia had helped dispel some of that.

The woman was scary as hell when she wanted to be.

He'd also learned a bit more about kink since they'd been together. Not enough to be entirely comfortable with it, but he'd never seen a woman or man leave the second floor look unhappy, as if they'd been abused, or... well, they all looked as though they'd thoroughly enjoyed themselves.

Olivia had been after him to take one of the introduction classes. She thought he'd make a "good Dom," whatever the hell that meant, but Nick always refused.

For one, he wasn't sure he could bring himself to spank a woman. Boss one around? Sure. He was bossy—he owned that—but hurt her? The very thought made his stomach tighten to the point of nausea.

Second, he was interested in Avery, his sous chef, who not only went toe-to-toe with him in the kitchen but knew what went on upstairs as well as he did and had never brought it up as a point of interest. If she had, he might be more predisposed to learn more about it, but right now, he was just fine without knowing.

Heading upstairs, Nick nodded to Freddy, who was manning the desk outside the Marquis' main room where the stage was. Dressed in a pink suit that clashed violently with the red-and-black décor of the room, Freddy looked entirely at home. The blond grinned and finger waved at Nick before returning his attention to the computer in front of him, probably going over the reservations for the evening.

From here, everything looked like a normal hotel lobby, although decorated a bit more boldly than most hotels. However, behind the door to the right of Freddy's desk, things got wild.

Shaking his head, Nick knocked on the door to Olivia's office and waited until she called out, 'Come in' before opening it. That hadn't always been the case. For the first few months, Nick would knock and immediately open the door. That had ended the day he'd discovered his brother and Olivia didn't always remember to lock the door when they were enjoying their intraoffice romance.

He'd seen his brother's junk plenty of times as a teenager and really didn't need to see it as an adult. He hadn't been able to look Olivia in the eye for weeks after seeing her boobs.

Opening the door, he found his brother was there as well, although fully clothed and sitting across from Olivia's desk, doing something on his phone while she worked.

Looking up, Olivia's silvery grey eyes locked on him, and a thin smile curved her lips. She was a stunningly beautiful woman with red hair and creamy skin that looked good in the red suits she often wore. Not that Nick was a fashionista, but he knew redheads supposedly didn't look good in red—Olivia defied that stereotype with ease.

"Hello, Nick, to what do we owe the pleasure?" There was a slightly sardonic note to her voice, as if she was inwardly laughing at him. She'd sounded like that ever since he'd walked in on her and Luke. Apparently, she'd found it hilarious, especially his reaction.

Taking a seat in the chair next to his brother, Nick gave Luke a quick smile before turning his attention to Olivia to ask about the wine shipment. Of course, because Luke was there, they chatted for a few minutes after business wrapped up.

The dinner hour was fast approaching, and Nick felt the urge to get back downstairs, although he knew his staff would have everything handled. He was the control freak Avery often accused him of being, and being away from the kitchen during a busy hour made him itchy.

"I'd better get back to work," he said, getting to his feet. Luke reached out so they could fist bump, causing Olivia to roll her eyes at him.

"Talking to me doesn't count as work?" Olivia teased, clearly amused.

"Never." Nick winked at her, which made her laugh, and Luke shook his head in amusement.

Sauntering back to the door, Nick opened it and stepped into the lobby of Marquis' second floor, then came to a grinding halt. Blinked. Surely, he wasn't seeing what he thought he was seeing...

"*Avery?*"

His buttoned-up—though still sexy as sin—sous chef was standing in the middle of the lobby of a sex club, dressed as if she belonged there.

The tank tops she wore under her chef coat had revealed she was curvy, but the corset pushed her breasts up into a deep cleavage that wasn't possible with mere fabric. It also pulled in her waist to improbable proportions that made him want to rip the damn thing off so she could breathe again.

Uh-huh. Sure. That's *why you want to rip it off her.*

The black leather skirt hugged her legs and was so short, he was pretty sure if she bent over, it would roll up to her waist. His dick pulsing at the idea, Nick shifted his stance uncomfortably, hoping his erection wasn't obvious. Fortunately, his drawstring pants were loose in the crotch. Three cheers for chef pants.

She stared back at him, eyes wide with horror, lips dropping open in shock at seeing him. The two women behind her, Domi and Rae, he'd met when Avery recently started hanging out with them.

"What are you doing up here?" he asked without thinking, even though he knew—*knew*—there was only one reason for her to be on the second floor of Marquis dressed like that. His brain couldn't quite believe what his eyes were seeing.

"What are *you* doing up here?" Her voice was higher, squeakier than normal, as if she couldn't believe she was seeing him, either.

"I had to ask Olivia a question." Nick raked his hand through his hair. "Do you... do you do this?" He gestured toward the door to Marquis' real entrance, where the shows were put on.

AVERY

Shit, shit, shit! What do I do? The wailing in the back of her brain was incredibly distracting, but she couldn't quite make it go away. Panic. That's what she was feeling. Straight up panic. It was too late to run, even if she wasn't wearing ridiculously high heels, which would probably cause her to trip, fall, and break her neck if she tried to dash down the stairs.

Pressing her lips together, she straightened, gathering her courage.

I have nothing to be ashamed of.

Behind her, Domi and Rae moved up on either side of her for support.

"I used to," she answered Nick's question. "I used to do 'this.' Be submissive. Kinky. I came here tonight to watch the show and get an idea if it's something I still want." Her eyes darted to Freddy, who worked the front desk at Marquis. Nick's appearance had interrupted the conversation they'd been having. Should she admit she'd been trying to figure it all out in case she and Nick started dating?

She wasn't sure if Nick would be okay with her outing them as a couple, especially since they weren't really a couple, more like a possibility. She definitely didn't want to be outed where she worked, though there was no one from the kitchen up here right now. Freddy wouldn't rat her out. She hoped.

Although they might not be a thing anymore, not even the possibility of something. She couldn't interpret the expression on Nick's face, one she'd never seen before despite months of working together and flirting. He was silent.

She'd heard a few of the remarks he'd made about Marquis' second floor. They weren't derogatory, exactly, but it had been made clear he wasn't into kink and didn't really understand people who were. That was why she needed to figure out whether or not she still was.

Of course, because it was her, she had to run into him on the way in. There was no way to hide that she was one of those people he didn't understand.

He turned around, turning his back on her, and her heart sank. But then he marched back into Olivia's office. Crap, he wouldn't get her banned from watching the show or something, would he? He didn't have that kind of pull... except Olivia was his brother's girlfriend, and his brother did part-own the place.

"Nick?" She hurried forward, a small kernel of anger stirring in her gut. It wasn't any of his business what she did in her free time.

He completely ignored her as she came up behind him, addressing Olivia—who was sitting behind her desk, watching both of them like a hawk.

"Okay, Olivia, you're finally getting your way. I want to sign up for the Dominant 101 course."

Olivia's lips curved in a smile, and Avery gasped, her hands flying to cover her mouth.

What the...?

❧   I   ❧

NICK

This is a terrible idea.

"Seriously?" Avery's voice rose to a high shriek behind him, a reaction he'd never gotten from her in the kitchen, no matter how much he'd ticked her off—and he'd done plenty of that. Their arguments about food preparation and the menu could get heated, which was fun as hell. "Nick, you can't... you don't..."

Her insistence he 'couldn't' take the class made him want to do it even more. Luke would probably say that was to be expected. He claimed Nick had always been contrary.

"Yes, I can, and I'm going to." He glanced over his shoulder. "This is what you want, right?"

Avery was right behind him now, Domi and Rae only a few feet away, their heads together as they whispered. Both of them seemed unsure how to react. He'd only met them a couple times, but he knew they were kinky, submissive, and had made friends with Avery not long ago. How, he didn't know... maybe doing stuff on the second floor?

Fuck, he didn't like that idea at all. Had Avery been coming up here all this time, and he'd not known?

Putting her hands on her hips, Avery took a deep breath that drew his attention to the tops of her breasts as they heaved within the corset. Seeing the direction of his gaze, she blushed bright pink, but it didn't slow her down.

"This is what I *might* want," she stressed. "And you and I, well... we haven't... we aren't..." Her tongue flicked out, licking her lips as if to help her think of what she wanted to say.

"We aren't a couple?" He arched his eyebrow at her. "No, not yet." That was when he realized his decision had already been made. No, they hadn't done more than flirt and exchange a few hot kisses, but that was absolutely where he'd been heading. He hadn't admitted it to himself yet, but he would have never fooled around with a co-worker if he didn't want an actual relationship. It never ended well.

Not that any of his previous relationships had ended well, but that was probably why he'd been attracted to Avery. His previous girlfriends hadn't understood a chef's schedule or his dedication to his work and moving up in the restaurant industry. Avery did, although she didn't have any ambition to become an executive chef— he'd asked her once if that was what she was looking to do. She was happy being a sous chef. She understood his schedule because she worked the same one. Even though she didn't want an exec chef position, she understood the pressures he was under and why he was a workaholic.

He'd never tried dating anyone from work, but that might have been because he'd been working his ass off to move up in the kitchen and saw everyone else there as a rival. Now that he was in the top spot, all he had to do was prove he deserved to be there. Avery wasn't a rival. She was an integral part of the team that was helping him do that.

They could talk about work and food to their heart's content, and she wouldn't get sick of it—or him.

Avery gaped at him. Apparently, she hadn't been quite on the same page.

"You've never even asked me on a date." Rather than shrieking, she was whispering as if it was some kind of secret. Her hazel eyes darted back and forth, looking behind him, and it didn't take a genius to know she was looking to see Olivia's and Luke's reactions.

"Fine." Nick crossed his arms over his chest. "Want to go on a date?"

Instead of answering, Avery hushed him, looking as though she was going to have a conniption.

"Avery?" Domi stepped forward to take Avery's arm. She was a cute little thing, petite in every sense of the word, with tight, springy curls that bounced around her head with every movement she made. Behind her, Rae was glaring suspiciously at Nick, watching over both Avery and Domi with a protective gaze.

When Nick met her gaze, she tossed some of her long braids over her shoulder and crossed her arms over her chest. *Do not piss off the girl-friends.* He quickly turned his attention back to Avery. "Do you want us to stay out here with you?"

Closing her eyes for a moment, Avery reached up to rub the center of her forehead, a move Nick recognized from the kitchen, which meant he'd gotten on her last nerve, and she was doing everything in her power to hold back her desire to yell at him. As always, it made him smirk. Normally, she was so cool, calm, and collected, he considered it a badge of honor to get under her skin.

"Domi, Rae, why don't you two go inside. Freddy can show you to your seats." Olivia came up beside Nick, making him jump. He hadn't heard her approach. How the hell did she do that in heels on a wood floor? The office had a rug, but he was standing on the wood. "Avery will be in with you shortly, but I think it might benefit her and Nick to have a quick talk first."

AVERY

A quick talk? Avery wasn't sure that was possible. There was way too much to talk about.

Nick discovering she was kinky.

Nick suddenly deciding he was going to try being kinky, too.

Nick thinking he would try to be kinky because he wanted to date her.

She'd barely gotten used to the idea dating the executive chef at the restaurant where she worked wasn't the most insane idea in the world—this felt like they'd skipped a few steps. Getting into kink wasn't something someone did for a casual hookup or even after a few dates. Yes, they'd known each other for months, but that time had been spent working together, not dating!

"You've got this," Domi whispered in her ear, taking Avery's hand to give it a squeeze.

"If you don't want him, tell him. We'll back you up." Rae gave Avery's fingers a quick squeeze as well, her words making Avery stifle a laugh.

She was so lucky to have found the two of them.

"Come in," Olivia said again, gesturing impatiently. Nick had already moved into the space between the two chairs in front of Olivia's desk. His brother occupied one of them, which meant he was leaving the other one open for her.

Avery only hesitated for a moment before coming in and closing the door behind her. Before moving to take her seat, she let out all the air in her lungs, which felt great—she wasn't used to wearing a corset. As she did so, Luke gave her an encouraging smile that she returned.

It was funny how the two brothers could look so alike yet be so different. They both had the same darkly handsome good looks, and no one could mistake them for anything but brothers. They also had a similar air of confidence, but Nick's was far more hard-edged. Luke also looked way more relaxed and had a soothing demeanor, whereas Nick was always wound tight as a wire. Where Luke was a placid pool of calm, Nick was quivering with barely contained energy.

Yet something about Nick had always called to her, while she'd never been attracted to Luke, even though she thought he was very attractive.

Sitting down gingerly in the seat, she was very aware of Nick looming behind her. He probably had a fantastic view straight down to her boobs. She totally did not sit up straighter and take a nice deep breath when she realized that... at least, not on purpose.

Taking her own seat, Olivia looked across her desk at them, folding her hands in front of her.

"So... Nick, I take it your sudden interest in the Dominant's class is because you found out Avery is a submissive?"

Trust Olivia to stab right into the heart of the matter. Avery's cheeks flushed hot red.

"I'm not sure I'm really still submissive. That's part of why I—" Avery's teeth snapped shut with a click when Olivia transferred her steely gaze to meet Avery's. Oops. Avery's head dropped, and she studied her hands without even thinking about it.

"You're submissive, sweetheart," Olivia said gently. "That doesn't go away, even if you haven't been in a club or had someone to be kinky with for a while. It's possible to deny or ignore parts of ourselves, but that doesn't mean that part is actually gone. I'd hazard part of the reason you questioned whether you really are is you wanted to see where things could go with Nick, and you knew he's not kinky."

Avery bit her tongue. She'd heard Olivia was observant enough to seem psychic, but she'd never had it turned on her. She almost sagged with relief when Olivia returned her attention to Nick.

"Nick?" Olivia prompted him.

"Yes." Short, simple, succinct, as if it was the most obvious thing in the world. Yes, of course, his interest in taking the class had to do with his employee, who he wasn't actually dating.

Avery buried her face in her hands.

"Is there a problem with that?" he asked, sounding confused.

Dropping her hands, Avery twisted in her seat, as much as her corset would allow, to look up at him with exasperation. She pretended not to notice when his eyes dropped to her boobs before returning to her face.

"Is there? We're not... I mean, we've flirted. We've kissed. You *just* asked me on a first date less than five minutes ago, and I haven't even said yes... yet. Don't you think you're moving a little fast?"

"When I know what I want, I get it." He shrugged his shoulder. "I want you."

Now she was breathless for an entirely different reason. His unswerving confidence was part of what she found so hot, even when it was infuriating.

"Well, this should be fun," Luke muttered, but when Avery looked at him, he winked. He actually looked as if he was having fun watching her and his brother face off.

"I think the best thing we can do right now is give the two of you some space to talk. Then, Nick, you need to read over this, fill it out, and sign it." Olivia picked up a small folder on her desk and handed it to Nick, who stepped forward to take it, his brow furrowed.

"Have you been holding onto this just in case I finally decided to take the class?"

The look she gave him was withering. It wasn't even directed at Avery, and she still felt like shrinking into her seat. Nick was made of stronger stuff, though he took a step back and looked a little abashed.

"No, honey, I have a stack of them here because the next class starts on Monday, and I've been getting together the materials for the students." Olivia shook her head. "Though I'm sure it's tempting to believe the world revolves around you."

"Can't prove that it doesn't," Nick said with a wink. "You might have not known I was signing up today, but the universe was prepared for me."

Olivia's lips twitched, and she almost smiled. Had to admire Nick's balls.

"He's insufferable," Luke said, shaking his head. He caught Avery's eye again. "Are you sure you want him? You can do better. There's a bunch of Doms at Stronghold who already know what they're doing."

Avery laughed, more at the expression on Nick's face than at Luke's joke—his big brother clearly knew how to get under his skin.

"Let's give them a few minutes," Olivia said, interrupting what was sure to be an outburst by Nick. Getting to her feet, she shot Luke a stern look and crooked her finger. He stood, grinning cheekily, not at all put-off. Luke murmured something in her ear as they went to the door, which made her chuckle.

The door closed behind them, leaving her dressed in fet gear next to her boss and crush.

Great.

2

NICK

He had to sit down. Not because he was feeling weak or tired, but if he kept standing where he was, he would never be able to concentrate on anything but Avery's breasts. They'd been luscious when she'd been standing in front of him, but when she sat down, and he was standing behind her... well, his imagination took flight. There was a part of him tempted to see if he could literally dive into her deep cleavage and snuggle in for a good, long time.

Which meant he'd had a natural physical reaction he wasn't ashamed of but which might make her uncomfortable, considering the circumstances, and would be a lot easier to hide when he was sitting down. Thank God for loose chef pants.

Taking the seat his brother had vacated, he looked at Avery and saw her expression for the first time since they'd come into Olivia's office. Normally, she met his gaze easily, never backing down, but right now, she was staring at her joined hands where they rested in her lap as if she couldn't bring herself to look at him. Well, that wouldn't do at all.

"Avery, look at me." He tried to say it gently, but it came out as more of an order. It worked, though. She looked up and met his gaze, appearing a little more defiant. "If you don't want to date me, that's fine."

"It's not that." The words came out in a rush, then she hesitated, and something in his chest tightened. Yes, he could handle rejection and would never try to push a woman to date him, but that didn't mean he enjoyed hearing it. "Okay, maybe it is a little, but not because of you but because of our positions."

Nick raised his eyebrows, giving her a gesture she should continue. He wasn't entirely sure what she meant. Yes, they worked together, and that could go badly, but he saw it as more of a positive than a negative. With his exes, it had been hard to find time to be with them. With Avery, they were together almost every night of the week.

"I've never dated my boss, and I'm not sure it's a great idea. I don't want to mess up the dynamic in the kitchen, and I definitely don't want anyone to think I have my position because we're dating."

The very real concern on her face was the only thing that kept him from scoffing. Instead, he reached out to place his hand over hers, right over where her fingers were twined together, and he sensed her stilling. She'd been practically vibrating with nervous energy, which wasn't at all like her.

"Avery, no one is going to think that," he said gently. "You've been working for me for months. Anyone who thought you have your position because we started dating months after we started working together is an idiot."

"Yes, because the world is full of completely logical people." She sighed, only partially convinced. "It's not only that. Being kinky... it's not something you've ever indicated you were interested in. Every time you mentioned Olivia wanted you to take the class, you laughed. I don't want you to force yourself to do something because you think it's what I want you to do. That's not a good way to start a relationship."

Okay, that was a good point. He pressed his lips together, trying to think of how much he should say. Baring his emotions had never been a strong point, but he had a feeling Avery would not accept anything less than honesty, and he didn't have a good argument that it wasn't the whole truth.

"I have some concerns, but working here has helped. I'll be honest. I'm not sure I have it in me to hurt a woman. Olivia has wanted me to take the class for a while because she thinks it will help me understand kink better."

AVERY

Well, that was probably true.

A class with instruction and demonstration would be a lot better to explain to him it wasn't a bad thing to 'hurt' a woman if she was consenting, a masochist, and all the terms had been agreed upon beforehand. It definitely wasn't the first time she'd heard this misconception about kink. When she'd tried explaining it to other people, it was hard to explain with words. Most of the time, she ended up sending them to romance books. Lexi Blake, Cherise Sinclair, Kallypso Masters, BJ Wane... so many of her favorite kinky romance authors did a great job of explaining the difference between abuse and kink.

She pressed her lips together, not reassured about the whole executive chef–sous chef thing, though he made a good point that no one could say she was hired because they had a thing going on. She still didn't want anyone to know. The kitchen could be a competitive place, especially in restaurants like Marquis. Most of them were looking to move up from their current positions and eventually be in Nick's. She wasn't, but only because her dream was a little different—she wanted to own her own catering company.

"We have chemistry." Nick moved to the edge of his seat, so their knees were touching, his hand firmly holding hers. Whether or not he realized it, he had a dominant personality, and she had no doubt it would extend to the bedroom. That was a big part of why she was attracted to him. But someone could be dominant in the bedroom without actually being kinky, and that might be enough for her.

To have Nick *as* a *Dom* in the bedroom?

Her inner muscles clenched.

Good Lord, yes, please.

Fuck.

She couldn't say yes... not yet. That would be selfish and her getting everything she wanted. She didn't want to do that to him, although he might be curious and feel a little better about kink. He'd been working at Marquis long enough to see the happy couples and play partners, but that didn't mean it was for him.

"Let's look at what Olivia gave you first," she said, nodding her head toward it. If it was anything like the paperwork she'd received, there would be a list of limits. That might be enough to scare him off, then she wouldn't have to be the one to tell him, 'No.'

Letting go of her hands, he opened up the file and quickly thumbed through the documents while she tried not to miss the warmth of his hand too much. Craptastic. No matter today's outcome, work tomorrow was going to be hideously awkward.

"This is a lot, and I have to get back downstairs," he said, shaking his head and closing the folder.

Avery's heart sank in her chest. She hadn't realized how much she'd gotten her hopes up Nick would do the class and try out kink until he closed that door. Then he surprised her.

"How about we get together to talk through this after I'm done tonight?"

"I... uh, sure. Yeah, we could do that." The words were spurred by the disappointment she'd felt when she'd thought he was writing off the experiment.

"Great. Come down to the bar when the show is over, and I'll come out as soon as I can."

Before she could respond, Nick was on his feet, and Avery instinctively looked up at him. Cupping her chin, he held her in place as his lips descended. Heat and need rose fast, her body responding to his kiss. It was rough and deep, meant to claim and conquer rather than reassure, and it left her gasping.

Winking at her, Nick sauntered out of the room, leaving her staring after him, wondering what had just happened.

NICK

Taking a minute to go to the downstairs office, Nick safely tucked the file folder in with his extra chef coats. He liked to keep two on hand at all times in case something happened in the kitchen, and he had to go into the dining room—he had an image to maintain, and the white coats he wore picked up some stains throughout the evening. It was a shared office, so there wasn't a guarantee of privacy, but no one else should bother his chef coats.

Energy buzzed through him, even more than usual. Despite everything, he felt on top of the world.

Avery was going to give him a chance. He knew it.

He'd expected to be a little more hesitant about getting into all this domination stuff, but if it was what Avery wanted, he was going to make sure he was the man who could give it to her. Nick had always been a fast learner.

If he was completely truthful, he could also admit he wanted to understand the new world his brother had entered. It was hardly the first time his older brother had done something first, but Nick couldn't remember the last time Luke had done something that Nick hadn't understood. He was a little nervous about the idea of having to hurt Avery, but hey, what was the point of being the one in charge if he couldn't say 'no, we're not doing that?'

"Chef, I have a special request at table twenty-seven." One of the servers, one of the few he actually liked, came to a halt in front of him, looking a little nervous. Everyone knew he hated changes to his dishes. Nick put them together in a particular way for a reason, and that's how they were meant to be eaten. If someone didn't like part of a dish, they should order something else. Of course, that's not how most diners felt.

"What?"

Alanna tucked a strand of auburn hair that had fallen free of her ponytail behind her ear, apology in her blue eyes.

"They have a shellfish allergy, but they really like the look of the scallops and lobster. So, they were wondering if they could get double scallops and no lobster."

"Oh, yes, that's fine." Allergies were one thing he would never mess around with. "Put the allergy in all caps when you put in the order. Table twenty-seven you said?"

"Yes, Chef." Alanna smiled brightly at him and scurried off to put in the order. Nick went to his place on the line, joining the expediter, who was currently plating the food. George was efficient and very good at what he did, but on the weekends, it usually took two people to keep things moving as fast as Nick wanted.

"Keep an eye out for table twenty-seven when it comes in," Nick said, giving George a nod of greeting before turning his attention to Darnell, who was on the sauté station. "Shellfish allergy. They'll be getting double scallops."

"Yes, Chef," Darnell said without pausing his motion of basting the fish he was working on.

Rolling up his sleeves, Nick got to work.

At least, he tried. He'd never had trouble focusing on work before, no matter what was going on in his personal life, but tonight was different. He was supposed to be garnishing the dishes and handing them off to the food runners for the correct tables, but he kept thinking about how Avery had looked in that corset, the way she'd been almost shy, and wondering about that list in the office.

Wondering about the short glimpse of things he'd seen on it.

"Uh, Chef? That's for table thirty-two, and that one is for table fourteen." George eyed him warily as though he wasn't sure whether he should actually say anything. A little older than the other servers, in his mid-thirties, he was about the same age as Nick, which was part of why Nick enjoyed having him as expeditor rather than food runner on the weekends. He wasn't as intimidated by Nick as some of the others were and would speak up when it was necessary—although he'd never had to make as big a correction as just now.

From across the line, Darnell glanced up, frowning in Nick's direction. Not with judgment but concern, but it still didn't feel good.

"Right, sorry. Got distracted," Nick said gruffly, putting down one of the plates and handing the other one to George. "I need to run to the bathroom. I'll be right back."

He'd splash some cold water on his face and get his shit together. Time to get his head in the game. He'd see Avery later—after his shift and after the show she was watching.

3

AVERY

Thankfully, there hadn't been much time for Domi and Rae to interrogate her before the show started. She'd barely had time to put in her dinner order before the lights dimmed, the music swelled, and the room had fallen to a hush.

She gave them a quick summary of everything that had happened once they'd left her in Olivia's office. They hadn't had time to respond, which was good because she wanted to get her thoughts and emotions in order before she had to answer any of the questions she'd seen bubbling in their eyes.

She wasn't sure she had answers.

She wasn't even sure she would enjoy the show, especially since she was hungry at the beginning of it.

When Will and Gina came out—Domi whispered their names to her—she got caught up in everything they were doing. It was a flogging demonstration, and by the end of it, Will was using a flogger in each hand, moving around Gina in a circle while she hung from her wrists, her body practically shaking with pleasure.

It was beautiful.

It made Avery ache. Not just between her legs but over her whole body. She missed being flogged. Spanked. Dancing on the precipice of pain and pleasure, her body so caught up in the sensation, she could no longer tell which was which. Jealousy was the wrong word for what she felt; it was pure envy.

She wanted that.

Not with Will or a faceless Dom she hadn't met.

No, she specifically wanted it with Nick.

Who didn't even know if he was into kink.

God, she was so fucked, and not in the fun way. Though... maybe she could be if Nick actually went through with the class. But what if it turned out he really didn't like kink? Or he forced himself to do it because he thought it was what she wanted, then he resented her.

Just once in my life, could I choose the easy path?

Wouldn't that be nice?

Past decisions showed that wasn't usually how she worked, though. Heck, she'd moved to a new city, miles away from her friends and family, for a job. A decision none of them had understood. Though when it came down to it, none of them had really understood her.

She'd felt more accepted and supported by Domi and Rae in the first few months of their friendship than she had by her friends back home, who she'd known since high school. While she still loved those friends, they were leading completely different lives from her, and none of them seemed to understand why she hadn't wanted the same for herself.

Maybe Avery could have been happy getting married young and having babies, but it wasn't what she'd really wanted then, and now she was glad she'd made that decision. Instead, she'd gone to culinary school, started working in restaurants, and finally made the move up here to work at Marquis. Some of her friends back home seemed to take her ambition as a personal affront, as if they thought she was looking down on them for being stay-at-home moms, whereas she felt they started shutting her out when she hadn't become one.

As the show finished with a bang—literally—Avery squirmed in her seat. Yup, she wouldn't have missed out on this for the world. Olivia had been right—Avery was still kinky. She missed this. She craved it.

In fact, she would have given anything to be in Gina's position, with Nick working her over and finishing her off.

"Damn." Domi fanned herself as the lights came up, indicating the end of the show if the empty stage hadn't already done so. "That was... well, let's just say, Mitch is getting lucky tonight."

"Lucky." Avery wasn't kidding. Mitch, Domi's boyfriend and Dom, was an accomplished sadist. The two of them were adorable together outside the kinky stuff as well.

"Hey, maybe you'll get lucky, too," Rae said, winking at Avery before scooting her way out of the booth. "You're supposed to talk to Nick tonight after his shift, right?"

"Right..." Avery hadn't really thought about getting lucky. They were going to talk about kink and go over the hard limits list Olivia had given him. Did she want to?

Yes.

Was it a good idea?

Ugh. That depended on so many things.

"Scoot," Domi said, poking Avery in the side. Apparently, she was planning on following Avery out of the booth rather than taking advantage of the open side Rae had vacated. "Let's go downstairs and get a drink, so we can talk."

That actually sounded really good. It would be way too hard to concentrate on any conversation up here, where people still occupied several of the booths and were enjoying themselves post-show. The moans and gasps were a little distracting. That's where she was supposed to meet Nick, anyway.

They could sit in one of the booths downstairs, where the noise of the crowd would help filter out any of their conversation. Restaurants could be gossipy places, and she didn't want anyone overhearing what she and the others were saying. On the other hand... she looked down at her corset as they walked into the lobby. Dammit. She hadn't thought it through when she'd agreed to meet Nick at the bar.

"I can't go down there in this."

Domi and Rae paused, looked at her, then looked at each other. All of them were wearing clothes appropriate for the second floor of Marquis, but not so much the first floor. Well, Domi and Rae could get away with it in the bar. At another restaurant. Avery might be willing to try but not at *her* restaurant.

They'd done a good job of hiding her as they came in. She wasn't about to sit in the middle of the dining room.

"Oh right… shit." The look on Rae's face was hilarious. "I can't believe I've gotten so used to dressing like this, I sometimes forget it's not the norm."

"You all look gorgeous," Freddy said from his place behind the host desk, sounding amused. Avery jumped. She'd forgotten he was there. "Olivia has some wrap dresses in her office in various sizes if you'd like to change. I'm sure she'd be happy to lend them to you."

Domi and Rae looked at Avery expectantly.

Well, that would solve the problem, but she wasn't sure she wanted to ask Olivia for another favor tonight.

"You should go ask her. You're the one about to date her boyfriend's brother," Rae said, nudging Avery with her elbow.

"Why don't you go ask her? You've known her longer, and she was your teacher," Avery said, digging in her heels, looking back and forth between Rae and Domi.

"Yeah, which means we know exactly how scary she can be. She'll be nice to you."

"I'll go ask her," Freddy interrupted, rolling his eyes and grinning with amusement. "And just so you know, we submissives almost never need to be scared of her. The Dominants, on the other hand…" He winked at them, sauntering over to knock on Olivia's door.

All three of them watched him.

"Maybe she gets less scary the more you get to know her… or with long-term exposure?" Avery murmured.

"I think Freddy might be a special case. He's worked here a long time. Did you know he's a lawyer?" Domi asked, keeping her voice hushed.

Freddy opened Olivia's door and leaned in to say something to her before turning around and giving them a thumbs up.

Ten minutes later, they were downstairs in Marquis. It turned out he hadn't been kidding about Olivia keeping dresses for anyone who wanted to use the first floor and hadn't brought a change of clothes—

she'd had more than a few. She had an entire wardrobe in multiple sizes.

The blue wrap dress Avery wore didn't fit her perfectly, but it was good enough. Domi's was a little big, and Rae's was a little short, but no one gave them a second glance as they made their way to one of the booths on the far side of the bar. It was late enough in the evening the floor was clearing out, which would give them even more privacy.

Only a moment after they slid into their seats, one of the servers came by to take their order. While they waited for their drinks, they talked about Domi's daughter and how things were going with her boyfriend, Mitch, waiting by silent agreement to talk about Avery and Nick. Which was much appreciated since their server was Josie, one of the gossipiest members of the staff.

Once they had their drinks and Josie had walked away, it was on.

"Okay, so... how are you feeling?" Domi leaned forward, her hands clasped around the bottom of her beer glass.

Lifting the dry martini she'd ordered to her lips, Avery took a moment to let the burn glide over her tongue and down her throat while she thought about how to answer.

"Excited... nervous..." She sighed, putting the glass down and rubbing her fingers against the stem, not twirling the glass, but in the same motion. There was something soothing about it. "I'm really afraid of fucking up my job. I'm worried he'll discover he doesn't like kink... yet."

"Yet you want him." Rae nodded, sympathy emanating off her. "Sometimes, we want what we can't have, but what's the harm in trying?"

"Yeah, Rae, what's the harm?" Domi murmured, making Avery giggle. Rae's worst kept secret was she had the hots for Brian, one of the Daddy Dom members of the club, but she refused to acknowledge it.

Rae glared at her.

"If you remember correctly, I did try, but I decided it wasn't for me," Rae said tartly. Domi opened her mouth to say something—probably an argument—but Rae pointed her finger at her. "Besides, we're focusing on Avery right now, not me."

"Fine." Domi rolled her eyes. "But we're coming back to this, eventually."

Ignoring her, Rae twisted in the booth, so she could look directly at Avery. Making a face, Avery took another sip of her martini. It was a little disconcerting to have both of them so focused on her. She knew she was the third wheel in their bestie friendship, and she was okay with that. Partly because she was used to not having a best friend and partly because it was hard for her to open up to people.

Best friends tended to expect to be told all sorts of secrets. Avery didn't have any earth-shattering ones, but she wasn't great at sharing much about herself. Maybe because she got out of the habit back home when it seemed like anything she said was judged or misinterpreted. The kinksters in Atlanta she'd met had been friendly, but none of them had sucked her into their friendship circle the way Domi and Rae had.

"What's the worst that could happen if you and Nick do the class together?" Rae asked.

Avery's stomach twisted. Even making herself say the words was hard.

"He could decide things wouldn't work out between us because I'm messed up in the head for liking kink, everything becomes way too awkward in the kitchen, and he fires me." She kept her voice low, wincing as her eyes dropped to the table. Looking at her friends to see their reactions was as hard as saying the words out loud.

There was a moment of silence, then Rae reached over to touch Avery's arm gently.

"Sweetie, you know there's nothing wrong with you for being kinky, right?"

Avery straightened in her seat. Yeah, of course, she knew that, but... She'd only told one friend back home about her interest in kink. Shannon had stared at her in horror and suggested Avery see a therapist. After that, she hadn't tried to talk to any of her friends about it. Pressing her lips together, Avery nodded.

It wasn't her fault Shannon hadn't seen things the same way. They hadn't seen eye-to-eye on a lot of things before Avery left home. She hadn't realized how deeply that one had dug in until this moment when she admitted she didn't want Nick to think that.

"The job stuff is a little harder," Domi said thoughtfully, a finger tapping against her glass. She leaned onto her elbows. "Does the restaurant have a policy against fraternization?"

"No..." Avery drew out the word and made a face. "But if we started something, and it fell apart, he could make working here miserable for me."

"Do you think Nick is the type of guy who would do that?" The question was said with more curiosity than anything else. Domi's head tilted to the side, her curls bobbing slightly with the movement.

"I... no." Probably not. At least, she couldn't imagine him doing so. If anything, he'd be icy cold but civil. Polite. Which would hurt after how close they'd become and their current good rapport, but it wouldn't be unbearable. He wouldn't actually fire her because they broke up.

Considering he worked for Marquis, it didn't make a whole lot of sense that he would think she was sick in the head for liking kink, even if he didn't understand it. If he really thought people who were into it were sick, he wouldn't work here, no matter how much they paid him. And he'd probably be on a mission to rescue his brother.

Instead, he would be willing to try things out.

Shouldn't she be?

"You guys are making too much sense," she grumbled.

"Cheers to that!" Rae lifted her glass, filled with a pink Dirty Shirley Temple, and grinned.

Laughing, Avery lifted hers as well, gently clinking her glass with Domi and Rae's before taking another sip.

All three of them nearly choked when Nick suddenly appeared at the side of the table. None of them had seen him coming. One moment, no one was there, then he was there, like a freaking ninja. Was it already that late?

"Hi," Avery croaked, looking past him to the wall behind the bar. Just after ten. She hadn't been paying attention to the time, but even if she had, she would have expected Nick to come out closer to eleven.

Things had died down in the dining room, but service wasn't over yet, and he was a control freak who had trouble stepping away.

"Hey." His gaze flicked to Rae and Domi before returning to her. "You ready to talk?" There was just enough uncertainty in his voice to make her realize he wasn't as confident as he'd appeared earlier, which made her feel a little better.

"We'll go sit at the bar," Domi said cheerfully, scooting out of the booth, Rae following only a moment behind her.

"Just shout if you need us." Unlike Domi, Rae sounded threatening and narrowed her eyes at Nick before she went.

Nick slid into Domi's vacated side of the booth, setting down the papers he was holding. Avery had been so discombobulated by his appearance that she hadn't realized he'd brought them. She really needed to get it together.

$$\text{❦} \quad 4 \quad \text{❦}$$

NICK

As soon as Josie let him know Avery was in the dining room—any time any of the employees came in to eat, whoever was leading the line was given a heads up—the burning desire to see her had overtaken him, which was not his norm.

He'd always gotten a rush of pleasure knowing when Avery was in the dining room and had sent out food he knew she'd like—sometimes specials that weren't on the menu—but he'd never had the urge to run out to her. Especially when there were still tickets coming through with new meals being ordered.

On the other hand... George had this. Things had slowed down enough, it was more like a weekday night.

So, he'd clapped the other man on the shoulder and said he needed to talk to Avery. Surprise had shown in George's eyes, but he'd nodded and gotten back to work. He'd even seemed pleased Nick trusted him enough to leave him earlier than usual.

Something to think about. Nick wasn't entirely happy to give up control over the kitchen this early in the evening, but it would be worth it. He knew it the moment he sat down across from Avery.

"No more corset?" he asked, eying the deep vee of the light blue dress she was wearing. It looked nice against her dark blonde hair and hazel eyes, but it wasn't nearly as much fun as the corset, and he didn't think she was wearing it under the dress. Too bad.

"No. There was no way I was wearing that downstairs. We're lucky Olivia had clothes set aside for people like us." Avery took another sip of her martini, which was already getting down toward the bottom.

Josie walked up to the table just as Nick was eying Avery's drink, wondering how much she'd already had. The server eyed both of them almost warily. Nick had snapped at her a time or two for talking too much in the kitchen, and now she was walking on eggshells around him, which he was fine with.

"Do you want another one?" she asked Avery.

"Yes, one more, please."

"And you?" She looked at Nick, wariness still evident in her big blue eyes. Several of the men on staff had been suckered in by her beauty, and especially those eyes, but Nick had never had any trouble ignoring her attractions.

"Whatever's on tap. Shane will know. Just tell him it's for me."

Josie nodded, her eyes dropping to the papers he'd set in front of him before she scurried away. Fortunately, he had his hands atop them, so there was no way she'd been able to see what they were. Not that he should care what she thought, but if he was going to do this, he didn't want to shout about it from the rooftops, and that was what telling Josie would be akin to.

"Did you have a good time tonight?" he asked, keeping his hands on top of the papers since he knew Josie would be back in a moment.

"I did. It was... enlightening."

Avery's gaze shyly met his again, which he wasn't used to. It stirred new emotions in him. He'd never expected to feel protective of Avery, but something about her looked more vulnerable than usual.

"And enjoyable." She sighed, almost as though he was making her admit to something she wasn't sure she wanted to. There was a bit of reluctance in her answer, subtle but detectable to him. Something he wouldn't have caught if he didn't know her so well and wasn't focused on her.

Her expression became more closed when Josie reappeared at their table with drinks, looking at them curiously.

"Thank you, Josie." Nick gave her a look. "We'll call you over if we need you again." There was a clear dismissal in his voice. Josie took the hint, although she glanced back over her shoulder as she moved away.

Taking a sip of his beer while Avery polished off her martini, Nick opened the file. The contract for the club was on top. From what he could tell, it was mostly a non-disclosure agreement—which he'd already signed when he started working for Marquis—and a list of rules. The small packet under it had the more interesting stuff.

He pulled that one to the top.

"You might need to explain some of these," he murmured, pulling his pen from the top pocket of his chef coat.

AVERY

Oh good, that didn't make her feel like chugging her martini.

"Here?" she whispered, her voice hissing out in horror.

Blinking, Nick looked up at her. She raised her eyebrows and cocked her head to the side.

"You'd rather do this in private?"

"Yes. Yes, I would." Crazy man. She couldn't decide if he had no shame or was just ignorant about the kinds of things she'd be explaining to him. Maybe a bit of both. "We haven't even agreed we're going to do this, and you want me to explain... stuff to you." Her eyes darted around, but no one at the bar was looking at them. Still.

"Okay." Nick closed the folder and put his hands over it again, staring across the table at her.

His dark eyes pinned her in place, and she took a deep breath. She'd only had one martini so far, barely taken a sip of her second, but he'd made her feel completely off-kilter. Maybe it was a Dom thing, or maybe because this entire situation felt surreal, but either way, she needed to get a grip on herself.

"I can come over after my shift is done. Probably in about an hour."

"Come over?"

He raised his eyebrows at her. "For privacy. Or you can come to my place. Whichever makes you more comfortable."

Comfortable discussing kink and a relationship with him? Yeah, that would be nowhere. But... no. Private where she wouldn't have to worry about anyone overhearing if she wanted to screech at him or explain some of the finer points of edge play... Ack. Yeah. Privacy.

"My place is fine." She stared at him, trying to figure out what he was thinking and coming up blank. "So, we're really going to do this?"

"Yes, we are. I'm signing up for the class regardless, but I hope you'll be there to help me." His gaze was steady. Probing. He meant every word. He would sign up, even if she told him she wasn't interested in him.

From what Avery knew, he would need someone in class with him. The signup sheet for experienced submissives to pair with single new Dominants taking the class had gone around a month ago. If he didn't come with a partner, one would be assigned to him for the class, possibly more. Domi and Rae said the Doms switched off when they did their submissives class to make sure no one got too attached.

She'd been wrong when she'd told Rae the worst-case scenario. Worst-case was Nick taking the class without her and falling for both the lifestyle and another submissive because Avery had been too afraid to try.

Nope. Big nope. Everything could crash and burn, but it was still better to try than stand on the sidelines and watch someone else get what she wanted.

"Okay, we'll go to the class as a couple." Nick's lips widened in a grin, and Avery held up a finger. "On one condition—no one at the restaurant can know we're dating or have a relationship other than a work one."

"Done." Nick held out his hand. Pressing her lips together to keep from smiling—and failing miserably—Avery reached out and took it. It didn't matter that it was a handshake rather than a kiss. Just touching him and feeling his callused palm against hers set her body sparking with interest. "I'd rather keep the workplace professional, anyway. There's enough gossip going on around here."

Well, he wasn't wrong about that. Avery didn't want to add to it and was relieved he didn't either, no matter how blasé he'd been initially about having this conversation in public.

"My house when you're done?" she asked as he got up, taking his half-finished beer with him. She kept her voice low, though not quite a whisper.

Nick nodded. "I'll text you when I'm on the way."

He didn't ask for her address as he sauntered away, even though he'd never been to her house. Of course, he'd have it on file in the office.

As soon as he walked away, Domi and Rae abandoned the bar and rushed back to stand over her, demanding in low whispers to know what he'd said. Knowing they hadn't been able to hear, Avery felt better about whether anyone else had overheard her and Nick. Domi and Rae been sitting the closest and would have been trying to listen in.

Avery quickly updated them, then tossed back the rest of her martini.

"Let's get going," she said, hooking her arms through Rae's and Domi's. "We gotta get our clothes, and I need to get home."

"You'd better text us tonight after he leaves," Rae threatened.

"*If* he leaves," Domi tacked on with a giggle. Avery came to a halt, blinking, in the middle of the stairs.

"Shit... you think he might... shit! I need to get home!" She slid her arms from theirs and hurried up the stairs.

"What? Why?" Rae was right behind her, more curious than concerned.

"I need to shave!"

"You're wearing a skirt. Didn't you already shave your legs... *OH*." Rae's voice changed substantially when she realized.

Yup, there it was. Avery had been planning to go out tonight, not get laid, or she would have taken the time to shave both. Not that she was definitely sleeping with Nick tonight.

Just in case.

❧

NICK

If keeping his head in the game had been difficult before, it was fucking impossible now. Thank God it was the end of the night, and things were already settling down. Basically, he stood back and let George handle the plates going out while he pretended he was watching over everything.

In reality, with his arms crossed in front of his chest, he was staring at absolutely nothing. All he could think about was going to Avery's place tonight. When he'd made the suggestion, he'd expected her to change her mind and want to stay here. They could have gone upstairs to talk for more privacy... but either the thought hadn't occurred to her, or she preferred having him come to her place. Personally, he preferred the total privacy since he knew how skittish she was about doing anything on restaurant premises, but he hadn't actually expected to get it.

Not that he was expecting anything more than that, but he could damn well hope.

If he went home tonight with nothing more than a hot kiss from Avery, he'd be happy, but he was hoping he might get a little farther than that. They may have started officially dating tonight, but they'd been flirting and dancing around their mutual attraction for months.

"Uh, Chef?"

Crap. George was standing right in front of him, and Nick was pretty sure this wasn't the first time he'd been addressed.

"Sorry, I was thinking about tomorrow's special. Do you need something?" He would need to do a better job of covering.

"I think we're about done if you want to get out of here." George's hazel eyes were full of concern, and he lowered his voice a little. "Maybe get some rest."

Nick opened his mouth to say he was fine, then he realized George had the line handled. The restaurant would close soon, anyway.

Although he never left early, maybe this once, he'd give himself a break.

"Yeah, that sounds like a good idea. I'll see you tomorrow." Hiding his grin at George's surprise, Nick went to fetch the file. It was finally time to go through it with Avery.

5

NICK

Avery's apartment was a ground floor unit in a garden apartment building. In the darkness, there were a lot of shadows, but the main path was well lit, as was the interior of the building where the stairs were. After the long evening he'd had, Nick was glad she didn't live on the third floor since there was no elevator. He didn't feel like walking up all those stairs.

His feet hurt, as they always did at the end of a long night, but he was more energized than usual. Most nights after shift, he would go home and sit on the couch, unwinding from the long day. He'd have a meal of broth and bread with a beer to finish it, maybe a cup of tea, then stare blankly at the television until two in the morning, when his body would finally be decompressed enough for him to fall asleep. Basically, most nights, he had nothing to look forward to.

That wasn't the case tonight.

Knocking on Avery's door, he felt an odd mix of anticipation and nerves, but it was the nerves that knocked him off-kilter. Being around Avery usually made him feel the opposite of nervous. He hadn't felt nervous about going on a date with a woman since high school. It probably had something to do with the folder tucked under his arm.

He still wasn't sure how he felt about the activities listed on the forms. He'd looked at them again, using red lights and the streetlights to read on the way over. He hadn't been able to help himself. Every time he looked at the list, his eye caught something new and intriguing... or something new and slightly terrifying.

Anal play and sex.

That had been at the top of the list and something he was more than okay with, especially with Avery. She had a gorgeous ass, even in chef pants, and that was saying something. He'd love to get up close and personal with it.

Bondage.

Okay, he'd experimented in his early twenties, tying a girlfriend up. Didn't most people? He'd liked it—a lot—but after they broke up, he'd never brought it up with another woman. "I want to tie you up" sounded too threatening, whereas "I want you to tie me up" had been sexy, and he'd never been able to figure out how to make it sound sexy instead of scary coming from his end. No other girlfriend had made the same request, so that had been that.

Figging?

No idea what the hell that was.

Fire play? Knife play? Mummification? Piercings? Whippings?

Yeah, he could guess what some of those were, and there was no fucking way.

What if that's what Avery wants?

The little voice that whispered in his head was not helpful. He knocked on her door, shaking the thought away. Surely, she wouldn't want to do all those things. He tried to imagine Avery with naughty piercings.

Okay, he didn't hate that... as long as he didn't have to be the one to pierce her. He didn't have a needle phobia, but he also didn't like the idea of sticking one into someone.

The door opened, and the tension that had been slowly building while he thought about all the options relaxed as Avery peered up at him. She was now dressed in shorts and one of the tank tops she normally wore under her chef coat, showing off far more of her curves than he normally got to see. While the tank top was nothing new, the itty-bitty shorts made her legs look miles long.

"Hey." Her smile was lopsided, a little nervous as she stepped back to let him in.

"Hey." Aware he smelled like 'kitchen'—aka sweat and food—whereas her apartment smelled like lavender. So did she. Nick tried not to let it get him down. She'd known he was coming straight from work and what the end of shift smelled like. There was only so much deodorant and a spritz of Febreze in the car could do. He'd taken off his chef coat, but the t-shirt he'd been wearing underneath it wasn't exactly a bouquet of flowers.

"Want something to drink?" she asked, heading toward the little galley kitchen he could see off to the right. "I have water, beer, and soda."

"A beer sounds good."

"It's a mango IPA, is that okay?"

"Sounds good." He liked fruity IPAs.

While she puttered in the kitchen, Nick studied her apartment. To the very left of the entrance was her living space, with a couch and recliner. The couch, which would sit three comfortably, was facing a decent-sized television mounted to the wall. The recliner was right next to him, facing the huge sliding glass door and window that took up most of the far wall, which would give her a good view outside when the blinds were open, and the sun was up. A view of what, he couldn't exactly tell since the blinds were closed.

Behind the couch was her dining room setup, with a small table, four chairs, and a little buffet against the wall. To the right of that was a hallway, where the kitchen was located, and he guessed, led back to her bathroom and bedroom.

The only art on the walls were three movie posters of the original Lord of the Rings movies above the buffet. Raising his eyebrows, Nick moved closer to inspect them, setting the file folder on the dining table as he passed it. Avery was moving around in the kitchen. He glanced in, but she was behind the door to the fridge, and he couldn't see what she was doing.

"I didn't peg you for a Lord of the Rings fan," he said, shoving his hands in his pockets as he looked up at the framed posters.

"I like the movies, hated the books. Don't tell anyone." Avery came into the dining area behind him, a tray in her hands with his beer, two glasses of water, and a plate full of cheese, sliced meat, and crackers.

His stomach rumbled at the sight.

"Holy crap, you read my mind." Sliding into the chair closest to him, Nick grabbed one of the knives on the tray and sliced off some cheese for himself, placing it on a cracker, along with some of the meat. A little smile curved Avery's lips as she sat in one of the chairs next to him.

"I figured you'd be hungry at the end of shift. I always am."

"Thank you for thinking of it." Belatedly, he remembered his manners. Hunger made him forget them sometimes.

"Of course." She watched him shove the cracker in his mouth. Hopefully, that wasn't a complete turnoff.

⁂

AVERY

Holy crap, Nick was in her house, eating her food, looking both tired and sexy after a long day of work, and ready to talk about kink. She felt like pinching herself, except she knew this was real.

"Have you had a chance to look over all of that?" she asked, nodding at the folder as she picked up her own cracker, cheese, and pastrami. While she hadn't planned on having a late-night snack, it was weird sitting and watching him eat alone. She nibbled hers since she wasn't all that hungry after dinner at Marquis.

Behind her, her phone chimed from its position on her kitchen counter. Probably Domi or Rae texting her back. She'd let them know as soon as Nick arrived. She ignored it. They wouldn't expect her to answer until after he left... if he left.

Awareness of his presence in her apartment buzzed through her again. She was used to being here alone, and Nick seemed to take up so much more space beyond his physical body.

"Most of it," he said, after using some beer as a chaser for his food. "I need your help, though. What's with the hard limits list? I just pick and choose what I want to do, and they'll teach me in class?" Skepticism threaded through his voice, and Avery laughed.

"Not exactly. Everyone has limits and things they don't want to do. A soft limit means it's something you're unsure about or aren't really interested in but might do with the right partner. A hard limit means it's an absolute no, something you will not do. Honestly, most people think of them as pertaining to the submissives, but Doms have them, too." It felt a little odd to be talking about this so openly with someone who wasn't in the 'know,' but Avery thought it was a pretty good explanation. "My understanding of the Dominants class is anything you'd be interested in doing with a submissive, you have to experience yourself in the class."

Nick's eyebrows rose practically to his hairline. "Does that mean you'll be doing it to me?"

"Oh, no." Avery shook her head vehemently. Though the image that popped up into her head of a class where the submissives got to show the Doms exactly how some things felt... Okay, that was kind of funny, but she didn't think the reality would be. Avery had absolutely no desire to be dominant in the bedroom and have someone else rely on her to make all the decisions. She enjoyed being dominated and wasn't interested in switching. "I'm sure there'll be other Dominants going through it with you. Experienced ones. I'll be your practice dummy." He snorted laughter at her description, but Avery had a feeling it was pretty apt. She'd find out more once she signed up, but she was only doing that if Nick did.

"Okay, so, help me figure out what my hard limits are."

NICK

Going through the list of kinks with Avery was fun and something of a relief. It turned out they had quite a few hard limits in common.

Unfortunately, it wasn't all fun and games. Fire play and knife play, two things that should have appealed to him as a chef, sounded more dangerous than sexy. He ended up putting them down as 'maybes,' so they were a soft limit rather than a hard one because he could tell Avery was interested. Thankfully, she wasn't into the mummification, bodily fluids, or needles.

"So, that's okay?" he asked, marking them down as hard limits.

"Absolutely. The only rule will be not to kink shame," she said, nodding her head. Nick looked up from where he was crossing them off the list, raising his eyebrows. She grinned back at him impishly. "No yucking other peoples' yum. It's fine to say something's not for you, but not say it's disgusting, gross, or anything like that."

"Makes sense." Even if that was what he thought about some of it. Just looking at the word 'mummification' made him shudder. On the other hand, if it made someone else feel good, he wouldn't hassle them. He and his brother had gotten a lot of flak for being Star Wars nerds growing up, and he'd never understood why people couldn't let them enjoy what they enjoyed without being insulting about it.

Same thing here. Different strokes for different folks. He could adhere to that... easily.

At least, he hoped so.

It was harder when dealing with things like 'Consenting Non-Con' and 'blood play' than with a preference for movies. The 'Consenting' part was what he had to focus on. He might not get why someone wanted to do something, but as long as it's what they wanted, he would do his best to honor that. Or at least, ignore what they were doing and let them have their fun.

There were a few things he was less sure about.

"Whipping? What does that entail? Is that like flogging?" He could hear the uncertainty in his voice, which he hated, but Avery had been so enthusiastic about flogging, he didn't want to come at her with judgment in his voice on this one. Flogging hadn't sounded too bad, once she'd explained, but whipping? All he could think of was Indiana Jones and that bullwhip. That had looked fucking painful.

He wasn't sure he wanted to whip anyone. Spanking was going to be hard enough.

✤ 6 ✤

AVERY

"Whipping is exactly what it sounds like, using a whip rather than a flogger," Avery answered, keeping her tone light. It was one of those things that sounded scarier than it actually was, mostly because certain whips could be very painful and do real damage when wielded incorrectly. But that was the whole point of the class. "A lot of the Doms at Stronghold use whips."

"Is that like a bullwhip?" Nick's unease about the idea of using a whip was obvious, and Avery pushed down her disappointment. She didn't want to unduly affect some of his choices, especially not after she'd realized he was closely noting her level of enthusiasm for everything and had left a couple options open he'd been hesitant about on his limits list when she'd been a little too exuberant in her explanation.

"It can be, but that's only for very advanced users. More are about this long..." She held out her hands. "Still can be dangerous, depending on the whip and the force used, but it can also be really great."

"Is that something you like?" The dubious note in his voice made her sigh inwardly.

"*This* isn't about what I like. It's about what you like." She could live without being whipped. It clearly made him uncomfortable. "I filled out my sheet before I went to Marquis."

"Can I see it?" Nick perked up.

"No!" Laughing, Avery sat back, shaking her head. God, that was just like him. She should have expected his response. He had a wicked sense of humor, despite how serious he could be at work.

"Worth a try." He grinned at her, completely unrepentant.

Even though she couldn't stop smiling, Avery tried to give him a stern look.

"You need to be serious. Remember, you're going to have to try everything you say you want to do." She'd reminded him of that when he'd bypassed 'figging' without even making it a soft limit, but that was his choice.

Expression turning more serious again, he looked down at the paper.

"I'll mark it as a soft limit."

Avery's heart went out to him. He was trying so hard, and she could tell he wasn't comfortable. While his confidence had been one of the things that had initially attracted her, being the one to see this moment of vulnerability was even hotter. This was something not everyone got a glimpse of—in fact, she'd bet most people would say he didn't have a vulnerable side.

Sitting here, doing his best to keep an open mind despite the biases he was obviously struggling against, showing his hesitation and his concern... well, she found that hot. She had a feeling he was going to make a very good Dom. Considerate. Thoughtful. Focused on what his submissive needed instead of demanding that he was catered to.

Hopefully, the class would help him open his mind a little more. She got it. There were a lot of misconceptions about kink. He had some, which was why she hadn't told him about her involvement.

Avery scooted a little closer. She'd started off on his left, but as they'd gone through the list, she'd ended up moving around, closer and closer, thanks to her round dining table.

Turning his head to look at her, a little confused, both of them froze when they realized their faces were mere inches apart. He smelled like Febreze and food, but the combination wasn't bad. At least it was one she was used to since she'd done the same thing many a time when she couldn't stop for a shower after a shift.

"Avery," he murmured, his gaze dropping to her lips before lifting to meet hers again. The sensual awareness in his dark eyes made her insides quiver. "What are you doing?"

"Um... sitting?" Her voice was softer, breathier. Leaning in a smidgeon more, she tilted her head. She was topping from the bottom, but Nick wouldn't know that. It wasn't really topping from the bottom, though. She was just... encouraging. Tempting.

Offering.

"Mmm-hmm." He didn't hesitate, his hand sliding into her hair, pulling her lips the last few inches to his. Avery sighed with approval as he kissed her, happy arousal bubbling up from her core.

Whether or not he was a Dom, Nick was a take-charge guy, which flat out did it for her. Once he had an idea of what she wanted, he went for it, and right now, Avery wanted a hot, passionate kiss while she didn't have to worry about anyone seeing them, didn't have to keep her ears alert for anyone approaching.

Nick shifted on his seat, angling toward her and pulling her against him. Lifting her hands against his chest, Avery caressed the hard muscles beneath his shirt, enjoying being able to touch him. The material of his t-shirt was a lot thinner than his chef coat.

"Fuck." Breathlessly he pulled away, but not very far, still cradling the back of her head in his palm. "How far do you want to go tonight, Avery?" Uncertainty flashed in his eyes. "Do you want to wait until the class, so I know what I'm doing—"

Oh, hell no. She cut off that line of thinking immediately. There was no way she wanted Nick to feel as if he was less because he lacked the knowledge he was lined up to learn.

"Just do what feels right. The whole point of the class is to learn how to do the other stuff I don't expect you to know right now. I don't even want it. I want you." It was the truth. She smiled wickedly. "Give me the Chef Nick Evans experience."

Laughing, Nick's hands dropped to her waist and pulled her, twisting, so she ended up straddling his lap, trapped between him and the table. Hands on his shoulders for balance, she wiggled on top of him. Wow. His chef pants were loose enough, she'd never been able to get a good look, but Chef Nick was packing one hell of a sausage.

"I'm going to be the top student," he said, sliding his hands up her sides to cup her breasts.

Avery shivered, panting as her arousal soared under his touch.

"Of course, you will." That was the guy he was—driven, competitive—which meant a bit of her bratty side had to come out to play. "Because I'll be helping you with your study sessions."

He chuckled, but his expression settled into seriousness.

"You just wait, Avery. I'll be the best Dom you've ever had."

Before she could answer, he pulled her down for another kiss. Rather than argue she didn't think there was any such thing as a 'best' Dom, Avery gave herself over to the kiss. Arguing right now was pointless.

❧

NICK

Damn, it felt amazing having Avery on his lap, her soft thighs settled atop his, those short shorts barely covering her lower body as she squirmed on his erection.

He realized he was nervous as he cupped her breasts, squeezing them gently, then a little harder to make her moan. That was a new feeling. Nick couldn't remember the last time he'd been nervous about pleasuring a woman. It wasn't because Avery meant something to him —at least, that wasn't the only reason.

He wasn't sure he could give her what she wanted—needed—and he didn't want her to think he was lacking. It was something he hadn't worried about in a long, long time.

He pushed that aside.

Hell, he'd had no complaints. Avery wasn't expecting him to know the kinky stuff, but he meant it when he said he would at the top of the class. Even if part of him cringed at some things on the list. He'd figure it out.

Right now, he needed to focus on showing Avery everything he could do without all those bells and whistles. He could be a little more aggressive than he had in the past. That's what she wanted, right?

Sweeping his thumbs over her nipples, he teased the little buds to hardness through the fabric of her tank top. Avery arched her back, pushing her breasts into his hands, begging for more.

Pinching her nipples, a rush of hot arousal swept through his body when she moaned and rubbed herself against him, kissing him more frantically. He tightened his fingers, crushing the little buds, and felt his satisfaction surge when she whimpered and squirmed rather than pulling away or protesting.

Fuck.

She liked it.

If his dick was hard before, it was nothing compared to how it felt now. Nick had always had to rein in some of his impulses, pull back on things he'd wanted to do. He'd felt guilty about some of his fantasies because he wasn't supposed to want it, because his girlfriends *hadn't* liked it, so he hadn't bothered trying with the few hookups he'd had over the years.

Avery, though... Was this kink? He didn't know, but he was getting a hell of a lot more excited about learning.

Releasing her nipples for a moment before giving them another hard pinch, he pulled away from their kiss, sliding his hands down to her hips.

"Bedroom?" His voice came out lower than usual, almost a growl. Normally, he'd try to be more suave, but he was having trouble focusing.

"That way." She pointed over his shoulder, down the hall.

He'd really been asking whether or not she wanted to go there, but hell, that worked as an answer.

Moving his hands under her ass, he stood. The chair he'd been sitting in skittered back, and Avery shrieked, wrapping her arms and legs around him and clinging on for dear life. Chuckling, Nick turned and made his way down the hallway.

AVERY

Nick wasn't just hot; he was fun.

And rough.

And bossy.

Exactly the way she liked it.

Which was probably why she'd thought maybe she didn't need the kink. He was bossy enough in his own right, she might not have missed it, but she was glad, oh so glad, he was going to try.

She wanted tonight to know him—know what he liked, what he would do—before the classes started. She was pretty sure he was still going to be the best vanilla sex of her life.

Going straight to her bed, he tipped her back onto it, following her down. Avery gasped, squirming beneath him as his hands slid up her arms to her wrists, pinning them down on either side of her head, leaving her helpless beneath him.

Not kinky, my ass.

He didn't know he was, but Olivia was right. Ignorance or denial doesn't change a person's desires.

Right now, Nick was running on pure instinct, doing what *he* liked, and what he liked was to dominate.

"Fuck, I've wanted to do this forever." Hands sliding down her arms, he yanked down the front of her tank top.

Avery was a solid DD cup, but her breasts were rounded enough she could wear tank tops with shelf bras, no problem. When she wanted deep cleavage, she'd put a bra on, but most days—especially when she was at home—she was most comfortable like this, with nothing but the shirt's built-in bra. So, when Nick pulled down the front, her breasts spilled out, pink nipples hard and begging to be pinched.

She didn't even have to ask. He filled his hands with her breasts, his mouth unerringly going for one of her nipples. Avery gasped as the hot, wet heat closed around the turgid bud, throbbing pleasurably from being pinched. When his teeth closed around it, her entire body clenched with pure pleasure.

"Nick!" Her fingers threaded through his dark hair, holding him in place, as he sucked and nipped the tender flesh.

7

Avery's breasts were perfect. Soft to the touch, wonderfully heavy in his palm, and tipped with the sweetest tasting nipples he'd ever had the pleasure of devouring. He thrust against her, despite the fabric between them, enjoying the way she arched up beneath him to meet the thrust.

Fuck, he wanted to be inside her so bad.

He wanted his hands and mouth all over her.

He wanted hers all over him, but he wouldn't ask for her mouth today, especially not before he'd had the chance to shower.

That didn't mean he couldn't lick her from head to toe.

Moving his mouth from one breast to the other, he pinched the nipple he'd just abandoned between his fingers, twisting it as he bit down on the new one.

"Nick!" Avery shrieked his name, her fingers tightening in his hair, sending another surge of blood straight to his groin and his throbbing cock. He'd fantasized about hearing her say his name this way, and the reality did not disappoint.

Sliding his hands down her sides to the waistband of her tiny shorts, he yanked them down. Not to be outdone, Avery started tugging at his shirt.

Deciding to oblige, he lifted himself up enough to let her tug it over his head, which meant he had the opportunity to look her over. The tank top straps were around her upper arms, the top of it rolled under the creamy mounds of her breasts. Both nipples were dark pink from his ministrations, shiny from being suckled, and tightened into plump points.

The blue tank top was a band across her stomach, the only thing still covering her now that he'd pulled down her shorts and panties in one fell swoop. What he saw made his brain temporarily come to a grinding halt.

She shaved.

Or something.

Instead of a carpet to match the drapes, she had hardwood floors.

To be honest, Nick had never really cared one way or another about what women did with their pubes. Whatever made them feel good made him happy, but this was his first time seeing Avery's.

He could see *everything*—the swollen, pouty outer lips, the glistening pink between them, and the little nub of her clit at the top of it.

"Fuck, that's pretty."

"You say 'fuck' a lot for someone who's not actually doing it," she teased.

"Sorry, sweetheart, you're going to have to wait." Nick chuckled. "I'm starving."

Thankfully, she was already well-positioned on the edge of the bed. Nick dropped to his knees, pushed her legs wide, and draped them over his shoulders. Hands on her hips, he yanked her pussy to his mouth and relished his first taste of ambrosia.

AVERY

Nick's mouth was wicked.

With a small cry, Avery reached down to clutch his hair as his head moved between her thighs while he feasted on her pussy. There was no other word for it. He was licking and suckling, devouring her as if she was his favorite treat.

His tongue swiped up the center, teased her clit, then darted away to explore her sensitive folds. Hard hands on her hips held her in place as she writhed against his lips.

It had been way too long since she'd had sex. Her pleasure was already climbing, the sensations careening through her and sending her soaring. Everything Nick was doing pushed her toward the edge, faster and faster, like a freight train with no brakes.

"Oh God!"

He sucked her clit into his mouth, lashing it with his tongue, and did something with his lips that made them vibrate around the sensitive bud. Avery's orgasm crashed over her, her toes literally curling as ecstasy surged along her nerves.

By the time he finally let up on the hot suction, she was panting for breath and feeling utterly wrung out. Standing, he loomed over her, her legs dropping from his shoulders to his elbows, leaving her thighs spread wide. She could feel the brush of cooler air over her heated flesh, and she blushed, knowing he was looking at her pussy.

When he'd stood, he must have slid his chef pants off his hips because he appeared to be totally naked now. Bending her head, she could see the picture they made—her splayed out on the bed, him between her thighs, the thick length of his erection standing straight and hard against his body. It was darker than the rest of his skin, the mushroom head dark pink with the blood filling it,

"Condom?" His voice was hoarse, full of arousal and need. It flashed in his eyes as his gaze moved over her naked body, drinking her in and making her feel even more exposed and vulnerable... turning her on even more. Talk about a vicious cycle.

"There's some in the drawer." She waved her hand at her nightstand. "But... if you don't want to, I'm on the pill."

His expression...

"It's been a long time since I had sex, and I've been tested since then."

"Ditto."

It was nice to know they were in the same boat. She honestly wouldn't have expected that of Nick. He was hot as hell and definitely a sexual man. Avery had assumed he was getting it from somewhere these past months, even if she hadn't liked to think about it.

Letting go of her leg, he wrapped his hand around the shaft of his cock, using it to aim the blunt head at her pussy. The soft mushroom tip pressed against her swollen clit, making her moan and jerk her hips upward as he pushed down, rubbing along the slick folds and wetting himself in her arousal.

When he reached her opening, he thrust forward, pushing into her, and Avery gasped. Her hands lifted above her head, reaching for the sheets beneath them and clutching the fabric between her fingers. Even when she wasn't cuffed or tied, she loved having her hands above her head while a man was between her thighs. The position never failed to make her feel both submissive and hot as hell.

The pain-pleasure of being stretched open only added to her enjoyment. Nick pulled back and thrust forward again, his hands grasping her hips and pulling her against him as he buried himself inside her. Moaning, Avery wrapped her legs around his hips, clenching around him as he filled her. It felt like her nerve endings were on fire as every inch of him rubbed perfectly against her sensitized flesh. She was exquisitely sensitive in the wake of her orgasm, and as he moved inside her, his cock sliding partially out then back into her clenching channel, her pleasure was climbing again.

When it peaked, it would be explosive.

NICK

Holy hell.

Watching Avery while he fucked her was almost as enjoyable as the feel of her silken muscles squeezing him every time he buried his cock inside her. He'd only had sex without a condom with one other woman, a previous girlfriend years ago, and he'd forgotten how damn good it felt.

He could feel every inch of the soft walls of her pussy, the slickness coating his dick, and the quivering of her muscles around him. Avery arched, pushing her jiggling breasts toward the ceiling, her hands over her head. Nick could almost imagine cuffs around them, like the ones he'd seen on several second-floor Marquis patrons, holding them in place there, and his cock throbbed in response.

He liked the idea of her bound and helpless in this position, her body exposed to him, unable to stop him from doing whatever he wanted to her. Guilt followed swiftly on the heels of his fantasy before being pushed out of his head when she moaned his name again.

It'll be fine.

I'd never do anything to hurt her.

That the vow was made silently inside his head made no difference —he meant it.

His determination spurred him on.

He was going to show her how damn good it could be between them. Whatever he learned in the classes would be extra, the cherry on top of the sundae rather than the sundae itself.

"Oh, fuck... Nick... yes... harder..." Her breathy demands were pleading, spurring him on. Gripping her hips, he moved faster, harder, his own need rising as he gave in to the cravings of his body.

Hot need coursed through him, his balls tightening in anticipation, and when she screamed his name, her pussy spasming around him, he finally lost control.

"Fuck!" His guttural cry joining hers, he slammed into her, over and over, riding her through her orgasm while she writhed for him.

His knees buckled, and he fell atop her, catching himself and bracing his elbows on either side of her body, so he didn't crush her. Avery's arms wound around his neck, holding him close, and they panted together as her clenching muscles milked the last spurs of his pleasure.

Resting his head on her chest, Nick could hear the fluttering of her heartbeat as fingers stroked his sweat-dampened hair. His muscles felt twice as sore as they had before, and whatever energy was left had been drained.

He couldn't remember the last time he'd felt this damn happy.

AVERY

The sex was amazing. Update you tomorrow!

Quickly sending off the text while she was putting her phone on its charger, Avery turned off the sound. She didn't know if her friends would still be up, but if they were, she doubted they would be satisfied with that bit of info. They would have to wait.

Looking dubiously at the pair of sweatpants she'd given him, Nick held them up in front of himself, then looked back at her. She giggled. The bright pink was a little lurid, but it was her largest pair, and Nick was a lot bigger than her. It was the only pair that had any hope of fitting.

"Maybe I should sleep naked."

"Up to you. I won't judge." Yawning, Avery crawled onto her side of the bed, swiping the wet tendrils of hair off of her shoulder. She was exhausted. Between the show at Marquis, Nick coming over, the sex, then the post-sex shower to clean themselves, she was going to bed a lot later than she'd planned.

Not that she was complaining. Neither were her lady parts. Every part of her hummed with satisfaction. She had no doubt tomorrow she would be sore in the best way.

She wouldn't complain about a naked Nick Evans crawling onto her bed and pulling her into his arms. The little shriek when her wet hair touched his bare chest made her laugh.

"Holy crap, that's cold," he complained, even as he pulled her closer.

"You're the one who insisted I join you in the shower," she countered, snuggling in and rubbing her nose in his chest hair. Mmmm, he smelled good. Yeah, it was her soap, but it smelled different on him and was much better than the Febreze-kitchen combo from earlier.

"It wasn't a complaint, just a comment."

Avery snorted. He'd totally been complaining, but she didn't call him on it. She was too happy... and tired.

This still had the potential to blow up in her face, but right now, everything was perfect. She was pretty sure Rae was right.

This was worth a try.

❧   8   ❧

NICK

Coming out of the walk-in refrigerator, Nick almost ran over Avery, not realizing she was coming in while he was headed out. They careened to a halt, but not in time to keep from colliding. He reached out to grab hold of her to keep her from falling back when she bumped off his chest.

For a moment, they stared at each other. He hadn't seen her since he'd left her apartment this morning. Waking up next to each other had been nice and quickly turned *very* nice, but they hadn't had much time to enjoy the afterglow because she'd had to get to work, and he'd been kicked out.

After sending Olivia a scan of his completed list and signed contract, he used the internet to research kink, which had had some upsides and some downsides. Eventually, he'd decided it was better to wait for the class. He had watched TV until it was time for him to finally come to Marquis.

He'd known she was here, but she'd been on the line, and he'd been in the office doing admin things. Now, he had his hands on her again and couldn't help thinking about this morning and last night when he'd had his hands on her in a far different way. As if she was thinking the same thing, a hot pink blush rose in her cheeks.

"Hey."

"Hey." Avery blinked. Stepped back.

Nick reluctantly let her go.

Right. No one here was supposed to know what they were up to.

"I was doing inventory." He'd wanted to make sure they were properly stocked for the weekend and see if there was anything that needed to be prepped. Usually, there wasn't since the kitchen stayed on top of things, but part of the reason they did was he was so anal about making sure.

"Oh... um... I needed to get some mirepoix." The uncertain way she said it made the statement almost a question.

This was awkward. Everything had felt natural this morning when he'd left her apartment. This was the opposite, and he didn't know how to fix it.

How did they normally act around each other? It was as if he'd forgotten. Where should he put his hands?

He shoved them in his pockets.

"Gotcha. There's plenty." Ugh. Really? That was the best he could come up with? His voice sounded stilted and awkward.

"Great." Avery flashed him a smile that didn't reach her eyes, which were looking more panicked by the second. Yeah. They were terrible at this. "So, uh, I guess I'll see you in a bit."

"Right. See you on the line."

Then he did the worst thing he'd ever done in his life. He did finger guns.

Avery stared at him.

He stared back at her. Felt his face heating and turning red.

Retreat! For fuck's sake, run away!

Without another word—or inane hand gesture—Nick fled back to the kitchen, Avery's giggling following him the whole way. Well, the tension had been broken.

Finger guns? Really?

At least neither his brother nor Olivia was anywhere nearby. He'd never live it down.

AVERY

The cold air in the walk-in helped kick Avery's brain out of whatever mud seeing Nick had stuck it in. Thank goodness. That had been... painfully awkward, but giggling about his finger guns had relieved a lot of her tension. It was hard to feel like everything was too serious when Nick was doing finger guns.

Running into him, having him touch her, had brought up her new awareness of him and the change in their relationship, and she'd basically frozen. Hadn't known what to say. How to act.

Their relationship outside of the restaurant had changed so fundamentally, so intimately. They'd agreed they wouldn't change things in the restaurant, but how was that possible when things *were* different between them? Yeah. She hadn't really thought this through. Kinda too late to go back, though. On her break, she'd checked her phone and seen the email from Olivia confirming she'd be Nick's partner for his class.

Not that Avery wanted to go back.

Going forward and skipping the awkward phase to get to where they were comfortable working together again, without the tension and not knowing how to interact with each other, sounded pretty great. If only.

Picking up the big jug of mirepoix at the front of the shelf, Avery checked the expiration date—she knew she didn't need to since Nick had just done inventory, but it was second nature—and hefted it onto her hip, holding it with one arm. On her way back to the kitchen, she was surprised when Josie stepped out in front of her.

"Hey, are you okay?" The very real concern on Josie's face was confusing. Shouldn't she be?

"Uh, yeah? Why?"

"You're not in trouble with Chef? It seemed like you were in trouble last night." Normally blonde and bubbly, Josie shifted back and forth on her feet, her brow furrowed in worry.

Blinking, Avery thought back to the night before and how much

Josie would have been able to see of her and Nick in the booth—Nick coming out and kicking Domi and Rae to the bar, Nick with a file folder he didn't open in front of Josie, Nick stalking back to the kitchen after what had probably looked like a pretty intense conversation where they talked very low... Okay, yeah, she could see how Josie had come to the conclusion something might be wrong.

"Oh, I'm good, thank you." She smiled at the server, who looked simultaneously relieved and disappointed. Josie was a busybody, and Avery had heard some of the male servers say she had crazy eyes. She had always had the sense Josie liked her but also liked gossip, and Avery wasn't sure which one she liked more. "Nick and I just had a few things to talk about, but I'm not in trouble with him."

"Perfect Avery in trouble with Nick?" Chad, one of the fry cooks and possibly Avery's least favorite member of the staff, sauntered down the hall toward them. "Doubtful. Nick would never be disappointed in Avery." The way he said it made it sound like a bad thing.

"Nobody asked you," Josie snapped as Chad passed them. He sneered at her while his gaze dropped to where her shirt was unbuttoned, showing a bit of cleavage. Since they were between shifts, Josie hadn't buttoned up or put on her tie yet.

Chad was a middle-aged white guy, ambitious like everyone else in the Marquis kitchen, but he was also an ass and tended to be lazy. She often got the sense he thought he should be higher on the line because of his age and experience, even though he wasn't as good a cook as many of the other chefs. Not to mention, the whole being an ass thing. A team player, he was not, and the way he was looking at Josie, who was in her early twenties, made Avery want to kick him in his balls. Avery scowled at him, not that he noticed. He completely ignored her as he passed, which was about par for the course.

As much as he could ignore her, he did, even when she was the one running the kitchen. He worked marginally better with Lloyd, the other sous chef, probably because Lloyd was older than him and a man.

Wrinkling her nose, Josie stared after him. "Ugh, he's so gross."

While she couldn't argue, Avery hoped Chad hadn't heard Josie's statement. It might be true, but she didn't want to deal with the clash of personalities, especially on the weekend when tempers would already be high because of how busy the kitchen was. Chad would never mess with the food, but that didn't stop him from messing with the servers.

"Come on, let's get back to work," she said, walking down the hall and hoping Josie would follow. Thankfully, she did.

Returning to the kitchen proper, Avery lugged the jug of mirepoix to Alice, who was on sauté.

"Thanks." Glancing up, Alice flashed her a quick grin, and Avery relaxed. If Chad was one of her least favorite staff members to work with, Alice was one of her favorites. She was also in her forties, but unlike Chad, she was meticulous and proactive about her work, which was why she was on sauté.

"You took your braids out. I like the puffs." Avery studied the little poofy knobs decorating the top of Alice's head in lieu of the braids.

"Yeah, my scalp needed a rest. I might do something different next time. We'll see."

"Can't wait." She always enjoyed seeing the styles Alice experimented with.

"Avery, I need you over here," Nick called from the counter. He was bent over a piece of paper, probably whatever he'd thought up for tomorrow night's special.

"Yes, Chef," Avery said, immediately turning. It didn't occur to her until a moment later, she had answered him naturally, with none of the awkwardness from the walk-in. As long as she wasn't thinking, everything was totally normal.

Good to know.

NICK

Thankfully, the shift wasn't a total disaster when it came to him and Avery. She didn't mention the finger guns, he didn't do them again, and both of them settled into their normal routine while everyone else was looking on. Maybe a little more flirtatious than their normal routine, but not enough that anyone would notice.

However, their normal banter was tinged with the awareness the tension between them had already been satisfied once... and they could absolutely do it again tonight if they wanted to. Should he ask her? He didn't want to presume, but he absolutely wanted to do it again, and again, and again...

On the other hand, weekends were also the most exhausting shifts, and they'd be starting class on Monday.

As the shift wound down, he kept shooting her glances. He couldn't tell if she was ignoring him or deliberately making sure he couldn't catch her eye, but so far, she wasn't looking at him. She was focused on the checklist in her hand.

Nick stepped to the side, coming a little closer. A little closer. A little closer.

He bumped her hip with his.

Lifting her head from the clipboard, she finally looked at him with what was probably supposed to be a stern expression, but she couldn't quite hide her smile.

"Yes? Can I help you?" Her lips pressed together, only twitching a little, her hazel eyes dancing with amusement.

"Are you done? I want to talk over a few things... in the back office."

When her expression changed slightly to more repressive, he realized how it sounded, then shrugged. It was hardly the first time he'd said something similar to her, though it sounded far more suggestive now and less business-like, but oh, well.

"Give me five, and I'll meet you back there," she said, shaking her head, seeming to realize if she made a big deal out of his request, it would look more suspicious, not less. It wasn't like they'd never had a meeting post-shift in the office.

Nick absolutely would not do something at work with a co-worker. Probably.

No, definitely.

Too much risk of being overheard. The gossip around here was lethal. Everyone knew when two of the servers had hooked up in the bathroom between shifts last month. Those that had missed that day of work were filled in within twenty-four hours.

If he was going to keep his promise to Avery about leaving their relationship outside the restaurant, nothing could happen in the office.

He *was* going to take the opportunity to ask her privately if she wanted to be private somewhere else together.

❦ 9 ❦

Walking back toward the office, Avery tried to settle her nerves. Chances were, Nick wanted to talk about something to do with the shift. Or maybe have a private moment with her, but considering it was a shared office, she didn't think so.

As she approached the ice machine, Alanna suddenly burst out from the side of it, her face flaming bright red. Jumping back in surprise, Avery put her hand over her pounding heart. It wasn't uncommon for the servers to be back here, but she literally hadn't seen Alanna.

"Hi, Avery!" Alanna's voice was high, squeakier than normal, and she quickly rushed past Avery, headed back to the kitchen. What had gotten into her?

A second later, Avery realized exactly what had happened when she took two more steps and saw Jonathan, another server who was incredibly handsome with black hair and devastating blue eyes, leaning against the ice machine. He grinned at Avery.

"Hi, Chef."

"Hi, Jonathan." Shaking her head, Avery hoped Alanna knew what she was getting into, not just a workplace romance, but with Jonathan. He'd already been through Josie and another one of the servers, Delia. Delia seemed to have hooked up with Roger since then, but she still had eyes on Jonathan when she thought no one was paying attention.

Not my business.

That was another reason she didn't want everyone to know about her and Nick. When Jonathan had been dating Delia, everyone had known it. When he'd broken up with her and moved on to Josie, everyone had known about that, too. She'd actually thought Delia might quit for a while, but she'd stuck it out.

Funny enough, Delia and Josie had teamed up. After Jonathan broke up with Josie, almost overnight, they'd gone from mortal enemies to supportive sisters. Everyone in the restaurant had born witness to all of it, and all had opinions about it, which were often shared loudly.

Yeah. No, thank you. Avery did not need or want people watching her romance succeed or fail and didn't need to hear their opinions about it. Especially since she and Nick had the slightly more complicated position of him being her boss. When the servers hooked up, they were on equal footing. Things would be a lot more problematic if one of them got involved with a manager.

Yeah, maybe stop thinking about that.

She and Nick were different. They'd already agreed to keep work and relationship separate. There would be no between-shift bathroom sex with this chef. The very idea made her shiver. Marquis' bathrooms were kept pretty clean, but still. Not for her.

Knocking on the door, she opened it. Another reason nothing would happen in this office. She was hardly the only one with that habit, and locking the door would be suspicious as hell.

Sitting behind the desk, Nick looked up and grinned when he saw her. Avery shut the door behind her.

"Hey there," he said, getting to his feet and coming around the desk. Her eyes widened as he approached.

"What do you think you're doing?" she asked, putting her hands up in front of her when she realized he was coming in for a kiss.

Dark eyebrows rose quizzically. "Well, I was going to give you a kiss."

"Nope." She crossed her arms over her chest, shaking her head. "We said we weren't doing that."

"I've kissed you in the restaurant before," he pointed out, a smug smile playing on his lips. "It's not new."

"Nice try." Avery couldn't help smiling as she shook her head again. Maybe if she hadn't just walked by Jonathan and Alanna doing exactly that... but she had, and nope. It had been okay before she and Nick talked about keeping their relationship out of Marquis, but they'd had the conversation, and she was sticking to it.

"What did you want to meet about?"

⚜

NICK

Would a real Dom insist? Or sweep her into his arms and kiss her, anyway?

Nick didn't know, so he decided not to risk it since she seemed serious, despite the smile on her face. Ah, well, it had been worth a shot. He would have liked a kiss, but he understood.

"I wanted to see if you want to get together tonight... outside of the restaurant." He winked at her.

Avery's cheeks turned pink, which was damn cute, as her hand swept along her hair as if trying to smooth down the flyaways from her blonde ponytail. They flattened for a moment before drifting back up again.

"Oh, um... Yes. If you want to."

"Oh, I want to," he murmured, letting his gaze move up and down her body. It didn't matter that she was still wearing her baggy chef pants and coat. He knew exactly what was under them. "Your place or mine?"

"Mine." Pursing her lips to hide her smile, she turned around, shaking her head and muttering, "We're taking a shower first this time."

That sounded good. Get nice and clean, so they could get down and dirty.

"Works for me." Then he did something he'd wanted to do for months—he reached out and smacked her ass.

Avery jumped and spun around, her lips popping open in shock. Nick grinned at her and waited as they faced off for a long moment, Avery's cheeks getting pinker and pinker.

He wasn't sure what she would have eventually said, but he never found out because the door opened, and Gareth, the front-of-house manager for the evening, stepped into the office. The oldest of the managers, probably in his fifties, had salt-and-pepper hair with a grey beard, dark brown eyes, and a bit of a belly, though he was still in pretty good shape.

"Oh, hey, guys," he said, glancing up from his phone for a second before turning his attention back down to whatever he was looking at. Thankfully, his distraction meant he didn't see anything weird going on between Nick and Avery, even though Avery had jumped about a foot in the air and was bright red.

"Hey, Gareth. How are things? I mean you. I mean, how was tonight?"

Wow. Avery was terrible at this. Nick stared at her. Even Gareth finally lifted his head, his forehead wrinkled in confusion.

"Uh, excuse me, I gotta go. Exhausted." Avery darted out the door, swiftly closing it behind her.

Slowly, Gareth turned his head to look at Nick, his eyebrows raising. Their gazes met, and Nick crossed his arms over his chest, keeping his expression blank. He had absolutely no idea what he could say. It felt like anything would only make Avery's behavior seem more suspicious.

After a moment, Gareth coughed and looked down at his phone again, heading for the desk.

"I am Jon Snow," he murmured. In other words, he knew nothing.

"Thanks," Nick said before also vacating the office. Avery had already fled, but that was okay. He'd meet her at her place.

AVERY

After fleeing the scene, Avery went straight to her car, silently vowing to get better at acting. She'd done well during her actual shift. She'd only been thrown off because Nick had given her that little swat right before Gareth had come in. Who wouldn't have been flustered, given the circumstances?

She wasn't mad at Nick, exactly. At least, she hadn't been until Gareth had opened the door. If she was honest, she'd been turned on, which was why she hadn't been able to find the words to rebuke him. She still should have been mad. It had been a little easier to summon that emotion after Gareth walked in, although her embarrassment overwhelmed pretty much everything else.

"Argh." She banged her head against the top of the steering wheel to clear it. Not that it actually worked, but strangely she did feel a little better. Putting the car in reverse, she got out of there, making sure she was gone before Nick followed her out. Just in case anyone saw them leaving at the same time.

Well, hello there, paranoia. You look like fun.

Making it home in record time, she gave Rae a call as she was walking in the door. She needed to talk to someone who could talk some sense into her, and since Rae didn't have a kid or boyfriend, Avery figured she was more likely to be free than Domi. It made her feel like a terrible person, but she didn't want to infringe on Domi's night, especially because it was already pretty late.

"Hey, girl, what's up?" Rae always got straight to business when she answered the phone.

"Hey... I..." Avery's voice trailed off. She was full of worry and tension, but now that she wanted to tell Rae about it, she found she couldn't find the words.

"Everything okay?" The concern in Rae's voice came through clearly as if she'd been relaxing and was sitting up. "Nick didn't fuck up already, did he?"

That startled a laugh out of Avery.

"No... at least, well, maybe sorta? But not really."

"Very descriptive. Do Domi and I need to come over?"

"No, no," Avery said quickly, sitting on her couch. Rubbing her forehead, she leaned back and let her head drop. That felt good. "Nick's on his way over. He's following me home from the restaurant."

There was a tiny pause.

"Okay, so that's a good thing, right?"

"It is. I... before we left, we had a moment in the office. He gave me a little swat when I was heading out the door, and it surprised the hell out of me, but it was kinda hot, you know? I jumped, then turned around and stared at him. I couldn't think of what to say or do, so we stood there, staring at each other, then one of our managers opened the door and came in, and I freaked out, so I rambled at him... kinda like I'm doing to you right now, so I'm sure if he hadn't been suspicious something was going on between Nick and me, he definitely was after that." Avery took a deep breath, feeling lightheaded. That had been a hell of an info dump. She'd charged through it so fast, she was surprised Rae wasn't asking for a replay.

The pause this time was a lot longer. Avery nibbled on her thumbnail, waiting for Rae's reaction.

"I know you don't want anyone at work knowing, and I get that, but this manager—do you think he's likely to tell anyone?"

"Well... no." A little piece of the weight pressing down on her lifted. Gareth wasn't like that; none of the managers were. Though she was pretty sure they talked among themselves, they didn't gossip the way the others did. They only shared information with each other when it might affect the front-of-house staff—like which girl Jonathan was dating that week. They didn't bother worrying about the kitchen, leaving that up to Nick.

She relaxed a little more.

Even if Gareth realized something was going on with her and Nick, he had no reason to tell anyone, not even the other managers.

"Now that you've been in the situation once, you'll think of a million other ways you could have handled it, so if it happens again, you'll be prepared."

Rae made it sound so reasonable, Avery nodded along as Rae spoke before coming to her senses and shaking her head.

"It better not happen again. I'm going to tell Nick—spankings on the second floor only." The words had no sooner left her mouth than there was a knock on the door. Avery jumped to her feet, heart leaping up in her chest. "Crap, here's here."

"Go get him, girl! I'll talk to you later. We need to hang out soon."

"Definitely. Good night."

"Night!"

Hanging up the phone, Avery went to answer the door. Nick stood outside, a cocky smirk on his face. Jerk. It wasn't fair that he looked so damn good when he was arrogant.

His eyes lit up when he saw her, his face brightening, and for that one small change in his expression, she realized she would forgive a lot.

"Hello there." Stepping in, his hands cupped her face to pull her in for a kiss before she could respond.

Avery grabbed onto the front of his shirt, her lips parting beneath his as she stepped back into her apartment. The door slammed behind him.

❧ 10 ☙

NICK

It had been one hell of a weekend with Avery. They'd spent one night at her apartment, the other night at his house, and had amazing sex both nights, waking up in the morning next to each other. Eventually, they had to separate to get fresh clothes and go to work. She'd seemed a little nervous the first time Gareth came through the kitchen, but that hadn't lasted long.

Now, it was Monday and time for his first class on how to be a kinky Dominant.

There was a part of him that wanted to ask if she still thought he needed it. The sex was amazing. Did they really need the kinky stuff? He also knew that was coming from a place of fear, so he kept his mouth shut. Avery would be concerned about his wants over hers, and he didn't want her to feel like her needs weren't a priority for him. He would get over his discomfort with the class.

Walking up the stairs and seeing Avery at the top, waiting for him next to the front desk, helped. She was chatting with Freddy, who was also standing in front of the desk rather than behind it.

Both of them saw him at the same time. Freddy grinned at him, but Avery went from looking nervous to even more anxious. She clasped her hands in front of her, pressing them together as though she was trying not to squirm. Going to her, Nick reached out his hand for her to hold instead and noticed she relaxed minutely when he wrapped his fingers around hers.

"Hey, Freddy, are you part of the class?" Gossip from upstairs took a little longer to reach downstairs, and he hadn't heard that Freddy was seeing someone.

"I am. We have a hetero Domme in this class, so I volunteered as tribute." Freddy chuckled, then corrected himself. "Well, technically, she's a switch, but she's already taken the submissive class, so she's learning how to be a Domme."

"Uh-huh," Nick nodded his head, pretending he knew the terms. Domme was what Olivia called herself, so he knew that meant a female Dominant. He hadn't heard of a switch before, but from the context, he guessed it meant someone who could go back and forth between being submissive and dominant. He wasn't sure how that worked, but maybe he'd get a chance to see.

"Freddy was just telling me it's a pretty small class," Avery said with a smile, squeezing his fingers, trying to reassure him.

"Yup, three men and one woman."

"Wait, does the woman mean that Olivia will come in to teach?" Nick asked, his stomach suddenly churning. When he'd asked her, she'd told him she had mostly turned the classes over to others and wouldn't be there for much more than the first class. Definitely not for any of the experience classes where he'd been learning what certain things felt like for the submissive. That had been before he'd known there would be a woman in the class.

"No." Freddy chuckled. "Master Law and Mistress Julie will handle the classes. Though I'm sure we'll see Olivia. She might make herself scarcer since you're in this class. I know she won't want to make you uncomfortable."

He could only hope so because he was pretty sure Olivia delighted in making people uncomfortable sometimes.

AVERY

The class comprised some people Avery recognized and some she didn't. She and Nick went in ahead of Freddy, who would be at the front desk until the last person arrived, so someone was there to welcome them. They found a semi-circle of chairs set around the circular stage in the middle of the room. All the lights were on and bright, very different from when she'd been here to watch the show.

A young woman sat on the far side of the semi-circle, in the very last chair, her head jerking up to look at them as they walked in. Beautiful, probably in her mid-twenties, her tanned skin and dark hair and eyes made Avery think she was probably Latina. That she was looking straight at Avery made her feel weird about sitting away from her, so Avery went to the chair next to her.

"Hi, mind if I sit here?" She gestured at the chair, aware of Nick hovering behind her. Given the choice, he probably would have sat on the other side of the circle, far away from the woman, but Avery felt rewarded when the woman smiled at her, relaxing a little.

"Sure. I'm Iris." She held out her hand, and Avery took it.

"Avery, and this is Nick." Avery shook Iris' hand and sat down next to her, allowing Nick to shake her hand as well before she had a thought. "Are you paired with someone? Should I move over?"

Iris shook her head and sighed, rolling her eyes. It made her look younger than she had a moment ago, more like an unruly teenager than a grown woman, one with a chip on her shoulder and something to prove.

"No, I'm here because Master Patrick thinks I need some more experience being submissive, and assisting with the newbie Doms will help me get a better perspective." She shrugged a shoulder, her body language screaming 'casual and indifferent' so hard, it was obvious she cared a lot more about what Master Patrick thought than she wanted anyone to know. Avery was pretty sure she must be talking about Patrick Murphy, the owner of Stronghold and one of the three owners of Marquis.

From what Avery knew, he was pretty hands-on in the club, but she'd only met him once or twice and had been intimidated as hell by the sheer aura of confidence and power that surrounded him; she'd barely been able to talk. The familiar way Iris spoke of him had her blinking in surprise, especially since she was pretty sure Iris wasn't the switch Freddy had mentioned.

"Do you know him?" she couldn't help asking. On her other side, Nick slid his fingers through hers, probably wondering why she was talking to this woman they didn't know, but Avery couldn't help it. As soon as their eyes had met, she'd felt how alone Iris was, and she hadn't wanted her to keep feeling that way.

"Yeah. He's friends with my brother, Andrew, who is also kinky and belongs to the club. It's one massively awkward situation," Iris smirked. Clearly, she was unbothered, but Avery bet it was awkward for both Iris' sibling and Master Patrick if they were friends. Master Patrick was in his thirties, so she was guessing Iris was a younger sister.

Yeah, she could only imagine how awkward that would be. Her own sister didn't know that she was into kink, and Avery was happy to keep it that way. Telling the one friend at home had been more than enough. Even when she'd lived in Atlanta, she'd kept her kink acquaintances separate from her friends, and she'd never been in a serious enough relationship that she would have to introduce them.

"Ha, sounds like my situation," Nick said, finally leaning forward to engage with Iris. "My brother belongs to the clubs, too, with his girlfriend."

"Yeah, but that's not the same as knowing your little sister likes to be tied up and spanked," Iris smirked. Avery got the feeling Iris was putting up a bit of a front, but she still liked her.

"No, instead, it's my older brother who likes to be tied up and spanked," Nick said, correcting Iris' obvious assumption that Luke was the Dom.

Iris' eyes widened in surprise, mouth popping open. Before she could respond, the door opened behind them, and the three of them turned to look.

A very handsome black man sauntered in. Shaved head, tall, thin but muscular, he was wearing a t-shirt that said, 'One Lab Accident Away from Being a Supervillain.' His gaze swept over all three of them, and he smiled, his expression barely faltering.

"Hey, everyone."

NICK

Feeling a little weird just sitting there as the other man approached, Nick got to his feet and held out his hand.

"Hi, I'm Nick."

"I'm Q. Nice to meet you." He moved in front of the seat next to Nick. Sitting down, Q followed before leaning forward to look at the women.

"This is my girlfriend Avery, and that's Iris."

Next to him, Avery jumped in her seat, startled. Amused, Nick shot her a look, and she gave him a wide-eyed stare before waving at Q. Chuckling at her reaction—what else was he supposed to call her— he took her hand in his.

"Hi, nice to meet you." As Avery greeted him, Iris murmured her own hello. "We're talking about how we knew about the class. Nick and Iris both have brothers who are part of the club. What about you?"

If Q was perturbed by the get-to-know-you jump into conversation, he didn't show it. Leaning forward, he rested his elbows on his knees so he could easily see both Avery and Iris.

"I have a friend who goes to Stronghold, and eventually, she convinced me I should check it out."

"Just a friend?" Nick asked, a little curious.

"Just a friend." Q grinned. There might have been a flash of something in his expression, but if there was, he suppressed it quickly. "She's married and has a kid with a guy she met at Stronghold."

They weren't able to talk much more when the door behind them opened again. Nick got to his feet, Q only half a second behind him. It was kind of curious Avery and Iris didn't feel the need to stand, but for him, it was both ingrained manners and wanting to see who was coming in to assess them. If he'd been sitting down, he would have felt like he was at a disadvantage.

A blonde woman walked in. Statuesque and curvy, she was dressed in a form-fitting blue dress, with a wide red belt that cinched in her waist and red pumps on her feet, giving her another couple inches of height. She was vaguely familiar, and Nick realized she'd been around Marquis before it opened when the first submissive class was held here —which meant she was probably the switch Freddy had told him and Avery about.

Nick couldn't remember her name, but before he could say anything, she came to a grinding halt, her eyes narrowing. Next to him, Q stiffened.

"You! What are you doing here?" Q barked out the question in a completely different tone than he'd been using. His relaxed demeanor had disappeared, and he had straightened to his full height.

The woman glared at him.

"Excuse me, Quinton? I'm a *member*. What are *you* doing here?"

"Quinton?" Iris murmured behind Nick, sounding amused.

"Don't call me that, Samwise," Q snapped. If anything, the blonde glared harder, putting her hands on her hips.

"Then don't call me that stupid nickname. We're not in high school anymore. Grow up." She muttered something under her breath that suspiciously sounded like 'ass.'

"I take it you two know each other," Nick interjected. Beside him, he could feel Avery growing agitated. Conflict didn't bother him the same way it did her, but he wanted her to be comfortable. Seeing Q and... whatever her name was, going at it the moment she came in the door would distress Avery.

As if remembering he wasn't alone, Q abruptly turned around and sat down, putting his back to the blonde.

"Hi, I'm Nick." He waved since the blonde didn't look like she was coming any closer. "This is my girlfriend Avery, and that's Iris."

"I'm single and ready to mingle," Iris quipped, getting a smile from both Avery and the blonde, though the blonde's seemed a little forced.

"I'm Samantha, but I go by Sam," the blonde replied, giving herself a little shake. She walked over to the other side of the circle to the last chair on that side, as far away from Q as she could get, then sat down primly on the seat, crossing her legs.

From his vantage point, Nick could see Q blatantly checking out her legs before averting his gaze. Whatever was going on between them, he was pretty sure it was more than just friction.

"Welcome to the party." Happily grinning in her seat, Iris seemed the only one unbothered by the odd little showdown between Q and Sam. Leaning back, she crossed her legs crossed like Sam, but her boot heel was bouncing up and down, jiggling as if she had too much energy to hold inside.

Thankfully, before they had to find something to say, the door behind them opened again.

This time, Nick didn't bother to jump up. He turned in his seat... and immediately wished he had gotten to his feet.

"Okay, everybody's here!" Freddy's cheerful voice preceded him and the last two arrivals, a stunningly beautiful redhead named Morgan. Nick recognized her because she'd recently started working at the front desk of Marquis' second floor. An absolute giant of a man, who he'd never seen, followed her. Nick fought back the urge to jump to his feet, so he didn't feel as if he was being loomed over, but it probably wouldn't have helped, anyway.

Nick was six feet and one inch and knew Freddy was only an inch or two shorter than him. Freddy only came up to the man's shoulder, so the guy had to be at least six-four, maybe more, and he was beefy as hell. There was no other word for it. He looked like the Mountain from Game of Thrones.

"Go sit down," Freddy said cheerfully, pointing to the three empty seats between Q and Sam. A frown flitted over his face for a moment before it disappeared, probably because it was clear Sam was on the outside of the group. They hadn't meant for it to be that way, but it looked bad. Nick winced inwardly, though he wasn't sure what he could have done.

"I'll be right back with Master Law and Mistress Julie." Freddy waved at them, then disappeared through the door. Sudden tightness clenched Nick's chest as Morgan and the massive Dom went to take their seats. Not because of them, but because he still didn't know what to expect once the class started.

He hated not knowing what to expect.

11

AVERY

With all the drama that had almost erupted between Q and Sam, everything else was almost anticlimactic after that. When Morgan and Connor introduced themselves, was it her imagination, or did Nick squeeze her hand a little tighter? Maybe because she couldn't stop staring at Connor. She'd just never seen someone so tall and muscular in real life. He was built like a linebacker or maybe a book cover model... for a really raunchy book.

They barely got introductions out of the way before Freddy returned with Master Law and Mistress Julie. Avery sat up a little straighter in her seat as the teachers came in. Yeah, technically, it wasn't her class, but she still wanted to make a good impression, and both of them were intimidating as hell.

Avery had met them both Master before. Master Law's real name was Lawrence, and he was a lawyer, which had led to the submissives dubbing him Master Law. From what Domi and Rae told her, he'd tried to fight it but had eventually given in rather than attempting to punish every submissive in the club.

Actually, she was surprised he hadn't been able to stamp it out. Not that he wasn't intimidating. He was. A bit taller than her, Filipino, a little grizzled, even though she was pretty sure he was only in his early forties, when he scowled, it was enough to make her want to hit the floor with her knees. There was just something too catchy about the nickname—and it fit him. Domi and Rae had told her he had a bit of a reputation as a hardass. Rather than leathers or fetwear, he was dressed in a dark blue suit with a striped blue-and-cream tie, which would fit right in at his office.

Mistress Julie was shorter than Avery by several inches, in her early thirties, and was as scary as Olivia. Her Japanese ancestry was clear in her features and the incredible length of long, straight black hair that hung nearly to her waist. Rae had whispered that when Mistress Julie put her hair in a ponytail, smart submissives ran for cover.

When she patted Freddy's cheek and smiled at him before he went to sit down in the last empty chair, he looked as though he might melt of happiness on the spot. Unlike Master Law, she had chosen to go full fet-wear, dressed in a shiny and slick catsuit that gleamed under the lights. Except for a large keyhole to show off a hint of cleavage, it covered her from her neck to her knee-high, laced-up boots with a spiked heel.

When the two Dominants got on the stage, looking over the semicircle of students in front of them, Avery pressed her hands and legs together and sat very, very still, clutching Nick's hand between hers.

If she had any doubts whether Nick was a Dom, it was cleared up when he glanced at her, clearly confused why she was freaking out. Obviously, they weren't having the same reaction to the Dominants in front of them.

"Hello everyone, and welcome to the Introduction to Dominance course provided by Stronghold and Marquis." Mistress Julie's voice was cool and composed, but she smiled like a shark, her dark eyes glinting with sadistic anticipation.

Nick was stupid if he wasn't at least a little scared.

NICK

"You have suspension down as a hard limit. Why is that?" Nick asked, trying to keep his eyes focused on the woman in front of him rather than where Avery was sitting with the massive Dom.

Even though she was his partner for the class, for today's activity—practicing getting to know their partner and talking about limits—the submissives were rotating through each of the Dominants so they could have four chances to work on communication with different people.

Not that Iris seemed submissive to him.

She was sitting back in the chair, now facing him, arms crossed over her chest, one booted foot bouncing up and down where her ankle was resting on her knee. Everything about her body language screamed, 'I don't want to be here.' Fair enough. Nick didn't want to be here either—at least, not with her.

"I don't like being tied up and hung out to dry," she said sardonically. It took Nick's brain a moment to register what she said, then he chuckled, yanking his gaze back to her. A tiny smile played on her lips. "Having trouble concentrating, Sir?"

"A little." He wasn't ashamed to admit it.

He was learning how to be a Dom for Avery and with Avery. Not to have to watch her be interviewed and talk about her sexual likes and dislikes with three other Dominants, even if one of them was a hetero woman who would have no interest in her. He was supposed to be giving this his all, and it wasn't fair to Iris or the other submissives to let his attention be so easily swayed—especially if he was going to be the best student in the class.

"I'm sorry for my distraction. So, you don't like being tied up at all or only if you're going to be suspended."

The way Iris' lips pressed together made him think it was more the former, but he wasn't sure she would admit it. Bondage was not listed as a hard limit on her sheet. She shrugged her shoulder as if she didn't care.

"It's not a huge turn-on for me, but it's fine if that's what you want to do."

Hmmm, definitely something there she didn't want to talk about. For the first time, Nick understood some of the reading material that had been sent home with him. His instincts were telling him there was something Iris was hiding, and even though she wasn't his submissive, and he had his own submissive, he wanted to get to the bottom of it.

It also made him wonder if there were things Avery had on her list that she wasn't talking about. She would be the last interview he did. Master Law and Mistress Julie had explained they wanted everyone to talk last to the partner they'd be working with the most, so they had some practice beforehand.

Inwardly, Nick had scoffed at the idea. He knew Avery so well at this point, he wasn't worried about interviewing her. Now, he was wondering if maybe he'd made that judgment a little too soon.

Part of him wanted to keep questioning Iris, but he wasn't going to be her Dom, and it wasn't his place. That was something else Master Law and Mistress Julie had made clear. Issues were for long-term partners to work on together, not short-term play partners. If you started working on an issue with a submissive, you needed to see it through.

That would not be Nick with Iris, but he hoped she'd find someone because there was definitely something going on there.

"Okay." He looked down at the list again. "You've marked figging as a soft limit. Any reason? Do you have something against ginger?"

Iris groaned, her head falling back. "This is so fucking awkward."

As if by magic, Master Law appeared beside them. Iris' head snapped back up, and she straightened in her seat, her jiggling boot coming to an abrupt halt. Damn. Nick wanted to learn how to do that.

"Is there a problem here, Miss Baez?" Master Law's deep voice was silky smooth and lethally controlled. Nick imagined that was how he sounded in the courtroom.

"Yes, talking about all this stuff with a stranger is really awkward." Iris lifted her chin defiantly, but Nick noticed she only met Master Law's gaze for a moment before her eyes dropped to the top of his tie.

"It is." Master Law nodded. "It's also necessary if you plan on participating in scenes with strangers. Don't you think so?" There was something in his voice that made Nick think there was a hidden meaning behind the question.

"Yeah, yeah, I know." Surprisingly, Iris looked at Nick apologetically, sitting up even straighter, her hands dropping into her lap, already appearing more engaged. Dammit. Why hadn't he been able to do that? Had he even been trying? He needed to get his shit together before Avery made her way back around to him. "Sorry, Master Nick. You were saying?"

Nick coughed.

"Uh, is there a reason you have figging as a soft limit?"

This time when Iris shrugged with one shoulder, the attitude behind it was entirely different from previously.

"It sounds really painful?" The lilt in her voice made it sound like she wasn't actually sure of what she was saying.

"Is that a question or a statement?" Nick's lips twitched, and he swore he heard Master Law chuckle before the other man turned away.

Iris scowled at him again, but her posture didn't change, even as Master Law moved back toward where Mistress Julie was standing on the stage.

"I hope you didn't list figging as a limit, so you can find out for yourself," she muttered.

That wiped the urge to smile right out of Nick.

❧

AVERY

Finally settling down across from Nick again, Avery tried not to feel too nervous, but it was hard. Talking to the other Dominants had been playacting. It had also been kind of fun, getting to know them a little and helping them when they stumbled over questions.

Samantha had had the easiest time of it, probably because she'd already been through the submissive training class. Q had stumbled over a few things, and she was pretty sure he'd blushed a few times, but he'd gotten through it. The massive Dom, Connor, was the one who had struggled the most. Avery had wanted to hug him when he'd sagged at the end of their turn, blushing a furious red and rubbing his face like he couldn't believe some words that had just come out of his mouth. He was like a massive, muscly teddy bear, and it was so freaking adorable. She wouldn't be surprised if he turned out to be a Daddy Dom, service Dom, or something along those lines. Stern but with a super squishy center. Once he got past his embarrassment, that was. She was looking forward to watching it happen.

This class was going to be more enjoyable than she'd thought. Though, sitting with Nick, she remembered it was also going to be enjoyable for an entirely different reason.

Sitting in the chair across from him was completely different from the others. He was just as new, but she'd been playacting with them, knowing the questions would lead nowhere, not really caring what they thought of her. None of that applied to how she felt about Nick.

"Hello." The half-smile on his lips was both welcoming and full of amusement. "Enjoying your evening so far?"

"It's been pretty good. I think it might have just gotten even better," she said flirtatiously, handing over her list of limits. His smile changed from half to a full as he took it from her, glancing at it. Avery had already shown it to him, but they hadn't really talked about it. Not the way she had discussed her limits with the other Doms tonight.

She wasn't sure what to expect.

Clearing his throat, Nick straightened in his seat.

"For the most part, we have a lot of our limits in common, but I want to make sure I understand why you have the limits you have so I don't accidentally trigger anything." He glanced up at her to check to see what she thought, and Avery agreed, silently impressed. She was pretty sure before tonight's class, he wouldn't have brought it up.

"You have verbal humiliation marked as a hard limit—what does that mean to you?"

"Oh... uh..." Avery blinked. That was something the others hadn't asked. They'd verified she didn't want to do name-calling, but they hadn't asked what she meant by it. "No name-calling. Um, things like that."

"Can you be more specific?" Nick's dark eyebrows raised slightly. "'Things like that' isn't very specific. When I talked to some of the other submissives, the examples they gave me weren't only name-calling. Would you object to being publicly called a naughty girl? Or a bad girl?"

"That's fine." Heat flushed through her from top to bottom. "I guess it's more like... anything designed to make me feel bad... well, except..." She stumbled over her words, realizing that wasn't specific enough either. Crap. She hadn't realized until this moment that she'd never tried to explain it to anyone. "I know that 'naughty girl' and 'bad girl' seem like they might be that way but... anything that's truly insulting. Like telling me, I'm naughty or bad in a scene doesn't feel like an insult. It feels like part of the scene. Telling me I'm bad for liking what I like or anything like that..."

She stared down at her hands, her fingers twisting in her lap. Everything inside her felt tight and unhappy at even saying it out loud. The voice in her head sounded exactly like Shannon when Avery had tried to talk to her friend about kink. It cramped her stomach and made her feel like crying and running. Ugh. She hadn't even realized the reason she didn't like verbal humiliation was it was too close to the things Shannon had actually said to her.

A large, warm hand covered hers and squeezed.

"It's okay, Avery. I think I understand the difference now. If I'm not sure about something I want to say in a scene, I'll check with you first."

"Thank you." She shook off the heavy emotions pushing at her and refocused on Nick.

"We'll talk about why you had that reaction eventually, though."

"It's because of some things a friend said to me when I told her about being into kink," Avery said hurriedly. She did not want him to think it was something bigger than it was. Not liking verbal humiliation wasn't uncommon, though she was aware she was a little more sensitive than some subs. "There's no big secret."

Nick eyed her for a moment, trying to decide whether or not she was telling the truth, then nodded.

"Okay, let's continue."

Later that night, Avery curled up against Nick's solid body, half-asleep but wanting to be as close to him as possible. He seemed to have the same thought, wrapping his arms around her and holding her close. Sleeping, she nuzzled his chest.

After the first class at Marquis, they'd both been turned on, barely making it through her door before they'd torn each other's clothes off and headed for the bedroom.

It had been vanilla sex, but she knew they'd both been thinking about all the things they'd talked through, all those 'yes' checked boxes on their limits list. A lot of her fears about Nick not actually being kinky had been soothed tonight. He might not be hands-on yet, but he was definitely into it, and she couldn't wait until they started actually *doing*.

12

AVERY

"I'm so glad you could come out tonight!" Domi bounced in the driver's seat as Avery slid into the car seat behind her, laughing at Domi's antics. Rae was in the passenger seat, looking just as excited. Both of them were dressed to go out, but not to Stronghold or Marquis.

They'd decided to have a kink-free night. It was the second Monday of Nick's Dom class, but she didn't have to partner with him tonight. Avery didn't have to work, so they were going to a local meadery. There had been a lot of breweries and wineries popping up in the area over the past few years, but meaderies were a little harder to find.

Avery loved the sweet alcohol made from honey and had heard Orchid Cellar's was good. Rae and Domi had been interested enough to join her—she thought they were indulging her rather than going for themselves and was really touched.

She hoped they'd find it worthwhile.

"I'm glad you two were willing to go try something new." Grinning at them, she smoothed the skirt of her little black dress down over her thighs. It wasn't a sexy little black dress, but it hugged her curves and made her feel good when she wore it.

"Honey, alcohol…" Rae shrugged. "Sounds like a fun combination to me." Half-turning in her seat, so she could look back at Avery as Domi pulled out to the street, following the GPS directions, she tilted her head questioningly. "Do you know what Nick's class is doing tonight? I'm glad we get to hang out, but I was hoping you'd have juicy details about what the class is like."

"Since we only get to know about the submissives class," Domi said, sounding only a little grumpy.

"We could always say we're switches like Sam." Rae looked thoughtful as if she might really consider it.

"You can, but I'm pretty sure Mitch would have something to say about that for me." Domi shook her head, her curls bouncing with the movement. Then she gave a little laugh. "Although, that could be fun, too."

"Masochists." Now it was Rae's turn to shake her head.

Avery sat in the back giggling at the two of them. She loved watching their interactions with each other. They were so similar in so many ways, yet so different in others. Rae turned her attention back to Avery.

"Sorry. So… did he tell you?"

"They're going over a lot of the basics." Avery couldn't stop from grinning, just like when she'd first asked Nick, and he'd given her the rundown. She didn't blame Rae and Domi for being curious. As excited as she was to go out tonight, a part of her was disappointed she didn't get to watch how tonight went for all the Doms. "Nipple clamps, spanking, flogging, and whips."

"Oh, man… to be a fly on the wall…" Rae shook her head. "It's not fair. The Doms got to watch and participate in our whole class, but you don't get to do the same?"

"It wouldn't be good for their authority." Domi snickered, turning onto the highway. "Mitch told me a little about their class. They really have to try every single thing they want to inflict on a submissive, and some of them don't take it all very well."

"Hey, if a Dom can respect me after I get a plug shoved up my ass, I can respect him for doing the same."

"Yeah, but it's one thing to know they did it and another thing to see it happen... especially if they don't react well." Avery was wildly curious and thought watching would be incredibly entertaining. Domi probably had a point about the effect on authority. Of course, she'd still respect Nick, but if he took it badly, and she showed any kind of amusement...

Not great for Domly authority and probably not good for subbies' bottoms.

"Bah, stop applying logic to the situation." Rae waved her hand dismissively. The sun was going down, but there was still enough light to see the twinkle in her eyes. "Anyway, how are things going at work? Still keeping things quiet?"

"Yes, and it's a lot better. No more awkward moments." Gareth had said nothing to anyone, and no one seemed to suspect. Granted, most of them were distracted by the drama swirling around Jonathan and Alanna. If anyone had wondered if George had a thing for her, it had been confirmed, and he was grumpy as hell about it. Though he wasn't nearly as bad as Josie and Delia, who were furious they'd been replaced. Avery wondered if they'd become friendly with Alanna after she and Jonathan broke up... although, he seemed pretty smitten.

Basically, no one was paying attention to what she and Nick were doing when everyone was being entertained by the front-of-house drama.

"It's been a great week. We've been taking turns sleeping over at each other's place every night."

A great week of fantastic sex, but she had to admit, she was looking forward to doing the kinky stuff with him. It was also one of the easiest relationships she'd ever been in. They worked together, left in their separate cars to whoever's place they were going, then took a shower and had something to eat before tumbling into bed and falling asleep.

Eventually, she hoped they'd go on an actual date, but at the moment, Mondays were the only nights they both had off at the same time. They had been eating breakfast and lunch together as often as possible, though they hadn't gone out anywhere.

On second thought, it might be for the best. As soon as she thought about going out with him in public, she started thinking about what would happen if they were recognized or ran into someone they knew.

Yup. Nope. Eating in was better.

❧

NICK

Standing next to Q on one side of the stage, Nick tried not to feel as though he was taking sides. Sam seemed like a perfectly nice woman. He'd just happened to arrive at the same time as Q. At least she had Connor standing with her, so she wasn't entirely alone, and she'd smiled back at Nick when he'd waved in greeting when she came in.

Of course, she and Q had glared at each other before Q had returned to the conversation he'd been having with Nick, pretending Sam didn't exist.

He really wished Avery was here. She was much better at the interpersonal relationship stuff.

Thankfully, Master Law came in a few minutes later, his expression unchanging as he took in the room dynamics. As at the last class, he was dressed in a suit. Nick wondered if he should dress up more. Samantha was also dressed as if she'd come from business-casual work, but Connor and Q were both in t-shirts, just like him. Well, Q's shirt declared he was 'Rebel Scum' with the Star Wars logo behind it, so not exactly like the plain shirts Connor and Nick were wearing, but close enough.

"Ready to get started?" Master Law asked, gesturing to the stage and the table, with apparatuses that they'd all been studiously ignoring. Not that anyone had said, "let's not look at all the stuff on the stage," but it had been an unspoken agreement.

Now that he had to look at it, Nick felt a stirring of discomfort. The past week with Avery had been amazing. Best relationship of his life, hands down. Everything had been easy. Natural. The sex was phenomenal. Did they really need to add stuff?

Stop being a chicken. You know she wants it. You need to at least try.

The last bit of his wavering resolve firmed up when the door opened a second later, and Olivia walked in with Luke, who was shirtless and wearing leather chaps and what looked like a speedo. Immediately Nick jerked his head back around and slapped his hands over his eyes.

"Uh, you okay there?" Q whispered.

"That's my brother," he groaned loud enough, Olivia chuckled. He knew it was Olivia because he knew exactly what it sounded like when she was amused at his expense.

The sadist.

"Get over it, Nick. You need to pay attention. Luke agreed to be our demonstration for the evening." Olivia's voice was far too cheerful.

Shaking his head, Nick let his hand drop. Letting her know she'd gotten under his skin would only make it worse. That was how she rolled. If he pretended he was unbothered, she'd stop ribbing him sooner. Of course, if he was actually upset about something, she wouldn't keep hassling him, but in this situation, there was no way he'd be able to pretend it was a real problem.

She was the mean older sister he'd never wanted.

Joining Master Law on the stage, Luke looked over his shoulder and winked at Nick, and at the moment, Nick realized his older brother wasn't wearing a speedo—he was wearing a banana-hammock thong. Nick made a gagging sound. Loudly.

"Alright, everyone," Master Law said, ignoring the antics going on around him. "Welcome to your first night of practice. Next week, we'll have the submissives in here for you to practice on, but tonight, you'll experience everything, so you know how it feels before you try doing it on someone else." He gestured at the four wood and leather structures arranged on the stage in front of the table. "These are spanking benches. We'll be using them today, and you'll all have a chance to be on one."

"Oh, yay..." Q muttered under his breath, quieting immediately when Olivia caught his eye and raised her eyebrows.

Connor's expression didn't change, and Sam looked completely undisturbed. Of course, she already knew what all this felt like, which made Nick wonder why she had to be here this week. Maybe to make sure she didn't miss anything or feel as if she wasn't part of the class. Or maybe she wanted the whole Dom class experience. Nick got that.

Even with the division between Q and Sam, there was still a feeling of camaraderie among all of them—especially now when they were all staring at the spanking benches, knowing they would be in the same position soon... ass up over those benches.

AVERY

Orchid Cellar Meadery was beautiful. The turn into the parking lot was a little steep because it was located at almost the top of a hill. There was the meadery building, then an actual house on the very top of the hill. Maybe where the owners lived?

The view was gorgeous. A big field and eventually, trees and greenery all around them. The sky seemed to go on forever.

"Oh, wow." Rae let out a low whistle as she stepped out of the car, looking around.

The meadery building was beautiful on the outside. It had a log cabin feel, and there was a porch with a gazebo, all of it strung with lights. Avery wanted to come out during the daytime so she could sit and really appreciate the view, maybe even watch the sunset. The last rays of lights were almost gone over the horizon, leaving them in the dark, but the meadery was lit up from within like a cheerful fairy dwelling.

"This is gorgeous," Domi said, shutting her door. "Let's go in, though, before I get eaten alive by mosquitos."

The fall air was getting chillier, but the mosquitos were still alive and biting, so neither Rae nor Avery argued with her.

The inside was as beautiful as the outside, continuing the log cabin feel but with lots of light wood, high ceilings, a gorgeous brick bar, and long tables. The wood gleamed under the lights, and what seemed like a big tree with no branches was in the middle of the room. Avery figured it must be the post to help hold everything up, but it looked like an actual tree, growing up through the middle of the building, which was really cool. Behind the bar, they could see bottles and bottles of all the different mead.

Several people were standing at one end of the bar, and one of the tables was taken up, but otherwise, it was pretty empty, which was expected for a Monday night. An extremely tall, slender man with dark blond hair that fell to his shoulders was standing behind the bar, talking to the other group, gave them a friendly wave when they walked in.

Going over, they stood against the bar since there were no stools. It was really a tasting bar. Domi scowled. At her height, it was uncomfortably high.

"Should have worn higher heels," she muttered, making Rae snicker. The knee-high boots she had on gave her an extra inch of height, but that wasn't enough to make a difference with the bar.

"We can sit at a table as soon as we get our mead," Avery said apologetically.

As if he'd heard her, the very tall man behind the bar walked over to them, still smiling. Avery's head tipped back. Holy crap. He was as tall as that Dom in the new class. A lot skinnier, but just as tall.

"Hello, welcome to Orchid Cellar. Have you been here before?"

"Nope, but I love mead. These two have never had any before."

"Well, you are in for a treat." His eyes lit up, and he practically rubbed his hand together. "Let me get you the tasting menu, and we can get started."

Avery couldn't help but grin back, sucked in by his obvious enthusiasm. It was clear he loved mead and couldn't wait to talk to them about it.

"He seems fun," Domi whispered without a hint of sarcasm. Apparently, she felt the same as Avery. "Does he have to be so tall, though?"

"Wait till you see the Dom who was in class last week," Avery whispered. She didn't think anyone cared about what they were saying, but she still didn't want to say 'Dom' too loudly in a public place. Just in case. "He's just as tall, but muscles everywhere, like a bodybuilder or something."

"Ooooh, scary?" Rae asked, perking up a bit. On Avery's other side, Domi rolled her eyes.

"Not really. I mean, when you first see him, yes, but he's a total teddy bear."

"Still... that has possibilities..." Rae tapped her finger against her lips, but their conversation cut off as the bartender returned, holding a small stack of menus and a bottle.

"This taste is on the house, so you know what you're getting into," he said, handing over the menus and picking up three glasses.

Ha. Talk about a metaphor. That's exactly what Nick was getting tonight. Avery hoped he was enjoying it as much as she was about to enjoy herself.

❧ 13 ❧

"**M**other fucker!"

Nipple clamps fucking hurt!

He glanced over at his brother, who was standing and watching with vast amusement on his face. Luke not only was wearing his clamps without protest, he'd *been* wearing them for the past few minutes while the students received theirs. Olivia had taken care of Connor and Q, while Nick had opted to have Master Law apply his.

Sam had reacted with what sounded like a sigh of happiness to having hers applied. Q had cursed under his breath, and Connor sounded like he was breathing hard... but Nick could barely contain another shout.

Fuck.

The damn things were throbbing. His nipples were two tiny points of pain on his chest, and not in a fun way—not that he'd ever thought anything about pain was fun. A part of kitchen work, yes, but actually fun? Nope. This wasn't changing his mind.

But Avery had marked down on her sheet that nipples clamps were a go.

He glanced at Sam next to him, trying not to be obvious since she was the only woman in the room who currently had her breasts out. Nick wasn't trying to ogle her chest, although she had a gorgeous pair. He was trying to understand her reaction. Her eyes were half-closed, and even though she'd obviously felt the pain—heck, her bigger nipples meant they were being pinched even tighter, right?—her reaction was so opposite of his, he wondered if hers was the typical submissive reaction.

No, not submissive. Masochist.

Like his brother.

Nick winced when he looked at Luke again. His big brother met his gaze evenly, still grinning with amusement.

I can do anything you can do, dammit.

Yeah, that brotherly rivalry was going to get him into all sorts of trouble in this class.

"Once you've applied the clamps, you need to keep a close eye on your submissive," Olivia said, walking up to Luke and patting his shoulder before turning her attention back to them. Beside Nick, Q was flexing his hands at his sides. Nick tried it to see if it helped. Maybe a little. It was distracting, at least. "Different people have different pain tolerances. Luke's pain tolerance is pretty high."

Nick made another gagging noise as quietly as he could so as not to draw Olivia's attention, but she still shot him a look. He endeavored to appear innocent. Next to him, Q was grinning but didn't otherwise give him away. On his other side, Sam still seemed lost in her own little world.

Her reactions were making him feel a lot better about putting clamps on Avery, despite how much he disliked having it done to him. This was probably good, though. If he'd only seen Sam's reaction, he wouldn't have realized how much the fuckers actually hurt. So, he got why Olivia was doing the practical demonstration.

"Some clamps will be easier than others. These tweezer clamps are often the easiest for men because of the size of your nipples, but we'll go over spring-loaded clamps, clover clamps, and clamps with weights as well."

Next to Nick, Sam winced when Olivia got to clover clamps and winced again at the idea of weights. Onstage, Luke appeared to be impassive, which meant Nick had to be as well.

It was going to be a long night.

❧

AVERY

She was having such a good night.

They'd moved to a table after tasting a few of the meads, each of them choosing a different one. Domi liked the sweetest one, Rae went for one that was heavier and more robust, and Avery liked the spicy one. Apparently, every Father's Day, the meadery made a batch with the spiciest rated pepper available—this wasn't that since it was a limited batch—but the ghost pepper mead was freaking delicious.

Hanging out with Rae and Domi, some amazing mead, and a delicious cheese and fruit platter—she was one happy camper.

"Okay, I am fully converted to mead." Rae sighed happily after taking a bite of cheese and another sip of her mead. "I cannot believe I've never had it before."

"It is kind of niche," Avery said with a shrug. "I have seen it at more beer and wine stores, but that's a fairly recent development."

"Well, I'm definitely taking some home with me," Domi said. "Especially since I can't have more than this one glass since I'm driving home."

"Good call. Maybe we can all get a bottle and have a girls' night in next time." Avery did like going out, but she didn't want Domi to feel left out.

"That sounds like a plan." Domi grinned before changing the subject. "So, what are the rest of the people in class like? You mentioned the tall Dom..."

"Connor."

"Connor, right? What about everyone else?"

"Well, you already know Freddy, Morgan, and Sam."

"I still can't believe she's a switch." Rae shook her head. "Did not see that one coming."

"I told you about Connor, the really tall one. There's also Q, who definitely knows Sam from somewhere, and they don't get along, but I don't know anything more than that." She told them about Q and Sam's reactions to each other.

"Samwise... that's from Lord of the Rings, right?" Domi's forehead wrinkled.

"Yeah." Personally, Samwise was one of Avery's favorite characters, but Sam had balked at the nickname, so she knew Q hadn't meant it in a favorable way. "Then there's Iris. She seemed really nice. She's a submissive and said she's the little sister of someone at Stronghold —Andrew."

"Woah, Master Andrew's little sister?" Domi sat up straight, her eyes widening.

"Have you met her?"

"No." Domi glanced at Rae, who shook her head as well. "But Master Andrew is Mitch's mentor, sort of. When Mitch wants some advice, he usually goes to Master Andrew or Master Michael, but usually Andrew. I'm having trouble imagining him letting his little sister play at the same club as him."

"I'm not. All these Doms are control freaks," Rae pointed out. "He probably prefers her at a club where he knows she'll be safe. Even so, that's so..." She shuddered. "I cannot imagine going to the same club as one of my siblings. What if we accidentally saw each other getting freaky?"

"Well, Luke and Nick will be at the same club..." Avery's voice trailed off as Domi and Rae considered that fact.

"I think it's the opposite gender thing that squicks me out," Rae said after a moment. "It would be one thing to see my sister there but my brother? Nope. Nope, nope, nope. I haven't seen him naked since he was a little boy, and I'd like to keep it that way."

Avery and Rae laughed, but she could see what Rae was saying. There was something different about the sibling relationship. Maybe it was a societal thing, but that was how she felt, and obviously, Rae and Domi agreed.

"Master Patrick's sub is his best friend's little sister." Domi grinned. "Which is probably why she usually wears a t-shirt around the club."

"Yeah, that's even weirder." Rae shook her head before refocusing on Avery. "Anyway, Iris is cool?"

"I didn't get a chance to talk too much to her, but yeah, she seemed fun. She reminded me a bit of you, actually." When Rae raised her eyebrows questioningly, Avery smirked. "Very sassy. She said she was volunteered to be a submissive for the class so she could get more practice. I get the feeling she's had some issues being on her own without supervision."

"Well, if she's interested, see if she wants to hang out," Rae said, and Domi nodded.

Pausing for a moment, possibly partially fueled by the mead buzz she had going, Avery went ahead and asked.

"Not that it's a bad thing at all, but... are you two looking to make friends for a particular reason? I'm thrilled you reached out to me, and I think it's great that you want to befriend Iris too, but I feel you two would have been perfectly happy on your own."

Avery really didn't begrudge them. She was happy to have friends, and Rae and Domi had proven to be good friends. Sure, there were times when she was a little envious of how close they were, but they'd been friends for years, and it showed. Hopefully, she'd be there with them one day—although they might be even closer by then, if that was even possible.

The two of them exchanged a look. Sometimes, they were like a couple in that whole managing to say volumes without speaking a word to each other.

"We got a talking to from Freddy," Domi finally admitted, heat filling her cheeks. "We hadn't realized it, but we were so involved in being besties, we really shut out a lot of people at the club. It was eye-opening, and we didn't want to be unfriendly."

"Then you showed up and were completely awesome and..." Rae shrugged. "One thing led to another." Her smile faltered a touch. "I hope you don't feel like a third wheel. We don't mean for you to be."

"I know you don't, and I usually don't. When I do, it's only because you two have known each other for so long, and I just met you. I don't expect you not to talk about the past, even though I wasn't there. You're great at including me," Avery said hurriedly. She didn't want to make them feel bad. She'd wanted to satisfy her curiosity but felt like she'd made things awkward. "Next class, I'll see if Iris wants to hang out with some other submissives. I got the feeling she feels a little out of place in the club."

"Good, then she'll fit right in with Rae." Domi elbowed her friend, cackling. Rae rolled her eyes. "Seriously though, we can be the misfit bunch. Sounds like fun."

"Sounds like something a masochist in a kink club would say," Rae muttered.

❧

NICK

He'd thought putting clamps on was bad—taking them off was so much worse. Unexpectedly so.

Sam let out a hiss of breath as she removed hers, which set the stage for everyone else's reactions. No one wanted to be the first to yelp or whimper. Q clenched his jaw so hard, tears sprang into his eyes, and he had to wipe them away.

The tweezer clamps hadn't been too terrible, but the spring-loaded clamps were a whole other story. The next ones, the clover clamps, were supposed to be the worst?

Red hot pain flashed through him as he removed the clamps, but he breathed through it. Up on stage, Luke caught his eye and gave him a thumbs up. It was ridiculous to feel pride at his brother's approval over nipple clamp removal, but that didn't stop the emotion.

"Okay, before we do the clover clamps, we're going to give your nipples a rest." The evil smile Olivia gave them was not at all reassuring. "That means we'll do spankings next. We'll start off with Master Law and me administering them, then you four can take turns with our practice dummies and eventually on each other."

That didn't sound odd and slightly humiliating. Avery's face flashed in his mind. It was a good thing she was worth it; otherwise, he might tap out right now.

Well, maybe not *right* now while his brother was watching. He eyed the others. They were all into kink and had come to the class because of that, whereas he was doing it for Avery. Yes, he was interested now, but also he knew himself well enough to know he'd never be here on his own. He'd never have made that leap without Avery as motivation. Did that make it easier that they knew what their goals were? His only goal was making Avery happy. Maybe he needed to figure out what to do beyond that.

"Alright, Sam, you're over here with me," Olivia said, pointing to one of the spanking benches. Master Law stood beside the other, his arms crossed, looking formidable. Luke had ambled over to the side of the room. His nipples were no longer clamped, but like everyone else's, they were darker and looked angry. Nick suppressed the urge to rub his own. "Nick, you're with Master Law. Pants down, everyone."

He wasn't sure how he felt about going first, but he supposed getting this over with sooner rather than later wasn't the worst thing in the world. Following Sam's lead, he moved to the spanking bench, lowered his jeans, and draped his body over the leather padding, acutely aware of the watching eyes. He liked the audience even less than the rest of it.

Glancing over, he caught Luke's gaze. His brother must have seen something there because, after a moment, he headed to the door to the bathroom as if he needed to take a break at the exact moment that Nick was going to be spanked for the first time. Pure relief and gratitude for his brother's understanding filled Nick.

Maybe this wouldn't be so bad after all.

❧ 14 ☙

"When spanking, you always want to keep your swats below the submissive's hip," Olivia said, and Master Law put his hand on Nick's ass, right at the very top. Nick gritted his teeth. This was so weird. "The same goes for any kind of impact play. The curves of the butt cheeks are where most spankings will be centered, but sometimes, you can do the thighs or the area right under the cheeks because those are even more sensitive than butts."

Master Law's hand moved with each spot Olivia named, and Nick almost jumped when he felt the other man's fingers against the sensitive spot right under his ass. It was a very sensitive spot, and it felt extremely odd to be touched there, especially by someone he wasn't attracted to.

Fixing Avery's face firmly in his mind, Nick focused on why he was there. He'd promised her he was going to be the best student.

"You'll need to be more careful when spanking or otherwise punishing the more sensitive areas so you don't push your submissive beyond what they can handle." Olivia's voice changed, becoming icy, and Nick knew she would not be pleased to hear about any of them pushing their sub past their limits. "You also need to make sure not to go above their waist. We'll talk more about kidneys, where they're located, and why we don't use impact implements on them when we get to the flogging and whips. For spanking, you need to know if you feel bone, you've gone too high. Keep it focused on the fleshy part."

That made sense. The idea of flogging and whips still made his stomach twist uncomfortably, but hearing how safety-focused the class was made him feel a little better.

"Okay, Sam and Nick, we'll start with the center of your butt cheeks, then the undersides and the thighs so you can feel the difference. After that, Connor and Q will each take a turn, then we'll get you back here to demonstrate how build-up and a prolonged spanking feels."

Nick started to nod his head, but he didn't get very far before Master Law's hand came down hard on the center of his ass. He yelped, unable to hold back the sound, and heard Sam do the same from her perch.

Fuck.

Master Law had a fucking hard hand. He'd never been spanked as a child, at least not that he remembered, and that fucking hurt!

He flexed his cheeks.

"Relax." Master Law's voice was deep and firm, filled with authority as his fingers tapped against the clenched muscles. "Always wait until your submissive unclenches before administering a spanking. Clenching might make it hurt less, but that's the whole point of waiting."

Sadistic fucker.

Nick groaned inwardly. If this was what Avery was expected to do, he needed to do it.

The next swat caught him in the center of his other cheek. He instinctively flexed again before forcing himself to relax. At least this time, he only grunted instead of yelping.

"Now the more painful spots," Master Law murmured, and Nick

groaned under his breath. He also mentally thanked Olivia for putting him with Master Law. This would have been so much worse if he'd had to bend over bare-assed for his brother's girlfriend to spank.

The sharp swat on the crease between his ass and his thigh made him want to yelp all over again, but he bit back the sound, and it came out as an agonized wheeze. Still not at all sexy.

Master Law chuckled.

"I understand the impulse to hold back your voice. You'll have to decide whether to encourage your submissive to stay quiet or express herself." He slapped the other spot, and Nick held back his groan again before panting for breath and letting his head drop to rest on the leather padding.

Fuck, that hurt.

Some people found this sexy?

That's why you're the Dom. You're supposed to find doing it sexy, not receiving it.

Right. Okay. Except he was struggling with the idea of making Avery feel like this.

It wasn't the pain. Nick was no stranger to pain. He was a chef, for crying out loud. His entire life was about blisters, small burns, and cuts. He didn't have any hair on his forearms because it had all been burned off over the years. He could stand for hours, bend over a cutting board for hours, and do whatever he had to in order to get through the night.

Yes, this was an entirely different pain, and he could handle it, but he didn't like the way it made him feel. This wasn't pain to get a job done; it was pain for itself. That's where his brain fritzed.

"Now the thighs."

Two burning spots on the backs of his thighs later, Nick was happy to get off the spanking bench. Embarrassment burned through him when he caught Q's eye. Stiffly, he straightened, avoiding Q's and Connor's gazes. It wasn't until both of them bent over the bench, he realized they hadn't been judging him—they were both clearly apprehensive as they got into position. They'd been watching him because he and Sam were the only indications of what to expect.

He didn't feel any less respect for them as they got into position. Connor got on a different bench than Sam, which had already been adjusted for his greater height. If anything, seeing their serious dedication to learning how to properly 'play' with a submissive and now understanding how much of a blow it could be to both ego and physical nerve endings, he had more respect for them.

Oh. *Oh.*

When Luke came out of the bathroom and came to stand beside him, Nick was very aware of his own nipples and ass burning, knowing the spanking hadn't even been that intense. He had a feeling the 'prolonged' demonstration would be much worse.

For the first time, he felt as though he understood Luke a little better. Maybe he didn't understand what drove his big brother to do this, but now he knew how it felt. And it fucking hurt. Yet, Luke would bear it for Olivia, and deep down—even though he would never say it out loud, even though he didn't want to think about it—he'd judged Luke and had thought he was weak.

Now...

Fuck. Luke did what Nick wasn't sure he could do, regularly and with a smile on his face. It might not have been what Nick thought of as 'strength,' but it sure as hell wasn't weakness. The fact Luke could regularly submit like this to Olivia, submitting both his pride and his body, without it affecting his self-image... Okay, maybe that was how Nick defined strength. He was already struggling with doing it once.

"I can leave if you want me to," Luke murmured, so no one else in the classroom could hear. "I'll go hang out in the office until they need me for the next demonstration."

"You're demonstrating?"

"Yeah, flogging." Luke shot him a quick grin. "They figured you all knew what a spanking looked like, but they want to show you a flogging and the whips on a real person before showing you what it feels like."

Nick didn't hide his flinch, and Luke grinned even wider.

"Don't worry, Olivia told me she's going to leave you to Master Law and Mistress Julie."

"I'm not sure that's meant as a kindness," Nick muttered. "Master Law has a hard hand."

Though now that he could see Olivia spanking Connor and the pink spots that were already appearing on the man's pale skin, he wasn't sure she'd be any lighter. Ouch. Was that how hard he was supposed to spank Avery? Or was Olivia using more force because Connor was a man? He wished he'd been able to see how hard she spanked Sam to get a better idea of what a woman could handle.

"Is that how hard she spanks you?"

"She usually prefers a flogger with me, but when she does, yes." Luke sounded completely unbothered by the fact his girlfriend was spanking another man.

On the other hand, being spanked by Master Law had demonstrated graphically to Nick that kink didn't need to be sexual. From Olivia's expression and body language, there was nothing inherently sexual about what she was doing now.

After she finished demonstrating all the pertinent spots to Connor, Olivia straightened. Master Law had finished with Q as well, but the man was still on the spanking bench.

"Since you're already here, we'll do the prolonged demonstration," Olivia said before glancing over at Nick and Sam. "You two are up next."

"So, want me to stay or go when it's your turn?" Luke asked, keeping his voice low as Olivia and Master Law started spanking Connor and Q in earnest. The two men grunted when the swats landed, the sound of flesh cracking against flesh filling the room. The spankings were rhythmic and steady. Olivia and Master Law were clearly spreading the impacts over their targets rather than letting them all land in one spot.

Nick's jaw clenched and unclenched, his fists opening and closing as he watched. Fuck, that looked uncomfortable.

"You can stay," he said, surprising both himself and his brother. This was what Luke did. He would have to watch Luke be flogged and whipped. Asking him to leave would only make it seem as if he couldn't handle this, and he totally could.

Besides, if they would be going to the same club, they would see the other doing something kinky sooner or later. Might as well get used to it.

❧

AVERY

I'm here.

The text came in thirty seconds before the knock on her door, and Avery went hurrying to answer it. The door, that was.

Jerking open the door, she wasn't really sure what to expect, but a scowling, grumpy Nick wasn't it. He looked as if he'd had a rough night in the kitchen, not an enjoyable night at the club.

"Hi." She didn't know what else to say, so she kept it short and simple. Something in his expression softened, which was a relief, as he stepped up to give her a kiss.

"Hey," he murmured as his lips descended and covered hers as his hands slid around her.

Avery melted into him and felt him relax against her. She wasn't tipsy, but she still had a bit of a mead buzz going on—half from the alcohol and half from the sugar content.

When she slid her hands around him and up his back, he stiffened and flinched. She quickly lifted them up and away.

"Sorry," he said, pulling away from the kiss and wincing. "I'm still a little tender—they demonstrated the flogger and the whip on our shoulders."

"Yeah? How was it?" Avery stepped back into the apartment, letting him in, then closed the door behind him. Only then did she notice he was walking a little oddly—stiff-legged.

Pressing her lips together—it really wasn't funny, even though it made her want to laugh—she sat next to him on the couch, curling into his side without touching him. His arm went around her shoulders, fingers trailing down her arm and gently tracing little circles. Remembering his nipples would probably be tender, she rested her head in the crook of his neck.

"It hurt. It still hurts. You sure that's what you want?"

It was Avery's turn to stiffen and not because of physical pain. The dubiousness in his voice, as if he was having trouble believing she could actually want to be flogged and whipped...

"Yes."

"Hey, come here." Nick's arm pulled her back in, not into his side but onto his lap.

Taking a deep breath, Avery let herself relax against him. She felt bad when he winced again because she bet his butt was pretty sore too, but hey, she hadn't tried to sit on his lap. He'd put her there.

"I didn't mean to sound judgmental. It's hard for me because I went through it, and I know it's not what I want. I'm sore all over. Everything hurts. My shirt is rubbing the hell out of my nipples. And there is nothing less sexy than having my brother watch while some dude wails on me with a whip."

Avery laughed so hard, she snorted, leaning against Nick's chest. She could feel the vibration of his chuckles as his hands gently stroked the sides of her ass and thighs.

"Well, when you put it like that..." she said as her laughter subsided to giggles. "I promise it will be sexier when you do it to me, and I absolutely will enjoy it."

"Even the soreness after?" The plain confusion in his voice made her feel a little better. He wasn't judging her; he was trying to understand her.

Squirming around on his lap, so she could get a good look at him, she leaned forward and kissed the tip of his nose.

"Especially the soreness after. Every time I feel it, it will make me think of you."

His eyes lit up with both understanding and interest.

"That doesn't sound so bad."

"It's not." She grinned and pressed a kiss to his lips.

When she finally pulled away, Nick groaned, shifting beneath her, obviously trying to find a comfortable position. He looked at her with big, plaintive, puppy dog eyes.

"Will you think any less of me if I say I want to go to bed and cuddle?"

"Not at all." Avery grinned. "That sounds perfect."

Truthfully, her vagina could use a rest. The lingering soreness made her think of him, but they'd been having so much sex, she was hitting the threshold of whether or not it was pleasant. Cuddling and thinking about all the delightfully devious things he was learning how to do her while he recovered from his first experience of what a submissive went through sounded pretty darn good.

❦ 15 ❦

AVERY

Being home alone meant it was time to do laundry, especially because she only had one clean chef coat left. It was also an opportune time to get some things around the house done because Nick had had to go into work several hours earlier than her. While part of her wanted to be lazy and lie on the couch, she knew she needed to get stuff done. It wouldn't get done after work.

She'd gotten one day of rest, then the next day, it was like Nick had something to prove. Which she'd thoroughly enjoyed, even if she didn't know exactly what he'd been trying to prove—that he could give her multiple orgasms without spanking, flogging, or whipping her? Honestly, she'd been a little disappointed when he wouldn't spank her, explaining he'd be more comfortable doing it for the first time with some supervision, but he made it up to her with his fingers, mouth, and eventually, his cock.

During round two, when she'd been on her hands and knees, he had gotten a couple of swats in, hard enough to make her clench and moan. That had been more than enough to whet her appetite and make her look forward to next Monday's class.

When her phone rang, she glanced at the screen and grimaced when she saw it was her mom. Not that she didn't love her mom, but the parental guilt trip about having moved so far away was never-ending and never fun. However, she'd feel even guiltier if she ignored the call when she actually had the time to talk.

Besides, it would be nice to hear her mom's voice.

"Hey, Mom." She put the phone on speaker and set it on the coffee table next to where she was sitting on the floor, folding the most recent load of laundry to come out of the dryer. It was still warm, which was one of her favorite things. Sometimes in the winter, she wanted to roll around in it. Sadly, she was an adult, so she resisted, but the impulse remained.

"Hey, honey, how are you?"

"Pretty good. Doing laundry since I don't have to be at work for a couple hours."

"Oh, that's good. You work too hard."

Yup, dig number one at her job. Avery sighed inwardly and shook her head. That hadn't even taken a minute.

"Are things still going well at the restaurant?"

It was a perfectly innocuous question, as long as Avery ignored the hopeful note in her mother's voice—hopeful maybe things weren't going so well, and Avery would decide to come back home, get married, and give her mom a few more grandbabies. Apparently, she needed at least one from each of her children to be satisfied, whereas Avery wasn't even sure she wanted babies.

"Yeah, it's going great. It's one of the best places I've worked." It was true, although there wasn't much to talk about when it came to the restaurant. "I got to go out on Monday. I went to a local meadery with a couple of friends."

"A meadery? That must have been fun."

"It was." Avery elected to ignore the note of disappointment in her mom's voice, but the guilt still simmered just below the surface. Maybe she should throw her mom a bone. "Um, so I've started seeing someone."

"You have? You're dating?" Surprise warred with happiness, then warred with more disappointment. Avery was sure her mom would rather she came home and met someone, but apparently, dating anyone was enough to perk her mom up, which was what she was hoping.

"Yeah, his name is Nick. He's a chef, too." She decided not to mention he was the executive chef, aka her boss, at the same restaurant.

"I guess that means he understands your schedule." Her mom's laugh was only a little forced.

"He does. He's at work right now." She smiled ruefully at the noncommittal noise her mom made. "He's even better in the kitchen than I am."

"Well, I doubt that." Her mom sniffed, sounding offended on Avery's behalf, which made her chuckle. She never doubted her parents were proud of her, even if they didn't particularly like her decisions. "When do we get to meet him?"

"We just started dating." She barely got the words out before her mom was already throwing another loaded question at her.

"Do you want to bring him home for the holidays?"

"Thanksgiving isn't for another couple of months—"

"Have you asked him about it? Does he celebrate with his family?" The questions were coming rapid fire, and Avery very much wished she hadn't brought Nick up. It was freaking September! Who asked about Thanksgiving now?

"I... no... We're not serious yet."

"Not serious? Avery, you are getting too old to be in a relationship that's 'not serious.' If you aren't going to be serious about someone, there's no point in wasting more time with them. Not at your age."

Oh, for fuck's sake.

"Mo-om. Sto-op." She drew out the words the same way she had as a teenager. In fact, she was feeling very much like a teenager right now. What was it about her mom that made her regress? "We're serious in that we're only see each other, but we're not serious in that we haven't been together for that long. I'll ask him about Thanksgiving by Halloween. Okay?"

The huffy sigh on the other end of the line indicated it wasn't okay, but at least her mom would compromise.

"If you say so, Avery."

"Thanks, Mom. How's Dad? Has he gotten his cholesterol tested lately?" It was a dirty move, but the one surefire way to distract her mom was to bring up her dad's health. Especially since he still wasn't following the diet she was trying to keep him on.

❧

NICK

Cuddled up on the couch with Avery after their shift, Nick rested his head on top of hers. They were watching a *Cutthroat Kitchen* rerun, which—since his first class at Marquis—he was seeing in a whole new light.

"Do you think Alton Brown is kinky?"

Avery laughed, her head moving beneath his cheek.

"Oh God, yes. Did you not think so?"

"I never really thought about it, but now it's kind of hard to ignore the... you know... handcuffs and spreader bars."

"Not to mention how often he refers to himself as Daddy."

Oh, holy shit. He hadn't even thought about that part.

"Maybe he's not, and kink has ruined our minds."

"Uh-huh," Avery snickered, not sounding convinced. "You keep telling yourself that."

"Are you getting sassy with me?" He tickled her, his fingers poking her ticklish spots. She giggled, twisting against him, trying to escape by burrowing into his side.

"Maybe I am... What are you going to do about it? Sir?" She gave a little shriek when his fingers found a sensitive spot, jumping up and landing on his lap, her knees slowly sliding down on either side of his thighs.

Fuck. She wanted to be kinky.

She'd been hinting, but other than a few swats during doggy style, Nick hadn't been able to bring himself to do more, hadn't been sure how to. One thing Monday's lesson hadn't included was 'how to start a scene with your submissive that doesn't feel awkward.'

Though he supposed that's what Avery was doing right now.

Could he spank her?

No. He didn't feel ready.

Maybe clamps? Clamps were their own thing. He couldn't make them worse or mess those up.

Her expression was growing tense, and she looked as though she wished she hadn't said anything.

Say something, dumbass.

"Do you have clamps?" He slid his hands up to her breasts, caressing them in case she didn't understand what he was asking. Under her tank top, the little buds of her nipples hardened, pressing against the fabric, and Nick's cock jerked in response. He ran his thumbs over the bumps, enjoying the way her back arched, and she squirmed on his lap. Her pupils dilated, the happy smile spreading on her face confirming he'd made the right choice.

"Yes, Sir."

Fucking hell. He wanted her to call him by his name because calling him Sir seemed demeaning, but he couldn't deny he got off on hearing her say it. Though since he hadn't asked her to, it was what she wanted, and he shouldn't feel guilty for enjoying it, right?

"Go get them." He tweaked her nipples through her shirt, hoping he sounded commanding. However, he sounded, she seemed to like it because she lit up from within. Smoothly, she got to her feet and sauntered toward her bedroom, which gave him a moment to compose himself.

What the fuck am I doing?

Shit. He should have planned something. Right? Was it okay to go with the flow? Why hadn't he asked any of these questions in class?

Because you hadn't thought of them yet.

Now he understood why there was a practical class with the submissives. When he'd thought about putting clamps on Avery, he'd been so busy worrying about whether they'd be too much for her or that he would remove them in time, he hadn't thought about the logistics of making putting them on her into something sexy.

It sure as hell hadn't been sexy when he'd been the one being clamped.

On the other hand, Samantha had still reacted as if it was sexy, even though there had been no foreplay.

Olivia had said foreplay would be good to help prepare Avery. Clamps were painful, but there was a place between pleasure and pain, especially for masochists. If Avery had her own clamps at home, she enjoyed using them. He hadn't, but she did.

Pain plus pleasure.

He could do this.

Foreplay. Clamps. Then sex. It was only one new element to their sex life.

When he thought about it that way, it wasn't such a big deal.

AVERY

Bad subbie, topping from the bottom.

Yeah, yeah.

She'd sensed Nick needed a little push, and it had worked, hadn't it? So, it wasn't really a bad thing.

Yeah, she knew a more experienced Dom would not only recognize what she was doing but wouldn't accept that excuse. She'd stop doing it as he was experienced to realize what topping from the bottom was. Besides, she might not need to do it ever again. He'd latched onto the suggestion right away, and once he'd realized what she was asking for, he'd taken charge.

Which was hot as hell.

She grinned as she opened her nightstand and scooped up her favorite pair of clamps—spring-loaded with rubber tips. They were adjustable, and when she'd first started using them, the tightest setting had been too much, but now, it was what she needed. It would feel so good to use them *with* someone again, instead of using them on herself while she went to town with BOB—her battery-operated boyfriend.

About to turn and head back, Avery paused and looked down at herself.

Nick hadn't told her to take off her clothes, but it would be more fun to go out naked. Give him a little surprise and hopefully throw him off a little, which would help him with his nervousness. It would be harder to be anxious if she was naked, right?

Stripping quickly, excitement was already humming through her veins. She knew it was the beginning, but she wanted to show him how much fun kink could be. The classroom was all about learning. This could be about pure play.

❧ 16 ☙

I t was taking Avery longer than he'd thought it would to get the clamps—although it wasn't like he knew where her clamps were. Left alone for a few minutes made him second guess everything.

Not what she wanted—he understood what she wanted—but he worried he wouldn't be able to give it to her. He didn't know what he was doing yet. Hell, they'd only had two classes, and they'd spent one of them talking. Nick hated feeling like he didn't know what he was doing, but he didn't want to let Avery down.

Maybe he should have told her he wanted to wait until class to try anything at all, but the nipple clamps seemed like something he should be able to do. At least, they had when he said it. Given a few minutes to himself, all he could think about was all the ways he might fuck up.

Putting them on wrong. Olivia had explained and demonstrated, and they'd even practiced on some bottle nipples, but that wasn't the same as a real nipple. A bottle nipple couldn't say 'ow' and let you know t you'd placed the clamp too close to the tip. Which was apparently a very real thing.

You'll practice on her on Monday.

Yeah, in a supervised class where someone can show me what to do ahead of time.

You're going to disappoint her if you back out now.

Crap. That was the real problem.

When he heard her returning, he twisted in his seat on the couch, still trying to figure out what he was going to do. The sight of her short-circuited his brain. The racing thoughts didn't grind to a halt. They flew off the racetrack as if there had been a mass collision that sent everything hurtling through the air.

Seeing her naked wasn't anything new, but he hadn't been expecting it. Turning around to see a naked Avery, when he'd been expecting a fully clothed version, sent the blood rushing back to his cock. His deflated erection went from zero to sixty so fast, he felt dizzy.

The seductive smile on her face as she slinked toward him contributed to the appeal. She knew exactly what she was doing and how he was reacting, which was fucking hot. The confidence she wore as easily as she wore clothing was one of the sexiest things about her.

He couldn't take his eyes off her as she came around the couch. Instead of climbing back into her previous position, she knelt at his feet. Knees apart, back straight, she lifted the hand holding the clamps, which were connected by a little chain.

"Sir." Her eyes were lowered, but the smile playing on her lips made it clear she was enjoying herself.

Fuck.

That shouldn't be as hot as it was.

AVERY

On her knees, excitement and happiness humming through her veins, Avery could barely keep her breaths even.

Olivia had been right. She'd been so right. Avery was submissive. Kneeling naked at Nick's feet while she called him Sir and handed him a pair of clamps to use on her... she couldn't remember the last time she'd felt this good. The last time something had felt this right.

Vanilla sex with him hadn't been bad. Not at all. It had been incredibly good.

But this... this was a different need. A different craving. One that vanilla sex hadn't satisfied. A need it hadn't been able to touch, much less fulfill.

"Uh, rise so I can..." Nick waved his empty hand, coughing before speaking again, this time with more authority. "Rise up, Avery."

Avery pressed her lips together against her amusement. She didn't find him any less sexy because of his moment of hesitation. Witnessing him overcome, hearing the change in his voice as he moved into a more dominant headspace was hot. Intimate. Something no other woman would get to see, no matter what happened between her and Nick.

Even if they didn't work out, this time with him, these moments were all hers. When it came to kink, he was a virgin, and she was so ready to pop his cherry. A moment of hesitation here or there was nothing but reminders he was new to this. She was going to thoroughly enjoy watching him come into his own.

Rising onto her knees, she glanced at him questioningly, her hands hanging loosely at her sides. The new position gave him much easier access to her breasts, and he leaned forward, using his free hand to cup one of them.

"When was the last time you used these clamps?"

Avery hesitated. Peeked at him again. His expression hardened, the look in his eyes suspicious.

"Um... Tuesday after you went to work."

"I see."

Her hands moved behind her back automatically, responding to the displeased tone of her Dom's voice. It didn't take a genius to figure out the reason she'd used the clamps—she'd been masturbating.

The gentle hand caressing her shifted, the fingers closing around her nipple and pinching hard. Avery moaned as the flash of pain and pleasure shot straight through to her needy core. Nick had been rough before now, but not so deliberately sadistic, and every part of her body happily responded to the difference.

"Naughty girl." His voice was low, rough.

Avery closed her eyes, taking in deep breaths as he tugged on her nipple. The desire and pain pulsed through her, making her muscles clench in anticipation.

"No more playing with yourself without permission."

"Yes, Sir." The reply was automatic, but the surge of pure pleasure at his command was a rush that came from deep inside, filling her up and sending her soaring. She'd needed this so badly. She hadn't realized how badly until this moment when it was finally happening. Her mind had hidden the problem because it had been too painful to acknowledge.

Another time, she might have been resentful at the command, but now?

Nope. Turned on. One hundred percent turned on.

Not that she should need to ask permission often, considering how high Nick's libido was. The only reason she had on Tuesday was she hadn't been able to stop thinking about everything he'd been learning in class. Thinking about what he was going to do to her soon, she had needed her clamps and BOB.

She had a feeling she wouldn't need BOB for a while after this. If Nick even gave her permission.

The idea he might not sent another fizz of excitement through her.

That was the reaction that occasionally made her question what was wrong with her brain chemistry. She shouldn't like being told if she could masturbate, right? It was a solitary activity for a reason.

And yet, she did.

NICK

Fuck, he was making this up as he went along, based on a few things that had been said in class, but if Avery noticed, she wasn't saying anything or reacting negatively.

And the way she looked at him...

Yeah, okay, he was getting why kink could be fun. He didn't think he'd ever had a woman look at him that way.

It was lust, but it was more than that—lust, trust, anticipation—as though she was hanging on to the edge of her seat, waiting to see what he would do to her next. Waiting for his command. He fucking loved it.

Cupping her breast again, he did his best to keep his expression impassive as his gaze flitted back and forth between watching where he was placing the clamp and keeping an eye on her expression to make sure he wasn't doing it incorrectly. Savage satisfaction filled him when she made a small sound in the back of her throat, eyelashes fluttering, her expression reminiscent of Sam's in class, but so much *more*. It felt as if all the blood that had rushed to his dick was pulsing there, making it hard for him to think.

Sliding his fingers along the chain to the other clamp, he used his free hand to pinch her unadorned nipple, making it even harder before placing the clamp on it, closing the rubber tips around her nipple, catching the plump bud in its grip, and crushing it. When he leaned back to admire his handiwork and the half-lidded expression on Avery's face as she panted, her lips parted, Nick had to admit he really fucking liked the visual.

The tips of her nipples peeked out from the black rubber surrounding them, pink, swollen, and rapidly darkening. According to Master Law, the clamps cut off circulation, trapping the blood in the nipples, which was why it hurt so much more when they were removed.

Granted, having them put on had hurt a whole hell of a lot, but Avery's reaction hadn't been anything like Nick's. Her expression was pained but also filled with desire, lust, and euphoria he'd never seen. A light in her eyes that hadn't been there until now.

The difference in their reactions was stark, and his cock was painfully hard at seeing hers.

Her tongue swept over her pink parted lips as her breathing evened out, sending another surge of desire through Nick, and he focused on her open mouth. Getting to his feet, he quickly shucked his clothing before sitting back down and reaching out to wreathe his fingers through her hair, pulling her head forward.

They'd played a little with oral during foreplay the past couple of weeks, but this was different. That had been in bed, mutual explorations of each other's bodies. This was Avery on her knees, nipples slowly darkening to red while she pleasured him with her mouth. Worshipped his cock with her tongue, her hands on his thighs, lips sliding down the shaft and swallowing him whole.

"Fuck!" Nick's head tipped back, falling against the back of the couch. The hot, wet pleasure engulfed him, and his fingers tightened their grip in her hair. She hummed, and the vibrations added to the sensations consuming him.

He felt powerful with Avery on her knees before him, moving her head in time with his hand, giving him her submission. And it was a gift. Avery was not the woman who allowed someone to boss her around, to control her this way unless she wanted them to. Knowing that and seeing how much she enjoyed giving up that control and letting him take the lead gave him an understanding into the lifestyle he hadn't had before.

It wasn't about forcibly taking control. It was about being offered control willingly, being trusted with it.

Some people might not handle that kind of pressure, but for Nick, the pressure was comfortable. He thrived in the heat and the stress, energized by it. Knowing he held the key to Avery's pleasure, that she wouldn't self-pleasure without his permission and would happily kneel and pleasure him without expectation of a return... That kind of trust, that kind of intimacy, was something he'd never experienced, and it was like a drug.

Now, he understood the euphoria he'd seen on her face because he felt it and wanted to share in it.

Pulling her hair, he lifted her head off his cock, tipping her back so he could look into her pleasure-glazed eyes, filled with heat and need. Her lips were still open, poutier, and swollen from use. Leaning forward, Nick took them in an aggressive kiss, pulling her toward him and using his other hand to leverage her onto his lap until she was straddling him the same way she had been—only this time, both of them were naked.

"Ride me, Avery. I want to watch you cum on top of me."

AVERY

She didn't need to be told twice.

Hands on his shoulders, she glanced down briefly to make sure she was in the right spot. His cock was pointing straight up, ready to impale her, his hands on her hips to help her lower onto it. Avery moaned, clenching as she found the tip and slid down.

Being on top was not one of her favorite positions outside of kink, but with someone like Nick, who was controlling her movements, even though she was technically in the power spot, it could be sexy as hell. Especially because it made his penetration feel so intense. Her muscles were tighter, clenching around him as she slid down, making him feel even larger than he did in other positions.

Avery was grateful for his hands on her hips, helping control her descent onto his lap. She moaned, squirming when he filled her, her body sizzling with pleasure. When he lifted one of his hands from her hip, tugging experimentally at the chain between her clamps, pulling on her nipples, she cried out and clenched around him.

"Ride me, Avery," he repeated.

Rising, he slid out of her, then she fell down on him again. Thighs moving, hips circling, she stared down at him while she did as he said. One hand on her hip, the other pulled and tugged on the chain, sending hot flashes of pain through her nipples. The pleasure and pain were mingling inside her, merging and pulsing to create a sensation unlike any other.

Nick used the chain to pull her closer, drawing her to him, so he could kiss her. Everything inside of Avery melted.

When his hands slid up to her breasts, cupping and caressing, she whimpered against his lips, then cried out when he opened the clamps and the blood began to circulate in her crushed nipples. He swallowed her cries as his palms covered the tormented nubs, warming and soothing them as her pulse pounded in her ears. All the while, she rose and fell on his cock, moving faster and faster, her need driving her toward the peak of ecstasy.

Closing his fingers around her breasts, Nick ended the kiss, squeezing hard, then shifting his grip so he could sweep his thumbs over her highly sensitized nipples.

"Good girl." His voice was rough, gravelly, and the accolade was the last thing she needed to tip her over the edge.

Crying out, pleasure ripped through her, ecstasy tinged with pain as he manipulated her nipples, making her writhe atop him, grinding down on his lap, her swollen clit throbbing with sweet release. She felt him jerk inside her, throbbing as each jet of cum spurted, filling her, adding to her rapture as he surged beneath her with his own climax.

NICK

Glancing at the clock, Nick scowled. Crap. He would have to finish working on the specials for this week after class—that or be late to class. Unfortunately, his relationship with Avery was a little more distracting than he'd realized it would be, and he hadn't thought about the specials over the weekend, meaning he'd given himself extra work for Monday.

There was a knock on the door, and it opened immediately. All the managers who shared the office knocked to announce their presence, then walked right in, so Nick was used to it.

He looked up to see Miles entering. Of indeterminate age, Miles was one of those guys who looked old and young at the same time. He was full of little contrary traits like that. Not many wrinkles, but his hair and beard were mostly grey, with only a little brown showing through. He was of average height and in good shape, but he also had a beer belly despite his muscles. He often seemed like he was off in his own little world, but Nick had discovered Miles observed far more than most people realized.

"Hi, Nick, how are you?" Miles smiled his usual warm and

welcoming expression. Out of the three front-of-house managers, he smiled the most.

"Doing good. I'm about done here if you need the desk. I may be back down later."

"After that class you're taking?" The tone of his voice didn't change, but Nick still froze. When he met Miles' gaze, the other man didn't seem at all perturbed that Nick was involved in the activities on the second floor, so that was good.

"Yes, after the class." Nick saved the document and got to his feet. He shook his head. He didn't believe for one second Gareth had gossiped, which meant that Miles—as usual—noticed more than anyone gave him credit for. Which tickled a thought in his brain. "Hey, do you know what's going on with George? He's been in a bad mood for a week now."

Normally, when George was on the expo line, he was fun to work with, plenty of banter and joking without interrupting the flow, but over the weekend, he'd been surly and grunted more than he'd spoken.

Miles snorted, moving around the opposite side of the desk, so he could replace Nick in the chair behind it.

"He's upset about Jonathan and Alanna."

"George liked Alanna?" Nick blinked in surprise. There was a bit of an age difference between the two of them, but when he thought about it, they did seem as if they'd make a pretty good match. On the other hand, despite his previous relationships with other servers, she and Jonathan seemed well-matched. Although he'd been brusque, George hadn't treated Alanna or Jonathan differently from anyone else.

"He'll get past it. Or he won't." Miles shrugged as he sat down. "We'll see how long Jonathan and Alanna last." His attention was already on the screen in front of him, totally focused. This was why people thought Miles didn't pay attention to what was going on around him.

Shaking his head, knowing better than to get caught up in the server drama, Nick headed for the door.

"Say hi to Avery for me."

Nick ground to a halt, hand on the doorknob. He looked back, but Miles was as focused on the computer as he was before.

"Ah, if you could not mention—"

"No one needs to know except you two." Waving his hand, Miles shooed Nick. "Go on, now. You don't want to be late."

Right. Nick sighed inwardly. No one except Miles and Gareth. Two of the managers had figured it out. Hopefully, they were the only two people who had noticed, but he couldn't worry about that right now. He needed to get upstairs to class. There would be plenty to worry about up there, like spanking Avery for the first time.

AVERY

Bent over the spanking bench in her bra and panties wasn't nearly as intimate or enjoyable as her interlude with Nick the night before. Her nipples were still extra sensitive today, which was nice, but it also reminded her how much more fun they'd had on their own.

Then again, she guessed this was supposed to be more educational than enjoyable, even if it was entertaining.

Directly in front of her were Connor and Morgan, and to say that Connor was struggling was an understatement. Across the way, Q had been having some issues, though she'd noticed he got better at putting some force into the swats he was giving Iris after Master Law had praised Sam for her swats.

Out of all the Dominants, Sam had the least trouble spanking with impact, and Freddy seemed to be enjoying himself.

Smack.

The impact of Nick's hand was minimal, leaving behind more warmth than sting, but it was better than the first few slaps he got in. The panties she was wearing weren't any good as a shield, so the tiny scrap of fabric didn't provide protection... not that she needed it right now.

"Harder, Nick." Mistress Julie's voice didn't leave any room for argument as she walked past him and Avery. Avery bit the inside of her lip to keep from laughing, which wouldn't help.

The frustration of the students in the room was palpable. All of them wanted to do what they were supposed to be doing, and they were worried about actually harming their submissive. Well, all except Sam, probably because of her experience on the other side. She'd started out a little hesitant but ended up getting into it.

Smack.

Avery gasped, her body jerking more out of surprise than pain, though that slap had enough force behind it to sting.

"Shit! Sorry!"

"No, that was good," she said, twisting her head to look over her shoulder. Any amusement she'd been feeling evaporated at the sight of Nick's expression. He looked more than frustrated—he looked unhappy. He wasn't enjoying this, not even on an entertainment level.

Dammit.

Her heart sank. Maybe this wouldn't work.

That would be okay, though, right? She could get by with clamps and bondage. They didn't have to do impact play.

"Harder, Connor. You won't break her. Morgan *likes* it." The hard crack of flesh against flesh that followed Mistress Julie's admonishment was accompanied by a low moan from Morgan. Avery's body clenched in envy, and a shiver went down her spine. "Isn't that right, Morgan?"

"Yes, Mistress." Morgan looked up at Connor. "Harder, please, Master Connor."

This time, under Mistress Julie's stern gaze, Connor gave Morgan a nice, hard swat, the sound nearly equaling that of Mistress Julie's demonstration. Morgan moaned again, lifting her bottom in the air. The hesitant consternation on Connor's face smoothed to relief.

Hmmm.

Avery looked over her shoulder at Nick again, wiggling to catch his attention, so he met her gaze.

"I liked that, Master Nick. Harder, please."

For a moment, she thought he wouldn't do it. His head lifted, and his eyes darted back and forth as if he was looking to see if anyone was watching him. Finally, he lifted his hand and brought it down on the opposite side of her ass, catching the other cheek directly in the center.

She let her head drop, moaning rather than crying out since she wasn't surprised this time.

"Yes, just like that." Normally, Avery wasn't a big talker during sex, but if positive reinforcement helped him feel better, she could do that. She could tell it worked with Connor—he was spanking Morgan audibly now. Mistress Julie's heels clicked against the wooden stage floor as she turned back to Nick and Avery.

As she approached, Nick brought his hand down again, hard enough to make Avery shriek. That was so much better. Her hips pushed up, hoping he'd bring his hand down again with the same force.

"Very good," Mistress Julie said approvingly, curving to move past them and over to Q and Iris.

⚜

NICK

If only Mistress Julie's approval made him feel better, though Avery's reaction did, a little.

She wants this.

Logically, he knew it. She'd told him, and he could see it in her body language.

Yet he couldn't shake the feeling he was doing something he wasn't supposed to. Guilt welled when he looked at the pink splotches on her ass, and his cock perked up.

Beating a woman isn't supposed to be sexy.

The problem wasn't that he disliked what he was doing but that he liked it too much. He didn't want to hurt Avery... yet he did. He wanted to slap her ass harder, to do it again and again until her ass was a bright, hot red, and she was crying out and begging him to stop. The idea made his cock as hard as it had been last night when she'd knelt in front of him and presented him with the nipple clamps.

Yeah, because you're a sick fuck.

No, I'm not. Do you think Q or Connor are sick fucks? Or Olivia or Law or Julie?

They seem like pretty normal people. You, on the other hand... you like this too much.

The internal war with himself wasn't going well. He hated the way it was making him feel. Hated feeling that when Avery made a noise, everyone was looking at him, judging him. Seeing him as a fucked-up piece of shit who enjoyed beating a woman.

It's spanking. It's different.

Is it, though?

Mistress Julie clapped her hands together. Standing in the center of the room, the shortest person in the room, she effortlessly drew all eyes to her with nothing more than that simple sound.

"Submissives, sit up. Dominants, stand behind them. Everyone, face me."

All the submissives moved, almost as one, getting into a sitting position on their spanking benches, facing Mistress Julie. Because of the angle of the 'bench,' the perch seemed a little precarious, but none of them spoke up to complain. Not that Nick could blame them for their silence.

"Submissives, close your eyes. Now, Dominants, I want you to raise your hand if you were worried about spanking your submissive too hard."

Gritting his teeth, not liking he had to admit to it, Nick raised his hand. He wasn't the first to do so, he realized with relief. Connor's hand had shot up, Q raised his hand at about the same rate as Nick, and even Sam raised her hand tentatively. Knowing they were all in the same boat, feeling the same way, made him feel a little better about his inability to reconcile what he knew with what he felt.

"Dominants, lower your hands. Submissives, raise your hands if you felt like your Dominant spanked you hard enough."

Not one hand went up. Freddy did a little waving thing in front of him, gesturing 'so-so.' Sam's face flushed red hot. Nick's stomach sank. Looking directly across the room at Q, he saw his own feelings reflected in the other man's expression when their somber gazes met.

The feeling of failure did not sit well. He could tell from the way

Avery's shoulders hunched forward, she didn't like not raising her hand but was too honest to lie to spare his feelings.

"Submissives, you may open your eyes." Mistress Julie smiled reassuringly at the subs, then raised her gazes to address the Dominants. "One of the things we'll be working on in this class is learning limits, emotional and physical, both your submissives' and yours. You should never push yourself into emotional harm because of your submissives' needs, but by that same token, you need to trust your submissive to know what their needs are. I don't think anyone in here got even close to a submissive using a slowdown word, much less a safe word."

Well, Nick felt called out.

Unfortunately, despite what Mistress Julie said, he wasn't sure it was going to get any easier.

❧ 18 ❧

AVERY

Well, that could have gone better.

Avery sighed inwardly as she watched Nick hurry out the door of the main room. She knew he had to get back to work and finish planning out the specials for the week, but she couldn't help but feel he was running away from her. Running away from the class. Not a great feeling.

"Hey, you okay?" Iris sidled up beside her, looking at her curiously. "Did Nick start spanking really hard or something?"

They hadn't gotten to flogging or whipping today, and Avery wasn't sure how he was going to handle that when they did. *If* he was going to handle it. All evidence to the contrary at the moment. Now, she did sigh aloud.

"No. I wish."

"Yeah, me, too. Although Q did get better." Iris' head tilted as she looked across the room to where her partner for the evening and Connor were talking to Mistress Julie. Morgan was beside Connor, one arm looped through his, the other patting his bulging bicep comfortingly. Sam stood off to the side, looking at her phone, but she kept glancing over at Mistress Julie as if she was trying to decide whether to join them. "I can understand why Connor was afraid to use too much force. He's built like Superman and probably could have broken Morgan in half."

Biting back the protest that Nick was really strong, too—he was, but no one in the class was built like Connor—Avery laughed. Poor Connor. If the Doms were struggling with not wanting to hurt the submissive they were working with, he would struggle the most. He really looked like he could easily break someone in half.

"Poor Connor." Avery shook her head and eyed Iris. "Hey, I hang out with a couple of other submissives from the club if you'd like to join us sometime."

"Who? Maybe I already know them."

"Domi and Rae."

"Oh, I've seen them around." Iris thought for a moment. "Domi is Master Mitch's girlfriend, right?"

"That's them."

"Yeah, I'd love to hang out with you all sometime. I haven't made too many friends at Stronghold." Iris shook her head. "I tried, but it seems like the majority of them have banged my brother and want to bring it up for some reason." She made a face.

"Huh..." Avery didn't know what to say.

"I mean, they don't come right out and say it. It's more like, 'Hey, nice to meet you, I know your brother,' and it's the way they say it, then I want to punch someone in the face... either them or him."

"You said your brother is Andrew, right? Isn't he engaged?" Avery blurted out. She was confused as hell. Yeah, she wouldn't want to know about his ex-lovers, but wanting to punch someone seemed a little extreme, especially since he was engaged. Did that mean Iris wanted to punch his fiancé, too?

"That's exactly why I want to punch them," she said, scowling. "He's a dumbass who lost the best thing that ever happened to him, then slept around with literally an entire kink club's worth of women. He's lucky Kate will touch his penis again, considering how much spelunking he did in-between."

Avery couldn't help it. She snort-laughed. Thankfully, it made Iris smile, and her expression turned rueful.

"Sorry. I get protective of Kate. I swear, if something happens, I will Lorena Bobbitt him for her. I'm pretty sure she's too nice to do it herself."

"Are they getting married soon?"

"December. They wanted a Christmas-themed wedding for some reason." Iris shrugged.

"Alright, everyone, you don't have to go home, but you can't stay here." Mistress Julie's voice didn't quite echo, but it was loud enough to make Iris and Avery jump.

They exchanged phone numbers in the lobby before heading home, which gave Avery an extra spring in her step. She'd made another new friend! The happiness that gave her helped wipe away the anxiety she had about Nick's abrupt departure after the class.

NICK

Arriving at Avery's apartment, for the first time, Nick hesitated before knocking. He wanted to see Avery but hated the way he felt. He'd been distracted the entire time he'd been working on the specials, unable to concentrate on food while his emotions warred with his desires, which warred with his logic.

He'd gotten it done, but it had taken longer than normal, and some part of him couldn't help but wonder if he'd been procrastinating to delay having to face Avery. If it was, it was dumb because as soon as she opened the door and he saw her face, he felt better. Maybe it was the way she lit up from within when she laid eyes on him, or maybe he felt as if he lit up the moment he saw her. Maybe a bit of both.

Either way, delaying seeing her again had been stupid.

"Hello there, handsome. Late night." It was commiseration, not a question. She on her tiptoes to give him a kiss, which he happily returned. Walking her backward into her apartment, he kicked the door shut behind them, his muscles relaxing with every step.

Holding her, feeling the press of her warm, soft curves against him, helped the tension melt away. How could anything be wrong when he had his arms around the woman he was falling in love with?

Holy shit.

The revelation was a kick to the gut, temporarily robbing him of speech, which might have been a good thing since he was tired enough to blurt it out otherwise. Not that telling her would be a bad thing. Would it? They hadn't been together for very long.

But they felt right. So right.

Even if some of the kinky stuff felt wrong.

Which... that might be a reason not to tell her yet. Not until he figured his shit out.

Lowering onto her heels, Avery sighed and hugged him, snuggling into his front. Nick hugged back, still reeling from his epiphany.

"It was a long night, but I finished the specials, and I think I might have some ideas for next week."

"That's good." Avery hesitated. He could see it in her face, the little hitch in her voice that indicated she still had something she wanted to say but wasn't sure she should. "Do you want to talk about class tonight?"

Did he?

Did he want to revisit his conflict and failure?

Not particularly, but he could tell Avery did. Maybe talking would make him feel better. He'd felt better *and* worse about spanking her harder after seeing none of the submissives had felt they'd been spanked hard enough. Doing it harder had worried him but knowing he hadn't done it hard enough had helped motivate him—knowing all the submissives felt that way kept him from being ashamed about not doing it hard enough.

"I'm sorry if it wasn't what you were hoping for," he said, deciding to get that out of the way first. "I know you and the other submissives said we weren't spanking hard enough, but I didn't want to hurt you."

"And I wanted you to hurt me." Avery's hands slid up his chest and around his neck, keeping him close. "I didn't want you to harm me, and there's a very real difference."

"I know. I did listen in class." He couldn't help feeling a little defensive. "I was trying."

"I know you were." Her tone was soothing, the same one she used in the kitchen, and he narrowed his eyes. She was managing him. At work, it didn't bother him so much, but he wasn't sure how he felt about it here. "I just feel like maybe it's different hearing it from me as opposed to Mistress Julie or Master Law."

"That's... true." It was a little different.

"I think it would also help if I could show you... really show you. Not like at class." Avery took a step back but kept her arms around his neck. He was big enough, he didn't have to move with her unless he wanted to, but he did. "I think you're not much of an exhibitionist, and it's hard to make it sexy when there's an audience, and you're under pressure, not to mention you're still learning, and there are teachers watching."

"So, you think I'd do better without the class?" Nick followed her with his hands on her hips, letting her lead him step by step toward the hallway. He had a feeling she was relying on him to keep her from running into anything, so he did his best to direct her away from the walls.

"No, I think the class is good and necessary for learning technique, but technique isn't everything." Avery's eyes sparkled as her fingers stroked the short hairs on the back of his neck while he maneuvered her into the bedroom. "For one, it's hard to demonstrate in class exactly how much I really love being spanked. However, here at home, I can absolutely show you."

Twisting slightly as she pulled away, she slipped between his hands. If only her brightly shining eyes could unravel the nerves slowly tightening his chest. Unlike before, this anxiety came from wanting to do a good job and nothing more. She was right—there was a lot less pressure here in the privacy of their bedroom. No one else watching or critiquing his performance. Even though he knew that second part was unlikely—the other Doms had been involved with their own subs, and most of Mistress Julie's attention had been on Connor—he hadn't been able to shake the idea.

Avery was wearing the same leggings and t-shirt she'd been wearing in class, but when she took them off, it was obvious she'd taken the time to remove the underwear she'd had on before he came over. As always, the sight of her stripping stirred his arousal, despite his nerves, and his cock eagerly jumped to attention.

Turning, she bent over the edge of the bed, presenting her bare ass. Not that different from when they did doggy style or earlier in the club, yet it was. It meant something different.

Avery was right—this wasn't at all like the class. Her movements were sensual, and the moment was intimate. When she bent over like this, he couldn't deny he wanted to slap her ass. Unfortunately, the guilt that welled up at the thought of how far he wanted to take things, how red he wanted to turn her skin, how much he'd wanted to go so much farther... that hadn't changed at all.

Looking over her shoulder, Avery raised her hips, teasing him with the perfect, curvy mounds of her ass. The pouting lips of her pussy were also visible, tempting him to slide between them. Why couldn't they just have sex? Why did he have to spank her first?

"We're going to play a game. You start off light, and I'll tell you harder until you get to my preferred amount of force for a fun spanking, then I'll say 'green.' Okay?" She raised her eyebrows.

'Green' was from the stoplight system, which had been explained during the first class. Red meant stop, Yellow meant slow down, and Green meant go. It was supposed to be an easy way to communicate between Dom and submissive. Everyone in the club knew the safewords, so if someone heard a sub say Yellow or Red, and the Dom didn't stop, they'd *be* stopped.

Here, Avery wouldn't have that backup. She was trusting him. With her body. Her pleasure. Her needs.

Taking a deep breath, Nick stepped forward, placing himself slightly to her side. He could do this.

⚜ 19 ⚜

The tiny smack Nick gave her rivaled some of the earliest ones he'd tried at Marquis. Avery did what she hadn't been able to do there for fear of embarrassing him. She snorted.

"Harder."

Smack.

Oooh, that was way better. Still way too light, but better, and many steps above his first swat. It stung a little, though not as much as she would like.

Avery wasn't sure this was the best way to do things, but she'd hated seeing how down on himself he'd been during class. The classes were public for safety reasons, and she got it, especially because private tutelage would be a huge time commitment, but it was clearly not how Nick was going to thrive. At least, not until he became surer of himself and trusted her to let him know when he was going too far.

"Harder."

There, hesitation this time.

She couldn't help but wonder if part of his problem was he was afraid of others seeing him take things too far instead of accepting that as part of the process. Sometimes, the quest for perfection could hinder itself when it came to practicing. He was very hesitant to hurt her, no matter how much she enjoyed certain types of pain.

Right now, she doubted they'd get to a point where she'd need to say Yellow, but she was pretty sure he'd be horrified if she did in front of an audience.

"Harder, Master Nick," she sing-songed the words, prodding at his pride and temper a little.

Smack!

This time Avery gasped, her body jerking as the stinging pain hit, then spread through her with warmth. She shuddered, fingers flexing in the sheets.

"That was pretty good," she finally said after taking a moment to enjoy the sting and the sensations that rippled through her in its wake. Her bottom lifted, begging for more.

"Again, please."

NICK

She had to be kidding.

Except she wasn't.

Nick had spanked her much harder to show her not to taunt him. That was something they'd gone over last week—not letting the submissives get away with bad behavior. It was supposed to have been a punishment swat, harder than the others... but she had enjoyed it.

Described it as 'pretty good' instead of painful, too much, or even 'great.'

Clearly, his expectations needed some reworking if he was going to give her what she needed.

She was right. It was a lot easier to do that without the audience. He wasn't sure he'd have been able to bring himself to spank her that hard at Marquis, even as a 'punishment.' He would have been too worried about what other people thought of him. Too worried about what conclusions they might draw about him. Even if they were all there for the same thing and focused on what they were doing. Hell, even if they felt the same things, which they probably had been since none of the submissives had been satisfied with their Dom's performance.

So, he did it again, this time allowing himself to slap her ass as hard on the left cheek as he had the right, watching the ripple through her flesh. She gasped again and lifted her hips back up, begging for more.

Now that he'd been encouraged, his cock surged from half-hard to rock hard as he watched her skin turn pink, much faster than it had during class because he was spanking her that much harder.

Smack! Smack! Smack!

She'd stopped telling him 'harder' but wasn't saying 'green' yet. Had she forgotten? Or had he not gotten there yet?

You're supposed to be the Dom. Ask.

"Avery, what color are you?"

"Green, Sir."

The answer came without hesitation, and the feeling of satisfaction that flooded through his chest was so strong, it was a physical sensation.

"More, please."

There was a note of pleading in her voice that called to his deepest urges. Nick raised his hand again and spanked her, a little harder than before, his hand moving over her luscious ass. He could already tell there was a huge difference between how he'd been doing it in class and what he was doing now.

Avery's skin turned from pale cream to hot pink, slowly darkening in places where his hand had overlapped the blows. Her ass jiggled with every impact, lifting right back into place to meet the next hard slap. Breathy moans punctuated the sound of impact.

He tried to spread the spanking over her whole ass, from the top, down over the softest part of the mounds, to just above where the curves met her thighs. Try as he might, he couldn't forget how much the 'sit spot' fucking hurt, so he wasn't ready to go there yet.

Not that Avery seemed to mind.

In their current position, and without her underwear on, it was obvious how much the spanking was turning her on. He didn't need verbal reassurance that she was enjoying the spanking. He could see it.

The cheeks of her ass were turning bright and dark pink. So, was her pussy, even though he hadn't touched it. The lips were swollen and puffy, the space between them glistening with her arousal. She was soaking wet.

When was he supposed to stop the spanking?

That was something they really hadn't gone over in class.

Before it becomes too much.

Not exactly a firm metric, but he got it.

When he'd first started cooking, there had been recipes to follow, certain amounts of ingredients, certain amounts of time... which was good enough for basic cooking, for getting the same results every time. Then something could change it. Different ovens heat at different speeds. Elevation changed how long something should be baked. An ingredient might not be available and require a substitution. And if you wanted to do something new...

Recipes were helpful, but they didn't account for individualized tastes, ovens, or locations.

Just like there was no metric for judging how someone might react to a spanking. Nick had hated every second, though he understood why it was required. Avery's reaction was completely different. He couldn't judge how much would be too much for her based on what he'd felt for himself.

What he could do was decide he'd had enough of spanking her, and now, he wanted to fuck.

AVERY

The heat spreading through her ass and along her nerves was like a siren song, calling to all of Avery's most secret impulses and desires. The ones she'd buried for so long were pushed away.

She'd missed this.

The intimacy. The pain. The pleasure. The rush of adrenaline that came from giving her body over to someone else's dominion. The trust it required.

She'd missed it so much.

Even as the spanking continued, verging on being too much, she didn't say anything because she didn't want Nick to stop. She'd needed this for too long. It was a treat she'd denied herself, and now her impulse was to overindulge to fill the well.

Then the swats stopped, and Avery moaned, panting as she assimilated the sensations. Reveled in them. Eyes closed, breasts squashed between her and the bed, ass throbbing from a well-administered spanking, she felt utterly perfect.

Nick made it even better.

Chef pants didn't have zippers, but she heard the swoosh of fabric as it fell from his hips to his ankles. A moment later, the blunt head of his cock probed her slick folds, sliding up and down between them and sending tingling pleasure to thread through the throbbing soreness from the spanking.

She leaned forward, toes pushing up, trying to line herself up with his cock. Not that Nick needed any invitation. He thrust, sliding into her hard and fast, hands smoothing over the hot cheeks of her ass before settling on her hips. Avery moaned at the extra sensation—her chastised skin extra sensitive to the hard knife calluses on his hands and the way the heels of his palms still pressed against her pinked flesh.

The inner muscles of her body clenched around him, and she moaned. The fullness of having his cock deep inside her, the way her hot cheeks pressed against his groin, his hands holding her in place and pinning her to the bed... was wickedly, deliciously submissive, and oh, so satisfying. He thrust, and Avery writhed, clenching and moaning, her body trying to push against him but held in place by his greater weight. She reveled in her helplessness beneath him.

Each thrust of his cock pushed another wave of pleasure through her, the friction hitting her in all the right places. His balls slapped against her clit, and his movements pressed her more firmly into the bed, the front of her mound rubbing against the corner and adding to the pressure on that sensitive organ. Avery moaned, arching her back, rubbing her nipples on the sheets.

Heat and need were flooding through her, but there was nothing she could do. No movement she could make. She was completely subjugated to Nick's will, his hard thrusts, his rhythm, and motion, all driving her wild. Each slap of his body against hers reignited the sting in her cheeks.

"Nick.... oh, fuck... Nick... please..." Clenching around him, she could feel her orgasm rising, each thrust almost too pleasurable to bear as his cock rubbed over her g-spot again and again. "Oh, please, Nick!"

Saying his name did nothing but make him move harder, faster, riding her for all she was worth until she was writhing and screaming his name with her face pressed into the sheets. It was everything she'd needed for so long. The waves of pleasure built upon each other until the ecstasy overwhelmed everything, bursting out of her in a white-hot supernova that seared her from within.

⚜

NICK

The ripples of pink flesh every time Nick slammed his cock deep inside Avery would be something he could never forget. He'd done that. Left his marks on her skin, heating it so he could feel it emanating from the surface of her skin against his groin. She moved beneath him, clenching and squirming, and the thrill of holding her in place was something he might be ashamed of later, but right now, it added to the eroticism of their joining.

She wasn't complaining.

Quite the opposite.

He knew exactly when Avery started to climax, her muscles spasming around his cock, making it harder for him to thrust as her body gripped him.

The way she cried out his name, along with her pleas, were making it impossible for him to maintain his control.

"Avery... fuck..." Those were the only words he managed to grit out between his teeth before his own orgasm exploded. Ecstasy throbbed through him, pulsing in time with each spurt of his cock. Physically it wasn't different from any other time they'd had sex, other than the heat from Avery's ass pressed firmly against his lower stomach, but it felt like so much more.

He emptied himself into her, yet he felt full in his own way, sating a craving he hadn't fed before. Breathless, he fell forward, bracing his elbows on either side of her but letting some of his weight cover her. He felt her sigh beneath him with happiness, her body still clenching around him as he softened.

As they cuddled on the bed, Avery's head tucked into his chest, his hand drifted down to her ass and squeezed gently. Testing.

"Ouch," Avery grumbled, and Nick winced, releasing the handful of flesh. Avery poked him in the chest. "That wasn't a complaint. I like knowing I'll be sore after."

"I'm not sure I do."

"Please." Avery snorted. "I bet I'm not even pink anymore. I won't feel a thing by morning." She sounded disappointed, even though it made Nick feel better.

Somewhat assuaged, Nick still took the time to push up and bend over to see if what she said was true. Yup, her ass barely had any blush left. He suddenly understood her disappointment because he kind of wished there had been a little more evidence of her spanking.

❦   2 0   ❦

From no friends to three friends. She was completely unsurprised Domi, Rae, and Iris were hitting it off. Iris was far more outgoing than Avery and fit smoothly into their little group as if she'd always been there. She had all sorts of fun stories to tell, thanks to her brother and soon-to-be sister-in-law.

At Iris' suggestion, they'd decided to meet up for Saturday brunch at Founding Farmers since evenings weren't so easy for Avery. Avery was enjoying the food, especially the red velvet pancakes that were the size of her head. Iris had ordered those for the table to share, insisting that they shouldn't miss out. They had ended up sharing most of the dishes since Iris was the only one who had been there before, and they all wanted to taste everything.

"Did you know Mitch was hired to be a stripper for a bachelorette party?" Iris' dark eyes sparkled with glee as their mouths dropped open in shock.

"What?! No." Avery glanced at Domi, who thankfully appeared to be fascinated rather than upset. Her makeup and clothes were toned down from her usual 'look' for brunch, though she and Iris looked as if they were cut from the same cloth. Both Latina, both wearing all black, both wearing more makeup than Avery or Rae.

In contrast, Rae was wearing a pink-and-orange flowered long-sleeved dress that matched the pink braids she had woven throughout her hair, and Avery was in a nice blue shirt and jeans. Domi and Iris looked ready to kick ass and take names, whereas Rae and Avery were more along the lines of 'ladies who brunch.'

"Yup. Kate told me. For Jessica, the one who has two husbands, Chris and Justin. They're both friends with Andrew. Her best friend knew none of the Doms would want a regular stripper there, so she asked Mitch to help them out."

"Oh my God..." Domi cracked up. "I am so making him show me his stripper moves."

"He'll enjoy that." Rae shook her head, but her eyes were dancing with glee as she nudged Domi with her elbow. "Think you can arrange a private showing for us."

"Absolutely not. He's all mine now." Domi stuck her tongue out at Rae. "Find your own stripper Dom."

"I can't imagine most of the other Doms doing that, even for a friend." Avery laughed. "Especially not for a friend." Mitch, she could absolutely see. He was a goofball of the highest order, despite being a sadist, and thrived as the center of attention. Plus, she would bet he was a good dancer.

Was Nick a good dancer? She wondered if she'd ever find out. Running a restaurant wasn't conducive to going out to dance clubs. Most places were still going by the time they left work, but usually, she was way too tired to enjoy it, and the idea of going straight from work rather than being able to go home, take a shower, and collapse, didn't appeal.

Ugh. She was getting old.

Stronghold had a dance floor. Maybe she could convince Nick to go with her sometime on a Thursday. It would be good for him to be in the club when other people were playing. She wasn't sure he'd watched a scene in person outside of what they were doing in class. Going to a show at Marquis might be good as well. He would probably feel more comfortable in a booth than where people could watch him.

A hand waved in front of her face. Avery blinked, and Domi's tanned palm came into focus.

"Earth to Avery, Earth to Avery, come in Avery." Domi grinned, taking her hand back when she saw she had Avery's attention. "How's it going with you and Nick? We need an update!"

She couldn't stop the smile that spread across her face. Nick was becoming a regular spanko. He'd even agreed to try out the flogger on her last night, despite the fact he hadn't practiced on her in class and wouldn't do so until Monday. Avery thought adding spanking to their private activities had given him confidence, and the particular flogger she had was very light.

"Good, it's going really well."

"Oooh, look at that smile," Iris teased. "I guess that means you two have been practicing at home?" She looked at Domi and Rae. "You wouldn't believe how hesitant the Doms were to spank us. Tiny slap, then 'oh, I'm sorry, was that too much?' Um... no, I would have made a noise if I'd felt it at all." She rolled her eyes as Domi and Rae cracked up. Even Avery couldn't stop herself from laughing. It might be disrespectful, but so true.

"Yes, we've been practicing at home, and Nick is much more comfortable without an audience." Avery shook her head. "He's such a perfectionist. I don't think he likes anyone to see him do anything other than his best. Add that to the worry he was actually going to hurt me... the class wasn't his best effort."

Iris snorted. "Yeah, they all thought they were going to hurt us. Talk about overestimating themselves." Her expression turned thoughtful. "Connor might have reason to worry. Hopefully, I'll get paired with him next time. I bet he spanks a lot harder than Q just because of physics."

"Or Samantha... she was doing a pretty decent job with Freddy."

"Yeah, but I think Olivia is trying to matchmake there." They sat straight in surprise, focusing on Iris, who snickered. "That's what Andrew said, though I'm not sure how well it will work since Sam is a switch and not a Domme."

"He's bi, right? Maybe they'll end up in a throuple. Or they could be a couple, and Sam could find a Dom to platonically top her. Sorta like what Kincaid and Zach have going on."

"Kink is so weird sometimes," Rae said, propping her elbows on the table so she could rest her chin on her hands. There was no judgment in her voice, more like she was adding commentary. "No one talks about vanilla relationships like this."

"We have different needs than the vanillas." Avery sighed ruefully. "I figured that out when my body lit up like a Christmas tree getting back into the kink stuff. I've gone without it for so long, I thought maybe I didn't need it, but I do." She sighed again.

"Is that a bad thing?" Domi asked, tilting her head at Avery.

"Not in and of itself," Avery replied after a moment. A small pit opened in the bottom of her stomach, and she recognized the fear but knew it wasn't necessary here. None of the women at this table were going to judge her. "I told one of my friends back home about me and kink, and she didn't take it very well. I didn't bother telling the rest of them. They're all very like-minded."

"Didn't take it very well?" Rae scowled. "Like it had anything to do with her."

"Forget her," Iris said, slinging an arm around Avery's shoulders on their side of the booth. "You're with us now. We're way better."

"Cheers to that." Domi lifted her glass, and everyone followed suit. At that moment, Avery knew she'd been right to leave home, no matter how much it bugged her parents. She was so happy she'd found these women. She couldn't ask for better friends.

NICK

The lunch rush was over, thankfully. Nick glanced at the clock on the wall. Only another couple hours before Avery arrived for the dinner shift. Working with his girlfriend was even better than he'd thought it would be. Sure, they stayed professional while they were in the restaurant, but he still got to see her a hell of a lot more than he would if they weren't working together. She made every shift they shared even better.

"Chef Nick! Your brother is at the bar and wants to know if you have a minute," Alanna informed him as she hurried past, flashing him a quick smile. From what Nick knew, she and Jonathan had a date tonight, both of them free for a Saturday night for once, and were rushing to get out of the restaurant. He didn't blame them.

It amused him how everyone knew everything that was going on with their relationship, but only the managers had figured out him and Avery. Maybe he should thank them. Everyone was so caught up in the George, Alanna, Jonathan love triangle, they didn't notice their executive chef was romantically involved with one of their sous chefs.

"Thanks, Alanna," he called after her, picking up the towel resting on the metal counter in front of him and wiping off his hands. She threw a thumbs up at him over her shoulder before disappearing out the door into the dining room.

Nick looked back over his shoulder at the cooks on the other side of the line. "I'll be back. Anyone need anything before I go?"

"No, Chef." It was like his own personal Greek chorus the way they all responded together. Nick waved his hand and followed Alanna's path out the door, twisting slightly to avoid George, who was on his way into the kitchen with a thundercloud expression.

Well, he was going to be fun to work with tonight.

Hopefully, George would eventually get used to it. In the meantime, there wasn't much Nick could do except to be considerate of why he was such a grump lately. It couldn't be easy watching Alanna and Jonathan as a couple, especially since George had decided to maintain his friendship with them both.

Dismissing the server drama from his mind, Nick headed to Marquis' bar, where his big brother was waiting. As always, Luke was dressed in jeans and his construction company's t-shirt, looking casual yet easily fitting in at Marquis. Maybe it was the windswept dark hair the two of them shared or the aura of confidence.

Now that Nick knew what his brother went through with Olivia on a regular basis, he was even more astounded by how supremely confident Luke was at all times.

Standing on the other side of the bar from Luke was Shane, one of the bartenders, chatting with him. Shane was older with a shiny bald head, a nicely trimmed dark goatee shot through with silver, and a smile that only quit when he needed to ream someone out. It didn't happen often because he was a quieter kind of guy, but Nick had seen it once when one of their male servers harassed one of their nonbinary servers.

Shane had followed Jeff into the kitchen and quietly and lethally verbally ripped Jeff a new asshole. Jeff had gone white as a ghost and immediately quit. Good riddance to bad rubbish.

No one had risked getting on Shane's bad side since. He was quiet and friendly, but if Nick ever needed to bury a body, he knew who his first call would be.

"Hey, Nick. The usual?" Shane smiled at him in greeting, already moving to grab a beer glass.

"Yes, thank you." Nick slid onto the barstool next to Luke. "What's up?"

"Wanted to check in. It's been a while since we've hung out and talked." Luke reached out to give Nick a half hug. Nick leaned in, his mind running over Luke's words. Hmmm, it had been a while. Normally, they tried to get together at least once every couple of weeks, but they hadn't done that since before the Dom class started. He'd been too busy with class, work, and Avery.

Damn.

Shane slid the glass of cold beer, fresh from the tap in front of Nick, then walked away. There weren't any other customers at the bar since it was the middle of the afternoon, but he must have decided Luke and Nick needed the space to talk.

"Sorry, I hadn't realized it had been so long."

"No worries." Luke pulled away, settling back in place with his half-finished beer. "I know you've been busy, and I'm happy for you. New relationship and all that." He grinned, lifting his glass to his lips for a sip while Nick did the same. "I remember the beginning of my and Olivia's relationship."

Wow. Luke was comparing Nick and Avery to him and Olivia... that was... fast? Was it, though? Nick already knew he was falling in love with Avery, even though he hadn't told her yet. Maybe he shouldn't be surprised his big brother already realized things were serious between them. Luke tended to be on top of things.

"I do, too. I remember having to take your dog for a lot of walks," Nick joked. Luke had called on him more than once to take care of Molly while he and Olivia first got together.

"If you ever get a dog, I'll be happy to return the favor."

Nick shook his head. His schedule was not conducive to a pet, especially not a dog. Maybe a cat, but even then... He couldn't keep an herb garden alive, so he wouldn't try with a living, breathing animal. Borrowing Molly was about at his level.

"How are things going with you and Olivia? Gotta tell you, the class is making me wonder how you do it."

"It's easy when you like it." Luke chuckled. "Well, easier. I had to let go of some ideas about what I was supposed to be and how I was supposed to act, but once I did, I was a lot happier."

"I get that. Sometimes, I get a surge of guilt with Avery, even though she says she likes it." Nick shook his head and took a large swallow of beer. Talking about his feelings was not his forte. "I still feel guilty."

"Do you like it?" As usual, his big brother went straight for the jugular.

"Yes, I like it." Nick made a face. "I think that's a big part of why I feel so guilty."

"Don't. I know, I know, easier said than done." Luke clapped his hand on Nick's shoulder. "I struggled a lot when I was getting into everything. I was ashamed of what I liked and felt as if I was enjoying something I wasn't supposed to."

"Exactly." Relief surged, tinged with surprise. He hadn't realized he and Luke might feel some of the same things, considering they were on opposite sides of the coin. Luke wasn't spanking Olivia; it was the other way round. Though... he could see how that could cause shame, too.

Why did this have to be so hard?

"It gets easier." Luke squeezed his shoulder. "Especially when you have someone to talk about it with."

"Right now?"

"Might as well. Shane won't judge. Right, Shane?"

"La, la, la, can't hear you," Shane replied, not looking up from where he was taking glasses out of the bar's dishwasher and drying them with a cloth.

What could it hurt?

❧ 21 ❧

AVERY

Walking into the kitchen, Avery finished buttoning up her chef coat as she looked around. Everything looked as if it had been cleaned up since lunch, and the chefs were doing their dinner prep. Not that she'd expected anything less.

"Hey, babygirl." Alice was on sauté and gave Avery a little wave as she glanced up from chopping garnishes. It didn't matter that Avery was technically one of her bosses. Alice had called her babygirl from day one. Avery had never been inclined to ask her to stop because she knew it was a measure of affection from the older woman. "How ya doing?"

"Good, thanks, you?"

"I'm here."

Avery snickered. That was the answer Alice always gave. For her, it meant 'I'm doing okay.' If she was having a bad day, she didn't hesitate to say so, but a good day meant she didn't complain. Winking at her as if she knew what Avery was thinking, Alice bent back over her garnishes.

"How about you, Darnell?" she asked their grill chef for the evening. He grinned and winked at her.

"Doing good."

Turning to the left, she sighed inwardly when she saw Chad at the fry station. He might not be her favorite, but she tried to treat him like everyone else, anyway.

"How are you doing, Chad?"

"Like you care." He snorted, wiping his hands on his apron, barely glancing at her.

Fine. Avery pressed her lips together. She should probably call him out for being so disrespectful, but it was the beginning of the shift, and she didn't feel like dealing with his temper tantrum throughout it. Some battles were more easily won by ignoring the person. Don't feed the troll and all that.

The pantry was empty. Sandra was probably getting something from the walk-in, so Avery turned away from that side of the kitchen rather than responding. Tying her apron around her waist, she glanced at the clock and frowned. Normally, Nick would be out here by now.

"Where's Nick?" she asked, directing the question toward Alice and Darnell.

"Out at the bar. His brother came by to see him," Alice told her, glancing up again. Something in her expression made Avery a little uneasy, not anything unfriendly, but it was *knowing*. Amused.

Stop it. You're imagining things. There's no reason to be paranoid.

Unfortunately, before that thought even finished, Chad snorted. Her head whipped around to face him, and the derision in his expression, the transparent animosity, made her step back.

"Shouldn't you know where your boyfriend is?" he mocked.

"I... he's not..." Avery stammered, but the words weren't coming. *Say something! Deny it! At least tell him it's none of his business!* It was as if her throat had closed up, and she could barely breathe, much less speak, as panic rose inside her like a tidal wave.

"Don't bother denying it. We all know you two are going upstairs to do freaky shit." He snorted again. "At least that explains how you ended up as sous chef."

His words hit like a punch to the gut, knocking the air out of her.

Not only did he know about her and Nick, he knew they were going to Marquis. Knew they were doing kinky stuff. She could only imagine what he thought they were doing and what he thought of her.

Not just him.

Everyone.

They all knew now.

The entire kitchen had come to a standstill while she gaped at Chad. It was like a bad dream, except she knew it wasn't. This was real.

Everything she'd feared at the beginning.

Everything she hadn't wanted.

It was real, and she had no defense.

They would all think she had earned her place on her back by doing freaky shit no self-respecting woman would do.

They would all think *she* was a freak.

They were staring at her. Waiting for her to stay something. To defend herself. To tell Chad he was wrong.

She couldn't.

It was all true.

A rushing noise filled her ears, and it felt as though time had slowed—stopped—and everyone was waiting to see what she did next.

She turned and ran.

Ran away from their judgment. Ran away from Chad's sneer. Ran away from being exposed.

Ran away from the roar of sound that swelled as soon as she reached the hallway to the back.

Ran out the service door at the back of the restaurant, like the coward she was.

❧

NICK

Shouting in the kitchen had Nick jerking his head up, and he wasn't the only one. It wasn't the usual shouting but didn't sound like an emergency. There was no panic, just angry shouting.

"What the hell?" Luke frowned, getting to his feet alongside Nick. Behind the bar, Shane had straightened, frowning.

Not bothering to answer, Nick bolted for the door. That was his domain, and if something was going on, he needed to know, especially since it wasn't just the bar that could hear everything. The servers, the hosts, and the few people who had trickled in early for happy hour were also staring at the swinging doors between the restaurant and the kitchen.

The only saving grace was so many people were shouting, individual words were hard to make out.

Shoving the doors open, one with each hand, Nick stalked through them to the center of the kitchen.

"SHUT UP."

Despite how many other people had been yelling, his dramatic entrance and command compelled them all to silence. From what he could see, it looked like Darnell and Alice had gotten into a shouting match with Chad, while Sandra, their pantry chef, stood frozen in the hallway that led to the walk-in, not sure if she wanted to come into the kitchen proper. Behind Nick, he could hear the doors flying open again as his brother followed him in.

"What the hell is going on in here?" His own temper was up. He'd been enjoying himself and was ticked off that his entire staff was unprofessional enough to scream at each other when his brother was there. Where was Avery? Why wasn't she taking care of this? Since no one was answering his first question, he gave them a follow-up.

"Where the hell is Avery?"

Relationship or not, he would have to ream her out about this. She should be on the clock by now and in the kitchen. A pang of worry hit him because it wasn't like her to be late, much less missing, especially without giving him a heads up. He was about to pull out his phone to check it, even though he knew he hadn't felt it buzz or heard it go off, when Alice and Chad started talking at the same time.

"Dickhead chased her off."

"She ran off. Hey! Don't call me a dickhead!"

"Then don't act like one, Dickhead!"

"Hey!" Nick half-shouted again, hopefully not loud enough to be heard in the dining room. Holding up his hand, he glared at both of them, then turned to Darnell, pointing at him. "Explain."

Chad mumbled something under his breath, and Nick had a feeling it was probably good he hadn't been able to hear the man. He was a good chef, but Alice was right; he was a dickhead. That didn't automatically disqualify anyone from the career. In fact, there were times Nick thought it might even be necessary, but it didn't make him easy to work with. Dickheads still needed to act professionally.

Unfortunately, Chad was the dickhead who thought he was owed something and rebelled against anyone being in a position of power over him. As long as he didn't act out, he would keep his job, but it didn't make him pleasant to work with.

"Uh, well, Avery came in and was asking how all of us were doing, then she asked where you were..." Darnell's voice faded, and his gaze cut over to Chad.

For a moment, Nick thought he was going to stop talking, but he shook his head. Clearly, Chad had done something, and Darnell didn't want to be a tattletale, but he'd been put on the spot.

"Chad said she should know since she's your girlfriend."

Shit.

Nick sucked in a breath.

How the fuck had Chad found out?

Not that it mattered.

"That's not all he said," Alice spoke up, glaring at Darnell, clearly displeased he'd left something out. Darnell looked away, unable to meet her gaze. When she was pissed, Alice was scary. "He said some shit about you two going upstairs, as if that's any of his business."

"It's all of our business if our sous chef got the position by spreading her legs," Chad shot back.

"Hey!" The word rang out from four throats at once, and Darnell was glaring at Chad with the rest of them.

A red haze settling over his vision, Nick took a step toward Chad, only to be jerked back.

"Don't. He's not worth it. Fire his ass. Keep your hands to yourself." Luke's voice was low and urgent in his ear. Nick realized his fists were clenched, and the urge to jump over the line and slam one of them into Chad's face was overwhelming. Luke must have realized that.

"You're fired," were the only words Nick could find. They were the right words, but that didn't help the way he was feeling, as if he wanted to explode all over the asshole.

"You can't fire me over telling the truth! I'll fucking sue!"

"Yes, he can," Luke said, stepping around Nick and bodily putting himself between them.

Normally, that would have made Nick furious, but right now, he was struggling to hold on to his temper and not get a physical assault charge. If Luke could actually form words, he was the better choice to confront Chad. Nick would rather punch him in the face.

"First, it's called at-will employment. Second, even try, and you will be slapped with a sexual harassment suit so fast, your head will spin. What you said to Avery was as egregious as it was untrue. The owners have been kept apprised of the relationship, which didn't start until recently, well after she was hired."

"Of course, you were 'apprised.' You're one of the freaks," Chad sneered. "I could tell everything about what goes on upstairs..."

"In which case, the non-disclosure agreement you signed can and will be used against you. Even if you find a lawyer to take you on, and that's a big if, you'll lose and pay out the ass for it. Then we'll still slap you with a sexual harassment suit. If you think I'm not willing to pay to protect my club, you're fucking wrong."

For the first time, a worried expression appeared on Chad's face. That it had taken so long showed how stupidly arrogant he was.

"You can't—"

"I can." Luke's voice brooked no argument. It was hard and uncompromising. That authority was part of the reason Nick had initially balked at the idea of Luke submitting to anyone. That wasn't who he was in public. He was like Nick—take charge, hold no prisoners, and fully in control.

Right now, Nick had never felt so out of control, which was why he was letting his big brother step in and handle Chad. Otherwise, Nick was liable to do a hell of a lot worse than merely fire him.

"It's Saturday night. You need me." Chad bristled.

"We really don't." Nick stepped out from behind his brother, shooting daggers from his eyes.

"I-I..." Chad's gaze darted around the kitchen, finding no sympathy from any corner. Even Sandra, who was usually friendly with him since they worked adjoining stations, wouldn't meet his gaze. "Fine. Fuck you all. You all know I'm right! Maybe that's not how she got her job, but... Ugh... Whatever." The supreme lack of logic in his conclusions was nearly as large as his lack of self-preservation.

Luke grabbed hold of Nick's arm again.

"Get out. Your final paycheck will be deposited. Do not come back for any reason, or you will be removed bodily from the premises." The threat was all the more impressive, delivered in Luke's low, silky tone.

Huffing, Chad stalked out—taking the more arduous way behind the line to avoid Nick, which was the smartest thing he'd done that day. Not that Alice made it easy for him. Her arms were crossed, and despite being almost a foot shorter, she was intimidating enough, so when he squeezed past her, he did his best not to even brush her.

They watched him go in complete silence.

It wasn't until he was gone, Nick felt something other than anger— a real and rising worry about where Avery ran off to.

❧ 22 ☙

Her phone wouldn't stop ringing. First Nick, then the restaurant number, as if she wouldn't realize it was still him. Then Alice's cell phone. Then Olivia's. Yeah, no way in hell was she answering that one right now. Even if she was pretty sure it wasn't Nick—he was bad enough—but the idea of Olivia being on the other end made her soul shrivel.

Everyone should make you shrivel right now.

You ran out on your job.

You are supposed to be the sous chef who runs the kitchen when Nick isn't there, and you ran away!

Why didn't you point out that you were hired way before you and Nick started seeing each other?

Why didn't you tell him you earned your place with your skill and work ethic, two things he doesn't do as well as you?

Why didn't you tell him it was none of his business?

Why didn't you tell him if he worked as hard as you did, maybe one day, he could be a sous chef, but if he kept making up excuses why other people were ahead of him in their careers, he would never get anywhere?

Yeah, why didn't you do that? That would have been a good one.

Why am I only thinking of all these options now instead of when they would have been useful?!

Screaming, Avery slammed her hands against her steering wheel, drawing a very odd look from the woman walking along the sidewalk in front of her.

"Sorry... sorry..." Avery shrank in her seat. This was what she got for driving to the nearest parking lot and pulling into a space that faced the sidewalk.

Maybe she should have gone home, but walking out on her job and going home felt more egregious than driving three blocks away and parking. Like, maybe she'd run out, but she hadn't run as far as she could have.

Yeah, keep acting like that matters.

Pick up the phone, you coward, or you're going to lose your job.

If she even had a job at this point.

She was sure her chances of keeping it were slipping through her fingers with every phone call she ignored, yet she couldn't bring herself to pick up the phone or read the texts dinging between calls.

Do I even want to keep the job? How am I supposed to go back there and face everyone when they all know? *How can I command any kind of respect when they know I get on my knees for Nick?*

In her position, she needed her coworkers' respect. She could still see the sneer on Chad's face, which had looked a lot like the disgust on Shannon's face after Avery had tried to tell her about kink. She hadn't dared look at Alice or Darnell, but she'd seen the shock on Sandra's face as she'd rushed past.

From the dead silence in the room before she'd bolted, it was hard to believe the others weren't coming to the same conclusions as Chad. Even if they hadn't, running might have convinced them.

Why did you run?! You should have stood your ground!

Too late now. She'd have to deal with the consequences. Eventually. When she got the courage to pick up the phone.

Which might be never.

A new ringtone sounded—Lizzo's 'Good as Hell,' which was so the opposite of what Avery was feeling right now, but the sound of it sent a surge of relief through her. It was Domi, Rae, or Iris.

Friends.

Real friends who wouldn't judge her and who would understand what was going on.

For the first time, she grabbed her phone, only glancing at the screen long enough to see Rae's face.

"Hello?"

"Hey hun, are you okay? I just got a call from Nick. He's worried as hell, and no one knows where you are."

Emotions surged, clamping Avery's throat shut again as misery, defeat, and the knowledge he must be so disappointed in her over-whelmed everything else.

She burst into tears.

⚜

NICK

It didn't matter that it was a busy-as-hell Saturday night, Nick kept his phone in his pocket, ringer on, and not one person blamed him. Not that it was a worthwhile effort at first. He'd tried contacting Avery every which way he knew how. He'd even sent Luke to her apartment since he couldn't step away from running the kitchen, but she hadn't been home.

Which left him wondering where she *had* gone, and he was worried as hell.

The rest of the staff was worried as well. Alice, Darnell, and Sandra kept shooting him glances over the line. Ravi, who had been called in to take over at the fryer station, knew something was up but not what and kept looking for clues from the rest of them. Add in a very grumpy George at Nick's side, and the entire evening was turning into a shit show.

Why hadn't she picked up her phone?

Had something happened to her?

He'd kept calling and texting from several phones. He'd even asked

Olivia to call her, thinking she might answer for another woman. In hindsight, that might not have been the smartest thing. Olivia was not only Avery's boss but a very intimidating woman.

Though it had given him the idea to finally call her friends. Thankfully, Olivia had those numbers. Domi hadn't answered her phone, but Rae had and promised to try to get in touch with Avery and find out what was going on.

Nick had given up on Avery getting back to him, but he was hoping Rae could hunt her down, then *she'd* get back to him.

Since Avery wasn't.

His feelings on that vacillated.

On one hand, he was furious with Chad and knew Avery would be upset about what Chad said and that their coworkers now knew about their relationship.

She'd run out on her job and wasn't answering her phone. That wasn't something that was acceptable under any circumstances, much less on the busiest night of the week. It was also incredibly unlike her. Not answering her phone might be explained by something terrible, and he was torn between hoping she was okay and wanting to spank the hell out of her if she was. Incredibly unprofessional on his part.

Maybe this is why people said not to mix business with pleasure.

"Here, Chef." Alice slid a plate onto the shelf in front of him, snapping him out of his thoughts. He needed to focus on work.

Why hadn't he thought about that when he'd decided to get involved with his sous chef? He'd thought about how great it would be to work together, so he didn't have to worry about her feeling as though she didn't get enough time with him, as he had in previous relationships. He hadn't thought about what it would be like if they had a fight or she did something unprofessional that required a warning on her record if not firing her outright.

Shit, would the others think she was getting special treatment if he didn't fire her outright now?

"Get your head in the game, Chef," George murmured, elbowing Nick in the side.

Crap. He'd just been standing there again, thinking instead of doing anything.

Getting two more orders into the hands of the food runners, he nearly jumped out of his skin when his phone buzzed. Yanking it out of his pocket, he saw it was just a text, not a call. At this point, he didn't care as long as it was about Avery, and she was okay. The pounding of his heart felt like it tripled when he saw the text was from Rae.

We've got her. She's safe. She won't be coming in to work tonight.

Nick blinked and re-read the text. Once. Twice. By the third time, his temper was up. What kind of shit message was that?

She's safe? If she was safe, why wasn't she coming in to work? Why wasn't she texting him herself? Why was she blowing him off? He wasn't just her boyfriend and Dom. He was her fucking employer.

He tapped out an angry message to Rae, then stopped. This wasn't her fault. She'd done exactly what he'd asked—found Avery and let him know she was okay.

It wasn't her fault Avery wasn't coming back as she was supposed to.

Deleting his response, Nick typed in *thank you*, sent it, and then shoved the phone back in his pocket. He would have to deal with Avery later. Hopefully, he would have calmed down by then.

AVERY

Sniffling on her spot in the middle of Domi and Rae's couch, with Iris and Rae on either side of her, she couldn't help but notice whatever Domi was working on in the kitchen smelled amazing. Her stomach rumbled, even though she would have sworn she couldn't possibly eat a thing, not while she was so upset.

At least she'd calmed down and wasn't still sobbing, but random bouts of tears kept welling up. She'd gone through half a box of tissues since arriving at Rae and Domi's. Mitch was there, but he was out back, playing with Domi's daughter, Ana. Avery had interrupted family night. Something else to feel guilty about.

"I can't believe he said that," Iris seethed. She squeezed Avery's hand. Rae was snuggled up on the other side of her with an arm wrapped around Avery's shoulders. "Want me to fuck him up? I know some people."

The way she said it made Avery think she wasn't kidding. There was something a little hard-edged about Iris, as though she knew how to get into trouble.

"No. I can't even be that mad. I knew what people would think if they found out about me and Nick." She'd known, yet let herself be convinced otherwise.

"Only people who aren't using their brains would think that," Rae countered. "Didn't you say he was a jerk? And that he thought he was better than he was?"

"Well, yeah, but—"

"Did anyone else say they felt the same way as he did?" Rae was ruthless in her cross-examination.

"Has anyone ever told you that you should be a lawyer?" Avery mumbled, dipping her head. "No, they didn't say that, but they didn't say they didn't believe it, either."

"Did you give them a chance to?"

Avery pressed her lips together. Damn it. Rae really should have been a lawyer. But she was making Avery feel a little better. Avery had taken everyone's silence as condemnation, but maybe she was a little oversensitive. Maybe they hadn't known what to say.

She sure as hell hadn't.

"No, but—"

"No buts." Rae held up a finger, shaking her head slowly, making Avery smile, which felt like a minor miracle. "You know what they say about assuming."

Coming into the room, the smell of something delicious and fried wafting alongside her, Domi put down a platter on the coffee table.

"*Tostones*. Start with these. The soup should be ready soon." She flipped around and headed back into the kitchen.

"Yaaaaaas," Rae said, letting go of Avery to lean forward and pick up one. "Ouch, ouch, ouch."

"They're hot," Domi called from the kitchen. "Maybe give them a second to cool."

"Nope." Rae bit the end off of hers and opened her mouth, fanning it as steam rose from where she'd bitten it. "Ah, it burns, but it tastes so good." After a moment, she seemed to realize Rae and Iris were staring at her. "What?"

"Doesn't that hurt?" Avery was used to burning herself on hot food but waited until it was properly cooled before trying to eat it.

"Ignore her," Domi came back into the room, dusting her hands off and shaking her head. "She thinks things are ready long before they are."

"It's not my fault things are Rae-Ready before they're other people ready." Rae took another bite of her tostones. "It's already cooling. The rest of you should be able to eat them soon."

"I should have left them on the cooling tray until they were actually ready. She does the same thing with cookies." Domi sat in a chair, giving Avery a rueful smile. "So, I say we eat comfort food, we drink, and we talk as much as you need to."

"Oh... I don't know..." That sounded amazing, but Domi had a daughter and a boyfriend, who were both home. Avery needed to talk to Nick, eventually, even though she didn't know what she was going to say to him or how to excuse herself. At least she had until the end of his shift to figure it out. "What about Mitch and Ana?"

"They'll play outside until it's time to come in and eat. Thankfully, she's old enough to do most of her bedtime routine on her own, but Mitch can help her with some of it. I'll pop out to do the rest at some point." The matter-of-fact way Domi laid it out made Avery feel a little better.

"Okay. Thank you... SO much." Tears welled up in her eyes again, but this time from happiness instead of the shame, frustration, and anger plaguing her. "You have no idea what it means to me."

"Hey, that's what friends are for," Rae said. "Now, we need to talk about why you didn't call one of us."

Avery blew out a long breath, using the time to think of an answer because the truth was, she wasn't sure. Now that she was here, it seemed like an obvious thing to have done. She hadn't thought. She'd reacted.

"I don't know," she finally admitted. "I panicked. I ran. Then I sat there, internally yelling at myself for running instead of doing anything, thinking about everything I should have done instead."

"Ugh, don't you hate that?" Domi groaned, leaning her head back. "I always come up with the best comebacks like three hours too late." Avery gave her a watery smile, feeling a little better. Domi was so sassy and snappy, it had never occurred to Avery that Domi also felt as if she didn't get to say what she wanted. "We'll use tonight to come up with the perfect thing to say when you see Chad again."

"If you see him again." Rae scowled. "Personally, I think his ass should be fired, and I will judge Nick if he doesn't do it."

"I should be fired, too." Avery rubbed her forehead, guilt welling up again. She'd left them short-staffed tonight. On a Saturday. And now sitting with her friends instead of doing the responsible thing—go back, face the music, and finish out her shift.

"Hey, you were verbally attacked, and this is self-care. You can't go back until you know how you're going to face that shitgibbon." Nodding firmly, Domi got up from her seat. "I'm going to check on the soup, then we'll figure out how to handle Chad."

"I still say we should key his car or something," Iris muttered under her breath.

$$\text{❧} \quad 2\ 3 \quad \text{❧}$$

NICK

The last ticket was being served up, and still nothing from Avery. He didn't take his phone out of his pocket again to look and make sure. Doing so to see an empty screen again would hurt.

Why wasn't she reaching out to him?

Even if she wasn't ready to as his employee, he was her boyfriend. He wanted to be there for her, and she wasn't letting him. She'd run away, which didn't say much about them as a couple.

Or maybe he was wrong. Maybe it said everything. Maybe this was another situation where he wasn't enough. Not around enough, not attentive enough, not dominant enough—he didn't know what box he'd checked off, but it seemed to be the story of his life with relationships. He was more than enough in the kitchen. He knew what he was supposed to do and what was supposed to happen. That was how he'd worked his way up to the position of executive chef.

When his phone finally rang, he pulled it out of his pocket, and when he saw Avery's name, he almost shoved it back in. Let her wait and see how it felt.

Only that he truly hated hypocrisy kept him from doing so. He would show her what she should have done all the times he'd called her earlier this evening—he picked up the phone.

"Hello." His voice came out as a short, sharp bark, and George glanced up at him, hazel eyes full of concern. One thing that had happened throughout the night was George had slowly gotten out of his funk as he'd watched Nick's mood deteriorate.

"Um, hi." Avery's voice was soft, hesitant. Which, oddly, made it harder to hold on to his temper. Now he felt bad for how he'd answered the phone. He was still mad and thought he deserved to be mad, but hearing her hesitation made him feel like he'd kicked a puppy.

Argh.

Not trusting what might come out of his mouth, he pressed his lips shut, waiting for her to say something.

"So, um, I'm sure you're wondering what happened..." Her voice trailed off, a bit of pleading imbued in her tone.

"The others told me what happened. I came in right after you left. Chad has been fired, by the way."

There was a moment of silence, then she sighed, and the sound grated on his nerves.

"That's... I mean... thank you. I hate you had to do that."

"That was the consequence of his actions." His voice was harsh. He turned away from George's worried expression to see Darnell and Alice were watching him. Great. Nick was tempted to abandon his post and head to the office where he could talk privately, but that would be extremely unprofessional, and on a night like tonight, he needed to be a good role model. Though talking on his phone with his girlfriend didn't really go along with that, but since she was also his sous chef, he could pretend that was the main reason. "I wish you had stayed around, so you could have been there for it."

"I..."

Another long pause and he got the impression she was searching for the words to explain herself. Determined not to speak first, he clenched his jaw so tightly, it ached.

"I'm sorry. I don't know why I ran. I really don't. Then once I did, it was so hard to come back... and every minute I stayed away made it harder."

"So, staying away completely and not coming into work at was the solution?" He couldn't keep the sarcasm out of his voice. Dammit. "It's Saturday night, Avery. We needed you."

"I couldn't face everyone... not after they knew."

Fuck. This again. Nick pinched the bridge of his nose and walked toward the hallway, so everyone wouldn't hear their conversation. They had cleanup covered, so they didn't need him.

"They don't care, Avery. You know how I know that? They told me. Gareth and Miles have known for weeks, and they didn't care."

AVERY

"Gareth and Miles know, too? Miles isn't even on tonight!" Avery's voice rose into a kind of shriek. She could feel her friends all staring at her... but she was freaking out. It was bad enough the kitchen staff knew, but she'd hoped the rest of the restaurant wouldn't find out. Vain hope, she knew, but at the very least, she hadn't expected it to spread so fast.

"He knew a while ago, he told—"

"And you didn't tell me?" The guilt that had been eating her alive diminished as anger took hold.

"What good would it have done? They wouldn't tell anyone, and you were already freaked out about people knowing—"

"Yes, Nick, for exactly this reason! If I'd known someone had realized, I could have been better prepared. I might not have been blindsided tonight. We could have done something, so maybe Chad would have never even known! There's a lot of good it could have done!"

"You're saying if you'd known two managers, who wouldn't tell anyone, knew you and I were dating, you wouldn't have had to run away tonight?"

The way he said it made her feel as if he'd stabbed her in the heart.

It was mocking, calling her out for the coward she was, but it hurt so much more than when she'd called herself the same thing.

"I'm saying I don't know, but some kind of warning would have been nice!"

There was a long silence on the other end of the phone. Avery would have sworn she was cried out, but she still had tears left, which were filling her eyes. The ache in her chest intensified, and she rubbed at the spot as if she could somehow make it go away.

She knew he was disappointed and probably angry as well—and had every reason to be—but she also felt betrayed. They'd talked about how she hadn't wanted anyone at the restaurant to know, and when Nick had found out someone knew, he kept it from her.

"I have to go. I have a shift I need to finish. We can talk about this later." He didn't even wait for her to say anything before he hung up.

Ouch. That spot on her chest felt as if it had been stabbed, as though fingers had wrapped around her heart, squeezing it painfully.

She wanted to say it had been below the belt but thought she deserved it. She *had* run out on the shift and hadn't gone back. She'd left the restaurant short-staffed on the busiest night of the week. The guilt would stay with her for a long time. That wasn't the employee she wanted to be, the person she wanted to be.

She regretted staying away tonight, but she'd needed the space. Time to breathe and regroup before facing everyone who knew things about her, she really wished they didn't.

"Hey, you okay?" Rae asked sympathetically, coming back into the room, Iris and Domi trailing behind her. They'd stepped away to give her a minute alone.

Avery nodded, then shook her head, her jaw clenched because she wasn't sure she could talk about it without crying, and she really, really didn't want to cry again tonight. Rae seemed to pick up on that.

"Okay, well, let us know when you're ready to talk about it. In the meantime, Iris and I can keep arguing about spooning."

Curiosity uncracked Avery's jaw.

"Spooning? Why spooning?"

"Rae doesn't enjoy being spooned." Iris shrugged. "I like it. I get snuggled, then if I feel like getting it on, I wiggle my butt until I get the result I want."

Rae snorted. "Sure, if that's the result you want. If I'm getting into bed, it's because I'm ready to go to bed. My sleeping cap is on, I'm tired, and if I lie down, I'm falling asleep. Then suddenly, boom, erection between my cheeks. No, thank you, Sir. If you wanted a piece of that, you needed to speak up before I turned off the lights."

Even Avery joined in the laughter. Personally, she saw both sides. Sometimes it was fun to have the little snuggle that turned into something, but other times... yeah. She was exhausted and just wanted to sleep. Not that she'd had that issue lately—Nick wasn't into waiting until they got into bed before he put the moves on her.

She sniffled again, and her friends eyed her, trying to decide if she was ready but stayed silent while Rae and Iris continued debating the merits and pitfalls of spooning while Domi refereed. Trying to pay attention, she giggled several times, but her mind kept moving to how Nick had sounded on the phone.

Mad—rightfully so.

Did she have the right to be mad? Maybe. Although she didn't have as much to be angry about as he did.

Yes, he should have told her Miles and Gareth knew, but maybe it had been better he didn't. Would it have really helped? Or would she have spent the past few weeks more and more anxious people would find out about them? She had a feeling it was the latter.

Instead, she'd had peace of mind while she and Nick grew closer.

Then blindsided by Chad.

Which would have happened anyway. There was no way she would have thought Chad would be the one to pick up on her and Nick's relationship. She knew Gareth and Miles would have never told him. They spent some time with the back-of-house staff, but not much, and they weren't friends with Chad. She didn't know how he'd found out, but it hadn't been through them.

From the reactions of everyone else in the kitchen, they hadn't known. She didn't know what had tipped Chad off.

Even if Nick had told her about Miles and Gareth, she would have still been blindsided by Chad tonight.

"Earth to Avery, Earth to Avery... you've totally zoned out." Iris jostled her with her elbow.

"Sorry." Avery sighed. "I can't stop thinking about what Nick said on the phone." Explaining, she was amused by the difference in their reactions. Iris appeared incensed on her behalf, Rae looked more worried than anything else, and Domi's expression was thoughtful.

"He should have told you." Iris crossed her arms over her chest. "He has no right to be mad at you."

"Well, that's not true." Rae shook her head. "He still has good reason, and you should definitely blame us for keeping you out of work."

"I'm not going to do that."

"But yes, he should have still told you. Trust me. Save your own butt. Put as much of the blame on us as you can."

"I... Oh." Avery's eyes widened. She hadn't thought about that aspect of the evening. "*Oh.*" She shook her head, misery welling. "I'm honestly not sure he'll think of that."

Which kinda sucked because a good, hard punishment would help relieve her of her guilt and would make her feel a lot better. It was what she would expect from her Dom, even if he wasn't her boss. She wasn't sure Nick was up to that or if he would consider it mixing business with pleasure.

"You'd better hope he doesn't," Rae muttered darkly. "Punishment spankings suck."

"She's not wrong. Makeup sex can be fun, though," Domi pointed out. She tugged on one of her curls, pulling it straight and letting it spring back into place. "I think you and Nick are going to have to talk things out."

Avery shuddered internally. Why did that sound so hard? BDSM was all about communication, but the very thought made her want to run. Like she had earlier tonight.

You've got issues, girl.

❧ 24 ❧

NICK

Scrubbing down the expo station until the steel surfaces gleamed and his arm ached didn't make Nick feel any better.

He was torn between feeling guilty he hadn't told Avery about Miles and Gareth, angry she'd walked out on the shift, and pure fury at Chad. Where the hell did that guy get off?

"Hey, Nick." Luke sauntered into the kitchen, though now he was wearing leather pants with his shirt, indicating he'd been upstairs at Marquis—where he likely hadn't been wearing a shirt at all. He kept his voice low, not that the others were listening. Sandra was busy cleaning her station, Darnell was already done and gone, and Alice and Ravi had their heads bent together, whispering. Probably Alice updating him on everything that had gone down tonight.

"When you're done, Olivia wants to see you upstairs."

Nick bit back a retort that he didn't need Olivia interfering in his relationship, but she had a right, at least when it came to Avery's employment. She was also a meddling busybody when it came to the submissives. He'd heard it enough times to have that fact drummed into his head.

"I'll be up in a minute," he said shortly.

Rather than respond, Luke patted his back and walked away, probably realizing Nick wasn't in the mood to talk.

Running the cloth he'd been using to clean an area already spotless, Nick scowled. He could have gone straight upstairs, but he wasn't in the mood to jump because someone else told him to. Not the headspace when going into a meeting. He needed to get a better semblance of control over himself.

Finally giving up on cleaning an already clean surface, Nick straightened up.

"I'm headed upstairs. Anyone need anything before I go?"

Sandra glanced up, shook her head, and immediately dropped her gaze again. Out of all the rest of the staff, she seemed the most disturbed by tonight's revelations. She said nothing, but that was how he knew. Normally, she was pretty chatty with whoever was working next to her, and she and Ravi got along well. She hadn't talked all night.

"We're good. One sec, though, Chef," Alice said, moving away from Ravi to the other side of the line, so only the expo window was between them. Unlike Luke, she didn't bother to lower her voice. "Don't be too hard on Avery, okay? She was in a rough spot and didn't know what to do. Chad was always a dick about a woman being in charge of him, and nothing anyone could say was gonna make that better."

"Oh?" Nick raised his eyebrow at her. "Would you have run?" Considering Alice was one of the few on the line who had the guts to yell back at him, he seriously doubted it. Then again, Avery did, too, and she still ran.

Alice snorted.

"Nah, but I'm old. When I was younger, I might've." Alice shook her head. "You're a white dude, hon. You have no idea what it's like for women, much less a black woman like me, to be faced with a big angry man, spewing hateful shit. Especially when it comes to something like sex, where women are judged all the time. Now, I think what you two get up to is between you, but Chad, and guys like him, are gonna judge Avery for what she's getting up to."

"But not me?"

The look Alice gave him was scornful, and he got the impression if she could reach the back of his head, she would have slapped it, boss or not.

"No, not you. When was the last time you were judged for having sex?" Now it was Alice's turn to raise an eyebrow, and Nick flushed. The answer, of course, was never. And he knew that wasn't true for women. "Mmm-hmm. Now, like I said, don't be too hard on our girl. Got it?"

"Yes, Ma'am." Nick nodded. He wasn't sure he could keep that promise, but he wasn't quite as upset with Avery as he was before Alice talked to him. Out of the corner of his eye, he could see Sandra watching them and realized she had been listening. Probably not a bad thing.

Gathering the remaining shreds of his dignity, Nick headed up to Olivia's office, waving at Freddy behind the desk, and knocked on her door. He only had to wait a moment before she called him in. Clearly, she'd been waiting for him, which wasn't at all unnerving.

"Hey," he said, walking in. Luke was sitting in the other chair. As Nick had thought, now that he was on the second floor, big brother wasn't wearing a shirt. Behind the desk, Olivia had on a shiny black outfit that fit her like a second skin. Her red hair fell around her shoulders in long waves. She was a gorgeous woman with incredible curves, but she was far too intimidating for him to be attracted to.

His brother, on the other hand, was gazing at her as if she was the most amazing thing he'd ever seen. Luke liked to live even more dangerously than Nick did.

"So, Luke gave me a bit of an update, but I'm assuming you've talked to Avery by now?" Olivia asked, elbows on her desk and hands clasped in front of her, waiting for Nick's brief nod before continuing. "Chad will need to be replaced, but I also wanted to talk to you about Avery, both as her boss and as her Dom."

Nick barely withheld his groan. That was exactly what he'd been afraid of.

"No offense, Olivia, but I don't want outside interference in my romantic relationship. That part should be between Avery and me.

Though you should know, I have no intention of firing her, though I understand it will probably be necessary to write up a report on what happened tonight." That would mean a black mark in her employment file, but Nick hoped these were extenuating never-to-be-repeated circumstances. Olivia, being Olivia, focused on the first thing he said.

"Normally, I would never interfere with someone's relationship," she said. Luke coughed. Olivia glared at him, a look that promised retribution and made Nick's balls shrivel, though Luke smiled serenely in response. "At least, not without being asked for my opinion, but in this case, your relationship is also part of your training program as a Dom, and the paperwork you signed means I need to be involved."

He opened his mouth. Closed it. Shit. There had been some language about the instructors acting as mediators, when necessary, hadn't there?

"Can't Master Law or Mistress Julia do it?" he asked plaintively. "Nothing against you, but it's a little weird having my brother's girlfriend involved in coaching me with sex stuff."

"Thankfully for you, BDSM isn't entirely about sex, and what I need to talk to you about has nothing to do with the sex part." Olivia's gray eyes were hard, her gaze unrelenting. Her fingers steepled in front of her and pointed at him. "Imagine if you were in Luke's position and was a submissive, not a Dom, and someone at work found out and announced that fact to everyone. How would that make you feel?"

Again, he opened his mouth, then closed it. Right on the heels of what Alice had said to him, Olivia's question held extra weight.

He'd never had to deal with anyone judging him for having sex, much less for the sex he'd been having. Nick remembered his own reaction when Luke had told him he was submissive, and he wasn't particularly proud of it. The class had opened up his eyes to how strong submissives were and had swept away a lot of his judgment, but he'd had them, especially when he hadn't understood.

How hard had it been for Luke to explain his desires?

How much harder would it be for a woman, especially one who was in a management position, for those under her to know she was sexually submissive?

It shouldn't matter, shouldn't change people's perceptions, but it did.

Nick pressed his lips together.

When he'd thought about Chad confronting Avery tonight, he imagined himself in her shoes and thought about how angry the situation made him. How enraged. He'd felt nothing but righteous fury. He'd put himself, as he was, in her shoes, not actually imagining what it had been like for her.

Olivia's question brought that home. What would it be like for his coworkers... no, because they weren't coworkers for him or for Avery - what would it be like knowing that the people he was in charge of at work knew he was sexually submissive? Especially the men, as Alice had pointed out. Would there be anger on his part? Yes. There would also be humiliation, shame, fear, and worry he wouldn't be respected anymore.

Knowing they all knew he was having freaky sex as a Dom was very different from them knowing Avery was having freaky submissive sex. Something he hadn't really appreciated until this moment.

"Ah, there it is." Olivia smiled with satisfaction, her hands dropping to the desk, looking very pleased with herself. "That's what I was worried about. Sometimes, it's hard for us Dominants to remember what it's like for submissives when their preferences are exposed. Especially for women, who feel as though they can't give up any of their control or power without betraying the sisterhood, or who are in a position of power outside of the bedroom. It shouldn't change how people think of them, but it does."

Nick's anger had already deflated, and now, he rubbed his forehead where it felt like a headache was growing.

What had seemed so cut and dry an hour ago was much less so now. Even an hour ago, it hadn't been completely cut and dry since Avery was his girlfriend as well as technically his employee.

"Well, fuck." That summed it up. "What do you think I should do?"

Sitting up straight, Olivia beamed at him, and Luke chuckled under his breath. Crap. Nick hadn't meant to say that. Yet... considering how Olivia cut to the heart of the situation, it would be foolish not to take advantage of her insights. There was a reason his instinct had been to ask her.

"I have a few suggestions."

❧

AVERY

When her phone buzzed, the bit of happiness Avery had started to feel curdled in her stomach, her heartbeat picking up and pattering non-stop.

"Is it him?" Domi asked, perking up where she was snuggled with Mitch. He'd been invited in to join them when the night had begun to wear on. Avery had felt bad about keeping him from Domi's side on one of their nights together.

"Yeah." She summoned the bravery to open the message, given a slight courage boost by her friends. She wasn't sure what he was going to say but hoped it wasn't too terrible. After reading the message, she frowned and went over it again. "He says he wants to meet me at Marquis on the second floor tomorrow afternoon."

"Uh oh," Rae murmured, making a spanking motion with her hand.

Avery frowned at her.

"He wouldn't. He can't, right? This was work and had nothing to do with our relationship." Her gaze skittered over her friends' faces before landing on Mitch. The big blond looked thoughtful, rubbing his chin. Normally a goofball, it was odd seeing him so serious.

"I don't know. If Domi did something detrimental to herself, whether or not I have any say, we'd still be having a... discussion." The smile that pulled at his lips was more sadistic than mischievous, unlike his usual smile. "I would say running out on him pre-shift qualifies. He may have taken care of it both personally and professionally."

Iris scowled. "That's not fair."

"Who says a Dom has to be fair?" Mitch asked, his expression lightening. He winked at Iris as he palmed Domi's ass. She elbowed him, and he made a grunting noise.

"You can always tell him no," Iris said, turning her nose up at Mitch and focusing on Avery. "You don't have to go."

No, she didn't.

She didn't really want to.

She didn't want to lose Nick, though, and Mitch was right. Theirs was both a professional and personal relationship. Nick was the Dom. If he wanted to talk about the personal part first, that was his prerogative.

"Look at her expression. She's going." Rae shook her head. "We'll pray for your ass, and I mean that literally."

That Avery could still laugh, despite everything, made her feel maybe everything would be okay. Taking a deep breath, she sent Nick back a text, telling him she could be there at two.

That should give her plenty of time to freak out beforehand.

25

AVERY

Not sure what to expect, Avery walked up the stairs to the second floor of Marquis. For the first time, she didn't hurry, didn't feel like she was sneaking around... yet it didn't matter. No one saw her, which made her wonder if the previous times she'd been anxious about going up to the second floor had been a wasted effort.

No. Chad found out somehow. For all I know, he saw me headed upstairs.

She'd probably never know, and right now, she didn't have the energy to hide.

Besides, in the middle of a Sunday afternoon, everything was pretty slow. There were only a few front-of-house people still on, and most of them were hanging out in the kitchen. By now, Avery had no doubt literally everyone in the restaurant knew she and Nick were a couple.

A freaky couple.

Stop it.

If you won't let anyone call Domi, Rae, or Iris freaky, don't do it to yourself.

Yeah, easier said than done. Why was it so much easier to stand up for her friends than for herself? If someone had said something like that to one of them, Avery would have been shrieking with rage, not running in fear.

Talk about frustrating.

When she reached the top of the stairs, no one was there. It was weird walking through the door into the club part when there was no one behind the front desk, but Nick's text had said to meet him inside.

Since she had a shift after this, and he hadn't told her what to wear, she'd gone with her chef pants, a tank top, and a light hoodie. Her chef coat was in her car, waiting for her to be done. Walking into Marquis wearing that was even weirder, but she hadn't wanted to come prepared for kink when she didn't know what she would get.

Maybe she should have asked, but she couldn't get rid of the niggling worry he was calling her in to break up with her, end their classes, or something like that. Iris had pointed out it would have made more sense to tell her to go to Olivia's office in that case, and it would have, but Avery was still worried.

She didn't want to lose Nick.

She didn't want to lose her job.

While she still wished Chad had kept his mouth shut and Nick had given her a heads up, when it came down to it, it didn't change what she wanted. Even if everyone in the restaurant knew. Even if they all judged her.

Okay, in that last scenario, she might end up wanting to eventually leave her job, but she wanted to stick it out for now. She loved working in the restaurant and with Nick. Heck, even though this might have been the perfect nudge to go out on her own and start her own catering business, that hadn't been a consideration.

She wanted to keep working at Marquis... with Nick. Hoping she hadn't lost her chance to do so, she lifted her chin, walked over to the door, and opened it.

The room was dark except for the lights in the middle of the stage, which were on. In the center of the stage was a spanking bench, Nick standing next to it, arms crossed, wearing leather pants and nothing else, looking every inch the hot Dom.

Dammit.

Avery wished she'd worn something other than her work clothes.

"Avery." He nodded his head, and Avery's palms went clammy. Rae might have been right about her needing to worry about her ass.

"Nick."

Instead of answering, he lifted one eyebrow. Shit. That wasn't what she was supposed to call him in the club, even if she was dressed for work right now.

"Sir." She blushed as heat filled her cheeks.

"Better."

Better? What else was she supposed to call him? Master Nick? Master Chef?

Probably not that last one. She didn't think he'd appreciate the pun, and she didn't want him to think she wasn't taking this seriously. She was, but she was really nervous, and her brain went to humor to alleviate the tension. The room setup was not helping.

Wiping her hands on her pants, she stared back at him, waiting for him to tell her what to do.

❧

NICK

The theatricality of this moment wasn't something Nick had been sure of, but he had to admit it was effective. Avery certainly seemed to think so. Her hazel eyes were huge in her pale face, and she was gripping the sides of her chef pants, watching him warily, like prey eyeing a predator they weren't sure was hungry.

"Come up here, naughty girl." The effect of those last two words on Avery was immediate and visible. Her already wide eyes got even bigger, which he hadn't thought was possible, and she shivered.

A moment later, biting her lip, she took a step forward. The wariness in her expression had increased tenfold. Part of him felt guilty, but mostly it was guilt about how much he enjoyed seeing the trepidation and fear in her expression.

Yesterday, along with her suggestions, Olivia had pushed the point that Avery would need several things—punishment to help her clear away her guilt and reassurance she was forgiven. She said it was up to him whether that reassurance became sexual and hammered home. The only reason he might not want to was some Doms saw pleasure after punishment as rewarding bad behavior.

What he did was up to him.

He wasn't sure how he felt about spanking her without it being sexual but also saw Olivia's point.

Right now, he wasn't sure what he was going to do after he was done spanking her. He'd wing that part, see what felt right.

Avery's little pink tongue flicked over her bottom lip as she stepped onto the stage. She was still pale and wide-eyed, but now that she was closer, he could also see the excitement in her expression. The anticipation.

When she was only a few feet away from him, he gave her another order, not moving from his wide-legged stance with his arms across his chest.

"Strip."

Coming to an abrupt halt, she stared at him for a long moment, then nodded.

"Yes, Sir."

A thrill went through him at the honorific and the way she immediately complied.

The hoodie came off first, revealing the blue tank top beneath it, then she kicked off her shoes and let her pants drop. In just the tank top and panties, she seemed to relax, as though she was dropping more into the submissive mindset with every piece of clothing she removed. Though she hadn't lost either the anticipation or trepidation, there was now a peacefulness to her expression as though she had accepted what was about to happen and felt good about it.

Yanking her tank top off, her breasts bounced free, and Nick's slowly growing erection pressed against the front of his pants. It was a lot more uncomfortable in tight leather than it had been in his loose chef pants.

Whatever you do, do it with confidence.

Reaching down, he blatantly adjusted himself and had to hide his grin when he realized Avery was watching him. She stared before giving herself a shake and moving to take off her underwear.

⚜

AVERY

Holy crap.

Nick was a Dom.

Like a *Dom* Dom. The hesitation that had been present before was gone. So was any uncertainty. She'd gone from feeling as though she was the one who knew what was going on to feeling as though she was floundering, and Nick was the confident, knowledgeable one.

This was not what she'd been expecting when she walked in.

It was so far from it, she felt even more off balance.

Nick had been working up to this point, but until this moment, she felt as if she was more in control than he was when it came to kink and sex. Now, she not only felt out of control but as though she didn't know what was coming next. Even with the spanking bench there, which would seem to indicate a punishment, but what kind? How hard?

How far was this new Nick willing to go?

Completely naked, she straightened to look at him, hands hanging loosely at her sides. Chewing the inside of her cheek, she knew she was doing a terrible job of hiding her nerves, but did it really matter at this point? Probably not.

"On the bench, Avery."

For the first time, she hesitated.

"Aren't we going to talk about... everything?" Her voice only faltered a little, but it was enough to undermine the firm tone she'd been trying to adopt.

"Oh, we are." The smile that curved his lips was more unsettling than reassuring. "As soon as you're on the spanking bench."

Evil, mean, bad Dom. What had she done?

On the other hand, what had she expected when she'd taken an already bossy, domineering Alpha male and introduced him to kink?

Yeah, but he didn't have to take to it so well or so fast.

Pressing her lips together, Avery knelt, her knees pressing against the leather pads, and draped herself over the bench. The last time she'd been in this position, in this room with Nick, she hadn't been intimidated, hadn't felt squirmy, nervous, or worried about what her ass was going to look like at the end.

She was now.

Gripping the handholds, she kept herself from wiggling around too much as Nick walked behind her. One callused palm caressed her upturned ass, which felt very, very vulnerable indeed.

"Okay, Avery. Let's talk. Would you like to start by explaining why you left the restaurant last night and didn't return?"

With the lights shining down on them, heating her skin, it should haven't been possible to feel cold, but she did. Cold, then hot, then cold again, goosebumps breaking out over her skin. The whole time, Nick's hand kept rubbing over her ass, getting it ready for her punishment.

The bastard.

Thankfully, after talking out everything with her friends last night, she had a semi-decent answer.

۞

NICK

He had to admit, while incredibly unprofessional, there was definitely something to be said for having this kind of discussion over a spanking bench. For one, it was hard to hold on to anger with Avery's beautiful ass and pussy tipped up for his perusal. Even harder after she'd put herself in this position, all the while not knowing what to expect from him.

"I freaked out and didn't know what to do. I felt like everyone was judging me or would because of what Chad said, and I couldn't make myself come back to face that. I was ashamed about not being able to come back, but not as ashamed as I felt about what he revealed." Avery's words came out in a rush, with an odd cadence, as if she'd practiced saying it.

Taking a long moment, Nick caressed her assed as he turned her words over in his head. They were an echo of what Alice and Olivia had said, all in different ways.

"And the longer I stayed away, the more ashamed I felt, and the more I was sure everyone would judge me for running, which made it worse, then I couldn't make myself come back at all."

"But today, you showed up here, ready for your shift?" It wasn't an idle question. He'd wondered when she walked in, clearly dressed for work.

"If I'm not fired."

"You're not fired." He gave her ass a little swat, enough that she wiggled, though she didn't shriek or even gasp. It should have been hard enough to sting with warning. "It's not even going on your official employee record. Olivia insisted, and I agreed."

From his vantage point, it was easy to see the relief that slumped her shoulders, the tension draining out of her body, relaxing her muscles. Satisfaction slid through him.

"Okay, so now that's out of the way—"

"You're not going to punish me? Sir?" she interrupted him.

Nick smacked her ass a little harder, enough to make her gasp and her fingers tighten on the grips.

"For interrupting me? Yes. For work-related issues? No. Not here. That would be incredibly inappropriate of me as your boss. However, I felt compelled to ask because it leads to my next question—why didn't you answer your phone when I called? Or text me back? Or any kind of communication?"

The muscles that had relaxed tightened again, but Nick's satisfaction didn't diminish.

That's right, sweetheart. I might not spank the hell out of you as your boss, but I sure can as the boyfriend you ghosted last night.

26

AVERY

Despite all the talking she and her friends had done last night, why she hadn't answered Nick's calls or texts hadn't really come up. And the 'why' to that was a lot harder to answer.

"I wasn't ready to talk?" It came out as a question rather than an answer, and the moment she said it, she knew it would not be enough.

She was right.

Smack! Smack! Smack! Smack!

The hard, sharp swats landed with intention, two on each cheek, rocking her forward as she gasped. The spots throbbed—he'd down his hand laid in the center of each cheek both times, a lot harder than he'd spanked her at home, much less in class.

"Ow!"

"Why didn't you text me back to tell me you weren't ready to talk?"

Smack! Smack!

"You left me hanging, wondering if something awful had happened to you."

Smack! Smack!

"All I knew was that you were upset, and you drove off. I was worried you'd gotten into an accident or something."

Smack! Smack!

"No! I mean, I'm sorry!" The sharp bites of pain were well-deserved. She'd known he'd been worried and upset, but she hadn't thought about that aspect of it. "I drove to a parking lot a few blocks away until I could get myself back together."

Smack! Smack!

"As nice as it is to know that now, it would have been a lot nicer if you had texted me yesterday to tell me."

He really had taken being a Dom to heart. Every swat landed in the exact middle of her cheeks, over and over, so even though it wasn't the hardest she'd ever been spanked, it was really burning. He was using enough force to sting, and adding to the same spot meant the burn increased that much more.

"I'm sorry!"

"You're certainly going to be."

The flurry of swats increased, landing in the same spots, making the center of her cheeks throb and flare with heat. Avery's fingers tightened on the grips, holding on for dear life and wishing she was cuffed or tied down. It would be a lot easier to keep her position. Instead, she had to use willpower and the perverse desire for penance to keep in place.

Even though it hurt, and the hot pain was building fast and furious, Nick coming into his own as a Dom was one of the sexiest things she'd ever experienced. Her pussy was quivering with anticipation, apparently confused that she was being punished, not played with. Tears gathered in her eyes, even as her arousal swirled in her core.

When Nick stopped spanking her and reached down to touch her folds, he could feel how hot and slick she was.

"Enjoying this, are you?" he asked, rubbing his fingers up and down her slit. He sounded amused. Avery whined, lifting her hips to get him to touch her more, but he was purposefully avoiding her clit, the bastard. "You know that's not the point of this."

"Then maybe you should stop," she sassed back.

That got a laugh out of him... right before he started spanking her again.

NICK

The two spots in the middle of Avery's cheeks were glowing bright hot pink. He felt the heat emanating from her skin when he'd taken the pause to check her pussy. She was soaked... and he was hard as a rock.

If he finished this punishment without sex, it would be a fucking miracle.

Seeing the twin spots on her cheeks darkening, he wondered if he should move some spots around, but he knew from the last spanking he'd given her, the effects hadn't lasted long. This time, he was determined to make more of an impression.

Because it was still a punishment.

Relationships were about communication, whether a work relationship or a romantic one. BDSM made the need for communication even more important.

He'd tried so hard last night to get in touch with her, to the detriment of paying attention at work, and she hadn't reached back. That had fucking hurt. He hadn't done anything to deserve that kind of non-response.

He realized that was something he should say.

"Finding out from your friend, not from you, that you were physically unharmed hurt my feelings."

He gave her another few hefty whacks to punctuate his statement. There was something extremely cathartic about being able to use a spanking to emphasize his points.

"I'm sorry!" She sniffled. "I didn't think about it like that."

"That's what hurts. It felt like you weren't thinking about me at all." His voice was a little hollow, but it was true. That had been the hardest part. Feeling as if he hadn't merited a text or a call.

"Not that!" Her head came up, her neck craning to look over her shoulder.

He glimpsed the tears that had rolled down her cheeks. Her skin was blotchy, eyes shiny, and she looked far more miserable than aroused. That was the real punishment, he realized—not the spanking but his hurt and disappointment. She hadn't really tried to stop the spanking, but now she was doing her best to reassure him.

"I didn't know how to explain myself, and it was easier to hide from you than to find the words. I felt as if I owed you an explanation."

"Perhaps as your boss, but as your boyfriend, I wanted to know you were safe, and it hurt knowing you were willing to talk to your friends but not to me." When she tried to rear up, Nick placed his hand on her lower back, keeping her in place. "No, sweetheart, I'll let you make it up to me, eventually, but first, we're going to get through your punishment."

AVERY

The firm, authoritative way Nick made his declaration, with his hand pressing down on her lower back, had Avery's insides quivering despite her emotions being a wreck. Of course, her steadily increasing arousal didn't help. She desperately wanted to turn around and hug Nick or at least touch him. Hearing the very real hurt in his voice had broken her heart.

She should have turned to him. She should have answered.

The combination of boss and boyfriend didn't make it easy, but she'd made everything harder on both of them by ignoring his texts and calls—not to mention hurting his feelings—which could have been so easily avoided. If he'd been upset enough to leave somewhere and didn't answer her texts and calls, then she finally heard from one of his friends instead... Well, she would have tried to be understanding, but yeah, that would sting pretty badly.

It might make her question why he didn't feel he could pick up for her, but he could for his friend.

Make her feel as if she wasn't the most important person to him. The most trusted. The one she could lean on.

She'd denied him that because he was her boss as well as her boyfriend. That wasn't fair and something they'd have to work out at a later time.

Although right now, Nick was doing a fantastic job of putting the two together.

Damn him.

"Time for the paddle."

Avery squeaked in dismay and gripped the spanking bench tighter, hugging it with her whole body, not just her fingers. Paddle?! On her already chastised cheeks?

This really was a punishment, yet the arousal still sizzled through her. Her body's reactions were so messed up.

No, they're not. They're just how you react, and once you accept that, this whole relationship thing will probably be a lot easier.

Eek. Okay, yeah. She had some internal work to do on herself, too.

If she hadn't felt such a keen sense of shame yesterday, she probably would have answered Nick's calls. She'd been ashamed both as an employee and a woman, which had as much to do with how she felt about herself as with what Chad had said.

That wasn't something she wanted to continue.

"I'm so sorry, Sir. I realized... I think the reason yesterday was so hard is there's a part of me that feels what Chad said is true. Not about how I got my job, but the way he said it... I know I'm a submissive, but sometimes, I feel ashamed of that, too. Like there's something wrong with me because I am." Saying it was hard, so very hard, but the moment the words were out of her mouth, intense relief swept through her.

NICK

Holy shit.

Nick dropped the paddle to the ground, making Avery jump and nearly fall off the bench, but it was okay because he was there to catch her. Not just catch her, but pull her to her feet, so he could see her face. Her beautiful, tear-stained face with her wide hazel eyes, red nose, and parted lips. Feeling her naked skin against him, her breasts pressing into his stomach, made his dick throb, but he ignored it.

"Me, too." Rather than understanding, he saw confusion, and he cleared his throat. "I mean, I feel ashamed, too. Like there's something wrong with me because of how much I enjoy spanking you and how much farther I want to go."

"There's nothing wrong with you," she said, a stubborn expression sliding over her face.

Nick raised his eyebrows at her. If there was nothing wrong with him, the one actually doing the spankings and other painful things, there was nothing wrong with her. She narrowed her eyes back at him.

"It's different."

"How so?" he challenged. "You're ashamed because you enjoy receiving pain, but that's as physiological as it is psychological. What does it say about my psychology that I enjoy causing it? That I like to hear you cry out, that right now I can look down and see your tears, and my dick is hard as a rock because I know I caused them."

Staring up at him, Avery bit down on her lower lip, trying to think of a way to argue with him. Ha. Good luck with that. He was right, and he knew it.

"Okay." She wrinkled her nose. "Well, it sounds bad when you put it like that, but I feel like I'm betraying the sisterhood and setting back feminism because I like to be spanked and submit to a man. Society sets us up to believe men are supposed to be dominant and taking charge of a woman is natural."

"Maybe it once did, but now, as a good man, I want to support women and feminism and your right to do whatever the hell you want to do, not boss you around and spank you, definitely not enjoy it," he countered. "And that's *after* I got past the idea a spanking is different from beating you."

It felt damn good to get this out in the open. He hadn't realized Avery had her own doubts about kink and her preferences. He'd felt as though he was playing catchup this whole time, trying to make himself into what he thought she wanted, and at the same time, make sure she didn't see his insecurities.

Knowing she wasn't as comfortable in her skin as she'd appeared, knowing she had the same doubts—though from the opposite side of things—made him feel so much better. Even though the other new Doms in the class were struggling with some of the same things, that was different from knowing his partner felt that way. Especially since he'd assumed Avery was all in, with none of the apprehension he'd felt about what they were doing.

They were more on the same page than he'd known.

"You are supporting me in doing whatever I want because I'm the one telling you I want to be spanked!"

"And there's nothing wrong with that, just like there's nothing wrong with me for enjoying it." For the first time, he really believed it.

Who cared what society said they were supposed to like and what they were supposed to do? Fuck Chad and the others in the world who would judge them for what they wanted to do.

They weren't hurting anyone—well, other than Avery and only because she liked it. Everything was consensual, which was the most important part. He was giving her what she liked, what she wanted and needed, which matched perfectly with what he liked, wanted, and needed.

"Maybe I'm wrong, but the way it was explained to me was feminism is about you getting to make your own choice. If you don't want me to do something, all you have to say is your safe word, and I'll stop immediately. I might be the Dom, but the only reason I'm in charge is you're willingly giving me the control, choosing to follow my commands, and want to submit in this sphere." The side of his lips quirked, threatening a smile. "In the kitchen, you're usually the one giving me hell."

"That's because sometimes, you act like you think you're fucking Gordon Ramsey," she muttered, but her cheeks had turned pink with happiness at his compliment. She seemed a lot calmer and happier. The tension had slid away from her muscles, and she was smiling.

Nick laughed.

"I don't think I'm fucking Gordon Ramsey. I think I'm fucking you." He laughed as she sputtered at the terrible pun before planting a searingly hot kiss on her lips.

When he pulled away, he spun her back around to face the bench and gave her ass a short, sharp smack.

"Now, back over that spanking bench. You have a punishment to finish."

❦   27   ❧

AVERY

Getting back into place on the spanking bench, Avery had a new sense of peace. Returning to kink had satisfied the need inside her, fulfilling her in a way she'd been missing, but this was a new level of contentment.

Nick didn't judge her.

Even though he was new to the scene, Nick didn't think there was anything wrong with her.

That he thought there was something wrong with him made her want to hug the hell out of him.

He'd made some damn good points. It was time to get Shannon's and Chad's voices—the voices of everyone who had ever made her feel bad about what she wanted—out of her head. They could live their own lives, doing what they wanted to fulfill their own wants and needs, but they didn't get to dictate hers. Everyone wanted and needed different things, which was a good thing.

Nick was her match. They wanted the same things, which may not be the same things other people wanted. If everyone wanted the same things, it wouldn't be special when they found their match because anyone could match anyone.

Even in her own head, it sounded a little loopy, like maybe she was drunk on happiness. Which she was, so that was fine. Nick was her perfect match for insecurities, kink, and love of food.

Unfortunately for her, the match for the kink part meant a very hot ass right now.

Avery squealed as the paddle landed. She got a glimpse where it laid on the floor, so she knew it was a rectangular wooden paddle, but that had been all she'd been able to see. Now, she knew it was long enough to land on both cheeks, covering both spots he'd been spanking and more.

It hurt like hell.

"Ouch! I'm sorry!"

"I know, sweetheart, four more, then you're done."

Four more... Avery whimpered. Though it was nice to know there was an end in sight, the knowledge also loomed over her.

Four more is really gonna hurt.

Her pussy clenched.

Thwap!

The sound of wood against flesh was deeper, meatier than hand to cheek, and she felt the blow reverberate through her body. Her cry turned to a whimper as she rocked on the bench, panting, tears sliding down her cheeks.

She was going to feel this tomorrow.

Part of her reveled in that fact.

NICK

The paddle was so much more effective than his hand.

It was also less tiring, far more effective, and meant his hand wasn't getting sore from spanking her. The knife calluses he had didn't protect them, though the handle of the paddle felt good in his palm, thanks to those same calluses.

Hefting its weight, he smacked her ass again, enjoying the sound of the impact and her cry immediately after it. Even better, he was enjoying it without the guilt that had been weighing him down. He could see how much more relaxed she was, despite him laying down a paddle over her already spanked ass.

The two spots where he'd been spanking her were now dark red in a sea of pink, and his dick throbbed at the sight.

Fucking beautiful.

Maybe some people would think they were a little messed up because of what they wanted, but he and Avery were messed up in the same way. They fit together. He didn't think there was anything wrong with Avery wanting what she wanted, which meant he needed to stop thinking there was something wrong with him for wanting those same things.

Just enjoy it.

He certainly planned to.

Another hefty whack of the paddle and the sound of her cry was like music to his ears, a high-pitched squeal, ending in a short sob— yet she didn't say her safeword. She didn't even say 'stop' or ask for relief.

She needed this. He did as well.

There was something beautiful about that complementary perverseness.

"Good girl," he said, crooning his praise and enjoying the shiver that went down her spine. "Last one."

She gripped, flexed, then relaxed, realizing he wouldn't use the paddle again until she did.

Thwap!

The impact caused her loudest cry yet. Nick bent enough to lay the paddle on the ground, undoing his pants as he straightened. The other wonderful thing about spanking benches, besides how well they positioned a naughty sub's ass for her punishment, was they also positioned her perfectly to be fucked.

Freeing his cock, Nick moved behind her, gripping her hips with his hands. He buried his length into her wet heat with one hard thrust that made them both groan. Avery's muscles quivered around him, squeezing and contracting, massaging the length of his cock. Holding it inside her, he let her adjust around him.

"Oh, fuck…" Her panted words made him throb.

The heat of her punished ass emanated off her skin, warming to his groin and adding to his arousal. When he looked down to see those pink and red cheeks snug up against his body, the visual was almost too erotic to bear.

Dragging his cock back, he thrust again, watching as those pink cheeks jiggled enticingly, rippling from the force of his thrust. He wished there was a mirror set up in front of them, so he could see the expressions on her face as easily as he could see her slick pussy and red cheeks.

Maybe he'd make that suggestion to Olivia.

For now, he gripped Avery's hips hard and braced his legs.

"You may cum if you can."

Pounding away behind her, he vented his frustration, fear, and all the emotions that had bottled up inside him on her slick pussy. If she came, she came. If she didn't, that was part of her punishment.

AVERY

The rough, pounding strokes of Nick's cock in and out of her body were driving Avery wild.

He wasn't trying to pleasure her, wasn't trying to make her cum, and she could feel the difference. Her body was being used for *his* pleasure.

Perversely, that turned her on even more. She whimpered as he rode her, every thrust slapping against her already stinging buttocks, adding another flash of pain while her pleasure surged higher. Her muscles clenched, trying to grasp his cock, but she was so wet, her movements didn't slow him in the slightest.

The friction, the sensation of him moving in and out of her, the slick glide of his cock hammering home, and the inconsistent stimulation of her clit, thanks to the position, was sending her soaring, but she didn't know if she was going to come in time. The uncertainty made her even more aroused.

Her body was hurtling toward the peak of her climax, but she didn't know if she was going to make it or not.

Every hard thrust slammed her against the bench, leaving her writhing and crying out, sobbing with the need for release, yet unable to exactly get the right stimulation. Her mound pressed against the leather of the bench, but whoever built it must be one hell of a creative sadist. They'd made it so she couldn't quite get the right spot, no matter how she squirmed against the padded leather.

"Please! Nick, please!" she begged as her muscles tightened and quivered from the tension winding inside of her and on the edge of snapping... but not quite making it.

Ignoring her pleas, his fingers dug in, and he moved harder, faster, and she knew he must be getting close to his own peak. Her time was almost up. Tears dripped onto the leather beneath her cheek as she cried out, squeezing her muscles tightly, knowing it would get him off faster but hoping it might do the same for her.

Avery cried out, half with ecstasy and half with relief as her pleasure reached the tipping point and carried her over. She spasmed, her orgasm throbbing with every hard thrust of Nick's cock, then he buried himself inside her as he grunted her name. With his hot weight draped over her back, against her ass, she felt him pulse inside her, adding to her own blissful satisfaction.

Every spurt of his cock sent another shuddering wave of pleasure through her, and his groin rubbing against her tender backside ignited more sparks of sensation. Closing her eyes, she sighed as the tension melted away, leaving her limp and satiated over the bench.

Gentle hands caressed her sides as lips pressed a kiss to the center of her back.

"Good girl."

NICK

Getting everything cleaned up didn't take long, then he snuggled in with Avery in one of Marquis' many booths. They only had half an hour before they were both supposed to be downstairs, but he was having trouble bringing himself to care. He was supposed to be the one in charge, but Avery had the ability to shift his priorities.

Something his previous girlfriends hadn't been able to do.

Maybe the problem hadn't been they were too demanding or didn't understand him. Maybe the problem had been he hadn't been willing to prioritize them.

He probably owed them some apologies. Now, he knew his priorities could shift, and he'd never really given them a chance to with other girlfriends. Maybe it wouldn't have happened at all if he hadn't spent so much time working with Avery. She'd gotten under his skin in a way his previous girlfriends never had.

It's called falling in love, genius.

Sometimes, the voice in his head sounded suspiciously like his big brother.

Avery stirred on his lap, then suddenly sat upright, nearly knocking her head into his chin. He barely reared back in time, then grabbed hold of her to keep her from tumbling off.

"Oh my God! What time is it? We have to get to work!"

Well, now he knew how his exes felt when he'd focused on work over them. Ouch. Where'd the post-coital bliss go?

"We have some time," he said soothingly, pushing his hurt feelings aside. Avery had no way of knowing what he'd been thinking. Besides, after last night, she probably felt the need to prove herself, both because she'd run out on a shift and because of the things Chad had said.

Snuggling with him on the second floor would not help her feel better about either of those things.

"How much time?" She still sounded panicked, though a bit of the edge was gone. Nick tightened his hold on her to keep her from wriggling around too much.

"Hey, look at me." Deepening his voice, he went for the 'Dom mode' thing Olivia had talked about. While he and Avery hadn't discussed being kinky outside the bedroom, there would be times when it might actually help her. Like when she was panicking, like right now. She turned her head, meeting his gaze, and stilled. It wasn't relaxed, but she wasn't quivering like a tuning fork anymore. "You won't be late, okay? I'll make sure of it."

There was the relaxation he'd been aiming for. Her shoulders slumped, her spine relaxed, and the wildness retreated from her eyes.

"Okay," she whispered.

Pulling her back into his chest, Nick nuzzled the top of her head with his lips.

"Just let me enjoy this for another few minutes," he whispered, holding her tightly.

Avery nodded, relaxing even more against him, curling into his lap like a kitten. Trusting him to take care of her, trusting him to make sure she wasn't late. Trusting him with her reputation and to keep her from the judgments of the others in the restaurant.

That meant the fucking world to him.

✺ 28 ✺

AVERY

Walking into the kitchen at Nick's side, her fingers twitched, wanting to reach out and hold his hand. She knew he wouldn't stop her, and the support would make her feel better, but she worried it could make everything else worse. She was lucky she hadn't completely ruined her career by running out and she had no idea how everyone would react to that, much less her and Nick. There was a black mark on her record, but Olivia had reassured her that it would be removed after a year assuming she did no such thing again. Avery had reassured her there was no chance of that.

At least they were right on time. Walking in together made a statement, even if they weren't holding hands. Her butt was still sore and stinging under her pants, but no one knew. It would be a stark reminder all shift—not to run out on him or her job again and how he'd embraced his Dom side for her. Yeah, it might have been there regardless, but she was the reason he'd chosen to explore it.

She shouldn't be ashamed of being with Nick or what they did together, and even if she still had some trouble feeling that with her whole being, she would fake it till she made it.

To her surprise, as they entered the kitchen from the hallway, everyone was in the kitchen waiting for them. The back-of-house staff, the front-of-house staff, the managers. Some had clearly finished their shifts, others were coming on, and some were dressed in regular clothes, indicating it was their day off.

They all burst into applause when she and Nick walked in.

"About time!" someone yelled.

Her jaw dropped open, and she swiveled to stare at Nick, not sure if she was angry at him for setting this up, only to see him staring slack-jawed at their audience. He hadn't known they were going to do this. Slowly, she turned back toward them, her fingers automatically seeking Nick's. When they touched, he grabbed her hand and gave it a little squeeze—which didn't go unnoticed.

"Kiss! Kiss! Kiss!"

She was pretty sure George started up the chant, the big jerk, but the others picked up on it fast enough, she couldn't be certain.

Before she could do anything, Nick lifted her hand to his lips and kissed the back of it.

"There, you perverts," he yelled over the laughter and boos that followed. Avery's cheeks flamed hot, and she was really grateful to him for not actually kissing her. "Now, get back to work."

"Man, I thought we were going to get to watch," Alice complained, walking by them to get behind the line. She bumped Avery's hip with her own, her eyes twinkling with amusement. "Isn't that what you two like?"

"I think we prefer watching. Are you volunteering?" Avery retorted.

It might not make sense to some people, but Alice's good-natured teasing was exactly what Avery needed to be comfortable again. That was how the kitchen worked. If Alice wasn't giving her a hard time—in a fun way, not the way Chad had—it would mean she was upset. Alice joking about it meant she really was unbothered. In case the applause hadn't hammered that home.

She worked with a bunch of crazy people, and she loved it.

"Good luck," Ravi said, clapping her on the shoulder as he went by. "He's a jackass."

"Hey!" Nick looked affronted, but he didn't let go of her hand.

Avery had to roll her eyes. "The truth hurts, huh?"

Something glinted in Nick's dark eyes as he leaned in closer, lowering his voice for her ears only.

"Careful, sweetheart," he murmured. "Or I'll hurt you." He winked. The back of his hand bumped into the side of her butt, and her cheeks turned bright red again.

Such a Dom.

NICK

After the show of support—Nick suspected Alice's unsubtle hand behind that maneuver, for which he was both exasperated and grateful —the kitchen emptied, and everyone got back to work. Several more people stopped to tell Avery and Nick they were happy for them, with a few choice words about Chad.

It didn't escape Nick's attention that Alanna was one of those or that Jonathan wasn't lingering by her side, whereas George was downright cheerful. Apparently, last night's date hadn't gone well.

Oh, well, not his business.

If Jonathan and his rotating dating life was an example of why some people shouldn't date coworkers, he liked to think he and Avery were an example of how to make it work. They'd been doing so for weeks.

Tonight, it was like last night had never happened.

There was a happy buzz in the air, though whether it was due to everyone's happiness for them or Chad's absence, it was hard to tell. Probably some combination of both.

Toward the end of the night, Olivia came in. Wiping his hands on a towel, Nick moved to where she was leaning against one of the counters, watching. The orders had slowed enough, Avery didn't need his help at the expo counter.

"Looks like everything went well," Olivia said. Since she was right,

Nick didn't begrudge her the smug smile curving her lips. "She seems pretty chipper."

"It did." Nick leaned next to Olivia, casting his eyes over the kitchen rather than looking directly at Avery. In case she looked up, he didn't want her to feel like she was under a microscope. "She is. Thank you."

"Oooh, was that hard to say?" Grinning, Olivia nudged him with her elbow. "It sounded like it was hard to say."

"Maybe a little. I'm not used to needing relationship advice."

"From what Luke's said, it's more like you're not used to being in a relationship where you'd want advice on how to prolong it."

Ouch. Avery was right. The truth did hurt.

"She's different."

"I think she's good for you and you for her." Olivia cocked her head to the side, blatantly studying Avery. If Avery noticed, she was masterful at pretending otherwise. Nick had the feeling she really was wrapped up in her work, focusing hard to make up for not being here last night. "She seems okay with you two being out in the open."

"Probably didn't hurt that we walked into a standing ovation." Nick snorted, shaking his head. He still couldn't believe it. It had been one hell of a show of support he appreciated.

"Oh, did you?" The lilt of innocence in Olivia's voice had him turning his head sharply to give her a look. She smiled back at him. "I gotta get going. Things to do."

She sauntered off before he could decide whether he wanted to thank or strangle her.

Well, at least now he knew it hadn't been Alice.

AVERY

This might have been the most exhausting weekend of her life.

Emotionally, not physically.

But she was ending it in a good way.

Almost everyone had come up to her to tell her they didn't care what she and Nick were getting up to outside work. Several of them had joked they had 'known it!' and thanked her for the money they'd won betting on her and Nick as a couple. She just shook her head.

She'd thought they'd been so much more discreet than they were. When she'd finally said as much, Roger had smirked and explained it was the blatant lack of romantic interaction between them that tipped everyone off.

"Everyone could feel the chemistry. It was just a matter of time," he smirked again. "You were fighting it, then you weren't, so we were pretty sure you two had gotten together, but no one could prove it." He went to settle up his bet with Jonathan.

Shaking her head, Avery finished up her shift, then texted Iris, Rae, and Domi with an update before heading to Nick's house. Her friends' responses had come in during the drive, and she'd snickered when she'd checked them after parking in his driveway.

Rae's response had been a predictable '*I told you so,*' whereas Domi and Iris were more, '*I'm happy for you!*'

"Does this mean we're going to drive together now... please?" Nick asked as he opened her car door. Avery grinned up at him, sliding her phone back into her purse.

"Yeah, that sounds nice." Much easier, for sure. Now that she didn't have to worry about people knowing about them, it wouldn't matter if they drove in or left together.

"Thank goodness." He pulled her against him, his hands sliding down to cup her butt, making her squeal and wriggle. The sides of his lips curved up in a sadistic smile. "How's your ass?"

"Still a little sore." Glaring at him, she was pretty sure he'd figured that out from her reaction. He just wanted to make her say it.

"Good." He bent his head to take her lips in a kiss, and she could feel the hardness of his erection growing between them, pressing into her as she kissed him back. Big jerk. When he pulled away, she was all hot and bothered all over again. When he turned her toward the house and gave her ass a little slap that stung like hell, thanks to how sensitive her skin was, she shrieked. "Now, let's get inside so we can shower and clean up."

It was a hot shower in multiple ways as Nick insisted on washing her, his hands lingering on all her most sensitive spots until she was practically panting. Not that she didn't get him back, wrapping a soapy hand around his cock and sliding it up and down the thick length several times before he growled and pulled away.

Freshly cleaned and rinsed, they rubbed each other down with the towels, still teasing, before stumbling into the bedroom and falling on his bed. Avery moaned as he nipped and bit her nipples, tormenting the tiny buds with his mouth. His hands slid up her arms to pin them down on either side of her head, wrists just above. Feet on the floor, he was at the perfect height and wasted no time sliding into her.

Gasping, Avery moaned and clenched around him as he filled her, her legs wrapping around his hips and pulling him deeper. The press of his body against hers made her ass bounce on the bed, awakening phantom pains from spanking and adding that little dash of sensation to her pleasure.

Unlike at the club, Nick took his time with long, slow, firm thrusts in and out of her body. His mouth worked over her breasts and nipples, teasing her with pleasure and sharp nips of pain while he fucked her. Whimpering, Avery writhed beneath him, her body urging him to move faster, harder, instead of his relentless, steady pace.

"More, please, Nick!" She clenched, her thighs tightening, pulling him against her, trying to quicken his pace with her legs. "Harder!"

"Naughty girl." He nipped the sensitive nubbin tipping her right breast, making her moan. Thrusting in deep, he filled her to the brim and rocked, his body rubbing against her sensitive lips and clit, sending hot pleasure shooting through her. His hands pressed harder against her wrists as he thrust, then ground against her.

Thrust.

Grind.

Thrust.

Grind.

Each time, he pulled away for the next thrust just before giving her enough stimulation that she could actually get off. Her body ached, cramping. It was a kind of edging she hadn't experienced and wasn't sure he even knew there was a name for what he was doing. It was both awful and wonderful torment.

"Nick! Sir, please!" The plea came out as a near shriek. His pubic bone ground against her clit again before pulling away, leaving her body humming and buzzing, tight as a wire about to snap. She wailed at the loss of contact, muscles clenching as she was left on the precipice of rapture.

Then he was pounding into her, hard and fast, and her voice rose in a shriek as ecstasy rose like a tsunami and crashed over her. Hot bliss sizzled through her veins, leaving pure pleasure in its wake as she lost herself in the mutual celebration of their love.

29

NICK

As far as Nick was concerned, one of the biggest upsides of being open about their new relationship was Lloyd telling him to just let him know if he and Avery wanted an occasional Thursday night off together. A weekend night off together was probably too much to ask—though Luke had hinted they might work something out by having a guest chef or something—but a Thursday every few weeks was pretty great.

It meant when she asked him if he'd be interested in going to Stronghold with her and her friends, he could say yes.

He had to admit, he was curious about Stronghold. While he'd eventually like to see one of the shows at Marquis, he felt pretty comfortable inside the building itself, on both floors. At least in the main room of Marquis. Thanks to the classes, he was spending plenty of time there.

Stronghold, on the other hand, was a mystery and one he was wildly curious about. What would it be like? Would it be full of people having sex? Whipping each other? Or more like a regular nightclub?

And which would he prefer since all of that made him uncomfortable in different ways?

Odd that he was the most comfortable with the idea of a club full of people whipping each other, but it was true. That was something the Dom class had really helped with and not just him. The past few weeks, the new Doms had become a lot more confident in their newfound skills. Well, most of them. Connor still struggled but was better, as long as one of the instructors was watching him. Nick had a feeling the big guy liked having the 'safety net' of an instructor's presence in case his own strength worked against him.

Nick wondered if he'd see any of the other Doms from his class at the club. Avery said they were going with Iris, Rae, Domi, Domi's boyfriend, Mitch, and his friends. He was a little nervous about hanging out with Doms, who knew what they were doing but figured it would be good for him. He could watch how they acted and take his direction from them.

Hopefully, he didn't embarrass himself, although Avery had assured him she was perfectly happy visiting and not playing.

"Are you ready?" Avery came out of the bathroom, taking his breath away at the same time all the blood rushed to his groin.

Getting ready had been no problem. He'd put on a pair of leather pants and a black shirt that hugged his muscles before sitting down on the couch to wait for her.

She'd been locked in the bathroom for the past hour, doing who knows what, but damn if he could argue with the results.

The soft waves of her hair had been pulled back into a ponytail, and she was wearing heavier makeup than normal, the black liner accentuating her eyes, so they appeared even bigger, but what really made him stare was her dress. The shiny black material hugged her body, outlining every inch of her curves clearly enough, he was certain she didn't have a stitch of underwear underneath, making the way her boobs were lifted even more gravity-defying.

"Holy shit. No, I'm not ready. I think we should stay here." His pants were uncomfortably tight in a certain area. When he went to embrace her, she giggled and came willingly into his arms, but she looked up at him with such pleading eyes, he knew he was going to give in, even before she opened her mouth.

"Please, Sir? I really want to go to Stronghold." She wriggled. "I promise you'll enjoy it."

"I think I'd enjoy staying home even more," he grumbled but gave her a chaste kiss, then helped her put on a long jacket that covered her down to her knees. It would help keep her warm in the chilly night air, as well as keep her decent until they got to the club.

Her happiness as she bounced to the car made him feel a lot better about the decision to go to Stronghold instead of staying home. Seeing her happy made him happy.

When they pulled into the club's parking lot, he stared. It was nothing like he'd expected. He'd known it wouldn't be like Marquis but wasn't sure it could be more different.

From the outside, Stronghold looked like a warehouse. Only the number of cars in the parking lot made it seem like it might be something else. The windows were tinted, so it didn't look as though any lights were on inside.

Hand gripping Avery's, he led her inside, thrown off enough to be unsure of what he'd find in there. The lobby reminded him a bit of the one at Marquis, though not as lushly decorated. It kept the industrial warehouse feeling. Behind the desk was a bubbly blonde who checked them in before they went through the door into the main part of the club, which was guarded by a massive bouncer. The guy was as big as Connor, though with a shaved head and dark skin. With his arms crossed over his chest, he was intimidating as hell.

"Hey, Master Jared," Avery said cheerfully, giving the big man a little wave as she passed. He smiled at her, his gaze sweeping over Nick before they went through the door.

"How many people do you know here?" Nick asked as they walked into the main room.

"Not that many," Avery admitted. "Rae and Dom talk a lot about the people here, so it feels as if I know them, even though I've never actually met them. I met Master Jared because he was visiting Olivia a few weeks ago when I had to go to her office for some paperwork."

Avery was a friendly person, so she remembered people.

Nick scanned the room and had to admit it was more like a dance club than he'd expected. There was a dance floor with a stage, though no one was currently performing. The music had a throbbing beat but wasn't so loud that it made conversation impossible, which he appreciated. The area just to his and Avery's left was filled with people mingling, sitting in the low chairs or kneeling on the thick carpet.

The kneeling made it different from a club.

On their right was a beautiful wood bar with erotic art hanging behind it and numerous bar tables scattered in front of it. Other than all the leather, it looked like it could be any dance club. He blinked as a woman walked by, leading a man who was crawling on a leash and wearing nothing but a thong and a hood that covered his entire head.

Okay, maybe not any dance club.

"Oooh, there they are!" Avery tugged on his hand, pulling him toward the bar.

AVERY

Nerves hummed through her veins as introductions were made. Nick wasn't the most social person, and she knew this wasn't his kind of scene. Pretty sure he hadn't been kidding when he said he'd be perfectly happy staying in tonight, she really appreciated he'd come out. Although it made her feel like she had to make sure he was having fun.

Thankfully, Mitch, Zach, and Kincaid were warm and friendly and seemed more than happy to add another Dom to their group. She was comfortable around Mitch since he was Domi's boyfriend, but she hadn't spent much time with Zach and Kincaid. They were both tall, dark-haired, and handsome and were in a relationship. She knew Kincaid was a detective, but she didn't know what Zach did.

Thankfully, she didn't have to find something for them to bond over. All of them had eaten at Marquis at one point or another, and them raving about the food not only gave them something to talk about but made Nick feel good. Starting out with a lot of compliments about his skills was a pretty great introduction.

"Aw, look at them making friends," Rae whispered in Avery's ear. "Did this feel like setting up a play date?"

Avery snickered. It had a little, and she imagined some of her anxiety was about whether everyone would get along.

"Shh," she whispered back. "Don't you dare let them hear you call it that."

As if sensing they were getting into mischief, Kincaid glanced over at them and raised one eyebrow. Avery and Rae smiled back with their most innocent expressions, which probably didn't fool him one bit.

The guys were having their own conversation, which had moved onto different kink, including Daddy Doms.

"Brian's here tonight. When he's done with his scene, he can explain better than any of us," Zach said.

Beside Avery, Rae stiffened, but when she glanced at her friend, Rae had already pasted a smile on her face. It was very different from her innocent one, her 'I'm perfectly happy and totally don't care Daddy Brian is scening with someone else' smile. This was the first time Avery had actually seen it, but she'd heard Domi's name for it and knew that's what she was seeing.

"Speaking of scening," Zach said as he got to his feet. "Amy's here. I'm going to see if she wants a scene." He turned to Kincaid, who was sitting on the barstool next to him. Since Kincaid was normally a little taller than Zach, their current positions put them at the perfect height to kiss. "I'll be back." Kincaid gave him a little pat on the butt, smiling fondly as his boyfriend walked off to scene with the woman.

Whoops. Avery could almost feel the confusion emanating from Nick. She'd heard about Kincaid and Zach's unique relationship but had forgotten to give him a heads up. He was probably confused as hell.

Turning back to the table as Zach hurried over to a petite, curvy blonde, Kincaid met Nick's eyes and laughed.

"I guess Avery forgot to tell you about Zach and me?" he asked.

"Oh, uh, well, she told me you two were together..." Nick's eyes darted around the table as though he was looking for someone to clue him in before he put his foot in his mouth.

"They are," Avery said in unison with everyone else. Domi snickered, leaning into Mitch's side.

"They're complicated," Domi teased.

"We are." Kincaid smiled calmly, catching Nick's gaze again. "We're in an exclusive relationship, but Zach is a switch. He's also a sadist. Doing scenes exclusively with me doesn't fulfill all his needs, so he sometimes platonically scenes with other submissives. Amy is engaged, but her fiancé is vanilla, so they scene together fairly regularly since both of them are otherwise romantically involved."

"That's... a lot of trust." Thankfully, Nick sounded more admiring than judgmental.

"Yes." Kincaid nodded.

"Oh, hey, isn't that Q?" Iris asked, going onto her tiptoes and distracting the flow of conversation. "I didn't know he knew Adam and Angel."

Avery had quickly discovered Iris knew what seemed like half the club.

"Let me guess," she said dryly, "more of Andrew's friends." Iris' big brother had a lot of friends at the club, though he wasn't here tonight. Apparently, he had ceded Thursday nights to Iris, Friday nights at Stronghold were his, and they bargained for Saturdays.

"Of course. Well, Adam is. Angel's his wife now, and she's friends with him, too, but mostly with Kate." Iris went up on her tiptoes and waved to the pretty brunette, who waved back before turning her attention back to Q. "I wonder how she knows Q."

"Connor just walked in," Nick said with amusement. "Seems like the entire class is showing up tonight."

Sure enough, Connor had walked in, but he wasn't alone. Master Law and another man were with him.

"Who's that with him and Master Law?" she asked. "He's not part of our class."

About Master Law's height—which put both of them at Connor's shoulders—he had the same dark complexion as Master Law but didn't look Filipino. Middle Eastern, maybe? Unlike Master Law and Connor, he had longer, slicked-back hair, which gave him another inch of height. The black glasses he wore with his leather pants and black button-down made him look like a bad boy professor.

"That's Master Asad," Mitch said. "The new Pied Piper of Pussy."

Domi choked on her drink.

"Excuse me?" Thumping her chest with her fist, she turned an incredulous gaze on her boyfriend.

"You know, the club player. First, it was Andrew, then it was me, and now Asad. Every club has to have one."

"Ew, don't talk about my brother that way." Iris covered her ears, making a face. "I don't want to hear about his man-whoring."

"Yeah, and I'm not sure I want to hear about yours." Domi elbowed Mitch in the side, but her admonishments did nothing to wipe the grin from his face.

"What? That was the whole reason you dated me," he teased. "Good sex, no commitment. Being bondage buddies was the start of our romance. You would have never been my friend-with-cuffs if I'd been a relationship kind of guy."

"He's got you there," Rae said, smirking. "Besides, you cured him of his pussy-hopping ways with your magic vagina."

"I hate all of you," Domi whined.

"Hey, I didn't say anything," Avery protested.

"Me, either," Kincaid chimed in.

"Okay, fine, I hate everyone except Avery and Kincaid. Does that work?"

"Mmm, hate sex." Mitch tipped his head to the side, staring off into the air, visualizing it. "Sounds good to me."

"I hate you the most."

"I can live with that."

As everyone laughed, Nick pulled Avery tighter into his side, chuckling.

"Your friends are insane," he whispered, his hot breath tickling her ear. Considering the conversation, she couldn't really argue.

30

NICK

When Avery suggested taking a tour of the rest of Stronghold, Nick agreed. As friendly as everyone had been, and as much as he was enjoying their conversation, he could use a breather. The main floor was not at all what he'd pictured, and knowing there were two more floors, he wanted to see what else the club offered.

"Up or down?" she asked. "Dungeon is downstairs, private rooms are upstairs."

"Up," he said. He'd seen the private rooms at Marquis, even though he hadn't spent much time in them, so he figured the Dungeon would be the bigger novelty.

He was both right and wrong.

The private rooms were different from those at Marquis. For one, they had windows with blinds that could be closed but currently were open. They could see everything that was going on inside. The rooms also had different themes from those at Marquis.

There was one that looked like a school locker room, another like an actual schoolroom, a private office, and one with a huge bed where multiple people were frolicking. There was that orgy he'd been wondering about. Nick watched, fascinated, but was pretty sure he'd never use that room.

Being watched by the instructors and other students during class had been bad enough. Total strangers? Not his thing. Although he had to admit, there was something stirring about watching. It made him feel a little hypocritical that he was enjoying watching when he didn't want to be watched but considering there was a movie theater where some people were watching a live feed of the orgy room, he couldn't bring himself to feel all that bad.

"You know what they need? A kitchen setup," he murmured to Avery as they headed back down the hallway. Several people were standing at the windows, watching what was going on in the private rooms, but none of them looked up as he and Avery passed by. "Some nice steel counters, spatulas, maybe some chocolate syrup..."

Avery giggled. "You should tell your brother that. Maybe he can set up something special for you."

Hell, that wasn't a bad idea, though he wasn't sure how many other people would have kitchen fantasies. Food fantasies, maybe... though he wasn't sure how they'd keep such a place hygienic. Maybe that was why they didn't have it.

Sighing inwardly, he held Avery's hand as they went down the stairs. Glancing toward the table where everyone had been, he could see Kincaid was still there, talking with Q, Angel, and Adam, but everyone else had scattered. He hadn't seen them upstairs, which meant they were downstairs.

"Ready?" Avery asked him, noticing his distraction.

"Yup. Let's go to the Dungeon." Wow. That sounded far more ominous than he'd intended. On the other hand, he didn't mind the effect it had on Avery. She tilted her head and gave him a sassy little look even better than her usual 'thanks.'

He was getting used to the skintight latex, but that didn't mean he'd stopped appreciating it.

Reaching the bottom of the stairs and looking around the Dungeon, it was more what he had in mind when he'd pictured Stronghold. There were spanking benches throughout the middle of the floor, St. Andrew's Crosses on the far side, and several alcoves where chains were hanging down. Thursday night was supposed to be less busy, but there were quite a few people occupying all the spaces.

To their immediate right was a small space with lots of couches, love seats, and armchairs scattered around, with a mini-fridge and a small stacks of blankets. He'd seen a similar space on the second floor, but it had been unoccupied. There were several people in this one, including someone he recognized—Morgan was cuddled on a Dom's lap, looking happily content. She didn't look up when he and Avery went by.

He didn't look at her for long, though, far too interested in everything else that was going on.

❧

AVERY

The Dungeon wasn't packed, but it had quite a few people in it. Avery sucked in a breath when she saw Master Brian giving Morgan aftercare and Rae and Domi on the other side of the room. Unfortunately, it wasn't crowded enough to block out the sight between the two. She could see Rae studiously had her head turned away from the aftercare area, but there was no way she'd missed Brian and Morgan's cuddle session.

Hopefully, she hadn't caught the end of their scene. Avery would have to catch up with her later.

"There are private rooms down here, too," Nick said, walking over to peer into the windows. For someone who didn't want to be watched, he had no problem peeking in, which amused Avery. She got it, though. Exhibitionism and voyeurism were two very different kinks, though some people had both, and they combined well for obvious reasons. "Oh, shit."

He turned around fast, which made Avery peek in and then laugh. Apparently, Mitch was running an interrogation on Domi—and it was going very well. She was hanging by her wrists from a chain in the center of the ceiling, clamps on her nipples, while Mitch held her up with his hands under her bright red butt and her legs wrapped around his waist, thrusting into her with vigor. They were so involved in what they were doing, they didn't seem to notice or care whether anyone was watching.

"Not ready to see people you know doing that, huh?" she teased. Nick's cheeks, already pink, reddened even more.

"Are you?"

Avery shrugged. "I'm not against it, but Mitch and Domi are a little hardcore for me. I like lighter play."

"That's good to know." His thumb rubbed against the outside of the hand he was holding as he turned away, his attention drawn to people using the spanking benches. Avery leaned into him.

"Do you want to try?" It was the equipment he was most familiar with, but she wasn't surprised when he hesitated, then shook his head. She hadn't expected to play tonight, but she hadn't wanted to make an assumption.

"For now, watching is good." His hand slid over to her waist and then down to her ass as they watched one of the submissives being spanked. He squeezed her cheek, making her giggle and squirm. "When we get home, though..."

NICK

While Nick had no interest in doing a scene at Stronghold, seeing how many different people were there—on a slow night, no less—made him feel a lot better about his own proclivities. Granted, he'd already made a huge step in accepting himself, but it was still good to see the many others involved in the lifestyle and know that he and Avery weren't alone. Not only that, they were barely dipping their toes in the waters of what was possible.

He'd learned needle play was definitely not for him or Avery. He'd watched, fascinated, but it hadn't been arousing—more like something he couldn't look away from because it was freaking him out.

It had made him feel a lot better about what he and Avery did. He got why she'd said Mitch and Domi were too hardcore for her. Nick knew he liked to cause her a little bit of pain, but he was getting a full demonstration of the different levels on display throughout the club.

Now he understood why Olivia had said it was important to visit Stronghold, not just rely on everything they learned in class, which were the things they wanted to do, not everything that was possible.

He also found out that the wax play looked a lot more interesting than he'd thought.

"Thinking about taking that off your soft limits?" Avery asked as they walked away from the table where a Domme was making art by dripping various colors of wax over her very happy submissive.

"Yes." He wasn't too proud to admit it. With his arm curved around her waist, he tilted his head toward her, lifting his eyebrows. "Any objections?"

"Nope. I like wax. Well, as long as I'm already shaved, I like wax."

Nick chuckled, but they weren't able to continue the conversation. Avery suddenly straightened, her head whipping around. Alerted, Nick's gaze followed to where Iris was facing off with a man nearly a head taller than her next to one of the St. Andrew's Crosses.

"Shit." Avery didn't wait for him, darting toward Iris.

Alarmed, Nick was on her heels. From everything he'd seen with Iris, she was mouthy, irreverent, and pretty hilarious most of the time, but right now, she looked pissed.

"You need to back off," the Dom said, his voice deep with threat as he loomed over Iris.

"You need to watch your mouth," Iris retorted. Despite being half-naked in a corset that pushed up her breasts and a short skirt that barely covered her ass, she didn't look at all submissive as she glared up at the bigger man. "You don't call people fat!"

The Dom's lips twisted in a sneer. "It's called humiliation play—"

Before he could finish his sentence, Avery was at Iris' side, tugging at her arm and trying to pull her away.

"Iris, come on. You're interrupting his scene." Avery's whisper was loud enough Nick could hear it as he came up alongside her. The Dom crossed his arms over his chest and glared at Nick as if this was all his fault, which he didn't appreciate. He scowled back. He didn't know what was going on and wouldn't speak up unless he knew.

One thing he did know was interrupting someone else's scene was not okay.

"But he called her—"

"Did she say her safeword?"

"No..." Iris' expression turned mulish. "But he called her fat and a piggie! And she's crying!"

Glancing at the submissive in question, whose very curvy body was on display, thanks to the St. Andrew's cross, Nick pressed his lips together. The Dom had said it was humiliation play, which was something Nick had put on his hard limits when Avery explained it. He had no interest in calling her names or making her grovel.

Seeing his look, the Dom scowled harder.

"I called her my fat little slut and my sweet piggie, both of which she *likes*." With more witnesses, his tone had turned defensive and louder, and more and more people around them were taking notice of the interrupted scene.

Shit. Nick hesitated. He didn't know what to do in this situation. The submissive on the cross didn't look as though she was in distress, despite her tears, and it sounded as if the words had been agreed on. She also wasn't speaking up either way, and Iris was clearly upset.

"What's going on here?" Master Law's familiar voice cut through the rising chatter around them, and Nick's shoulders relaxed in relief. He might technically be a Dom, but he didn't feel equipped to handle Iris all puffed up with self-righteous anger in defense of another woman and a Dom who probably had every right to be upset that his scene had been interrupted.

Iris and the Dom started talking, then stopped as soon as Master Law put his hand up. Wearing leather pants and a leather vest, with what looked like a badge on the left side of his chest, it took Nick a moment to realize it was the Dungeon Monitor outfit that had been described to him.

"Iris, you do not interrupt someone else's scene. Even if you hear the submissive use a safeword, you come and get one of us." He tapped the badge on his vest. "I know you know that. Come on. We're going to go talk to Patrick."

Crossing her arms, Iris didn't look as though she was going to do any such thing, but Master Law didn't give her a choice. Moving to her side, he wrapped his fingers around the back of her neck, marching her toward the steps. Only then did her posture slump.

Nick shot a look of apology at the Dom whose scene Iris had interrupted, but he wasn't looking at them anymore—he was already by his submissive's side, whispering something in her ear. From the way she was looking up at him, Nick didn't think they would have any problems getting back into their scene.

"Ah, crap." Avery deflated next to him, more so than he thought reasonable. Yes, Iris was probably in trouble, but she'd been trying to help, though she should have known better than to interfere with a scene. She was one of the submissives in the new Doms class because she was supposed to have experience.

"What's wrong? How much trouble is she in?"

"Probably a lot." Avery's worried hazel eyes turned up toward him. "She told us she was volun-told to be a submissive for the Dom class because she kept getting into trouble here. It was supposed to be a refresher for her on how things work in the club."

"That girl, man." Rae appeared beside Avery, shaking her head. "Did you see what happened?"

As Avery updated Rae, Nick looked around the room. Pretty much everyone had gone back to what they were doing, including the Dom and sub whose scene had been interrupted. He felt for Iris. Some of the stuff that happened here was outside of his comfort level, too. He didn't think he'd feel good hearing someone being verbally humiliated, but that was what they liked, and this was supposed to be a safe place for them to indulge.

Stroking his fingers down Avery's back, he couldn't help but think Master Law was right to come down hard on Iris. It was difficult enough to admit to wanting to do some of these things. Being interrupted because someone thought you were abusing your partner's trust instead of giving them what they wanted?

Nick's insides shriveled.

It looked like the couple had made a good recovery—in fact, the Dom was already taking off his pants. Nick had to give them massive credit. He wasn't sure he'd have been able to get right back into things so easily. It was a measure of how secure they were in their kinks and connection.

Even though he didn't share their kink, it felt like something to aspire to.

31

AVERY

Monday night with her friends when the Doms had their own class was starting to feel like a tradition, and one she was very glad about, especially this week. Iris hadn't wanted to talk on Saturday night after she'd finally been released from Master Patrick's office, but at least she hadn't been kicked out of the club. She hoped Iris might be a little chattier today because she was dying to know what had happened.

"It really wasn't that interesting," Iris said, rolling her eyes as she took a sip of her beer. They'd gathered at Rae and Domi's, which was empty tonight. Ana was with her dad, and Mitch was out with his friends, giving them total privacy and plenty of space to spread out the pizza they'd ordered. "Master Law was all 'blah blah blah, Iris was disrespectful,' then Patrick was all 'blah, blah, blah, Iris, how many times do I have to tell you?' He put me on server duty for the next month."

"That's not so bad." Rae looked surprised but impressed. She was sitting on the couch with Iris while Domi and Avery had taken the two armchairs on either end of the coffee table. "I thought it would be way worse."

"I also have homework." Iris made a face. "I'm supposed to spend an hour in the Dungeon every shift and take note of different kinks and how the submissive is reacting, not how it makes me feel. I get that, but like... ugh. My best friend growing up was a bigger girl. She had a boyfriend who called her fat and put her down, making her feel like shit. She ended up in the hospital with anorexia."

"Yikes. Is she okay now?" Domi asked before Avery could.

"Yeah, but she moved away. She couldn't stand to be in this area anymore. Too many memories." Even though Iris didn't say it, it was clear she missed her friend. Avery sympathized. Even though she was the one who had moved away from her friends, it was hard feeling alone.

"I should have walked away. It just... I don't know. I knew I should, then the next thing I knew, I was yelling at him." Iris shrugged one shoulder, but Avery got the feeling she was more upset about it than she was letting on.

"Next time, yell your safe word," Avery joked. "Then when the DM comes, make him carry you away."

"That could be fun." Iris perked up as Domi and Rae giggled. Then she made a face. "Well, as long as it's not Master Law on duty. I will be happy if I never see that man again."

"Yeah, you two are like... Law and disorder," Rae raised her glass, toasting Iris. "Get it? Like *Law and Order*, but you're disorder."

"My brother used to call me Chaos," Iris mused. "I think I like 'Disorder' even better, especially when it comes to Master Law. I swear, that man has no sense of humor. Does anyone know what kind of law he practices?"

They looked around at each other blankly. That appeared to be a 'no.'

"Well, at least I get a break from him tonight." Iris leaned back against the couch, letting her head drop back with relief.

"Do you know what they're doing in class tonight?" Rae asked, leaning forward to pick up another slice of pizza.

Avery pressed her lips together. She knew, but Nick hadn't been very excited. As open-minded as he was, she had a feeling he was going to struggle tonight. She didn't think he'd really like knowing she'd told her friends about it. Though they probably could find out, anyway.

"I do..."

"It's butt stuff night." Iris grinned at the look Avery shot in her direction. "What? This way, you didn't have to be the one to tell, so you can't be in trouble."

Well, she wasn't wrong. Iris being the one to tell wasn't Avery's fault.

Rae rolled her eyes.

"It's funny. They're all eager to put stuff in our butts, but when the tables are turned..."

"Hey, speak for yourself. Mitch enjoys a little back door action sometimes," Domi said, wiggling her index finger in Rae's direction.

"Ew, don't say things like that, then point that at me!"

Dissolving into laughter, Avery could only shake her head. Yup, she had found her people.

❧

NICK

Wiping his hands against the outsides of his thighs, Nick tried to pretend as if the idea of something going into his butt didn't bother him. The sweaty palms he'd just tried to dry on his pants indicated otherwise.

"They're enjoying this," Q muttered under his breath, glaring balefully at the center stage where Master Law and Mistress Julie were unloading a box full of new toys, still in their plastic packaging. As usual, Master Law was in his business suit. Today, Mistress Julie was wearing a pencil skirt and a ruffled top with three-inch spiked high heels. She looked like the hot librarian who would eat your heart out if you damaged a book.

They looked as though they were enjoying themselves, at least Mistress Julie did, as she glanced over at him, Q, and Connor every time she took out a new toy, wanting to see their reactions.

Sadist.

"Could be worse, I guess," Q mused. Nick had noticed he had a bit of a penchant for talking out loud, though he was doing so quietly enough only Nick and Connor could hear him right now. "At least Sam's not here to watch."

She'd been excused having already experienced this as a submissive.

The submissives were the ones who got things in the butt, which was why they had to learn how to do it first. Yeah, it made sense, but Nick had never had anything in his butt, never even considered putting anything in his butt. Okay, maybe back when he was a teenager, but he'd never actually done it. He'd outgrown the impulse—curiosity—not one he'd ever really thought would be fulfilled.

When Olivia sauntered in, Nick tried to shrivel into his chair. Oh, hell no. She caught his eye as she stepped onto the stage and smirked at him. Nope, nope, nope. He'd better not be paired with her.

The thought occurred, then he relaxed.

There was no way in hell Luke would be okay with that.

He was pretty sure.

"Who wants to be paired with me?" Mistress Julie asked, straightening and holding up a package with three butt plugs, starting with one that looked small and innocuous and ending with one Nick didn't want anywhere near his ass. On the other hand, having Mistress Julie was definitely preferable to Olivia being his instructor.

Unfortunately, Connor's hand had already shot up in the air.

"Good. Over here, please." Mistress Julie gestured to the spanking benches behind her, on the other side of the table. With the table and the Doms in the way, it was hard to see the setup, but Nick was pretty sure they were facing away from each other, so there was some mercy in that.

"Q, you're with me," Olivia said, curling a finger at him before smirking again at Nick. That meant he was left with Master Law, which was far preferable since he'd missed his chance with Mistress Julie.

Connor was already over his bench by the time Nick got to the other side of the table. Not to be outdone, Nick grit his teeth, pulled down his pants, and assumed the position. *Yeah, maybe don't think about it like that.* He could hear Mistress Julie murmuring something to Connor and Olivia talking to Q, but he couldn't make out what they were saying. It was drowned out when Master Law began talking to him, the Dom keeping his voice as low as the two Dommes.

"Now, the best thing you can do is relax. Take a deep breath. We'll start with the smallest one. It shouldn't hurt, though you might feel a slight ache." Master Law's deep voice was soothing. The sensation of something cold and hard pressing against Nick's anus was not. "Relax, Nick. Take a deep breath."

As the air left his lungs, the plug pushed in, and Nick clenched. The intrusion came to a halt but didn't go away.

Relax. It doesn't even hurt. It feels weird. That's nothing. You want to put your whole dick in Avery's ass. You're a hell of a lot bigger than this tiny plug. Suck it up, buttercup.

He relaxed, and the plug pushed in deeper.

Master Law was right. It didn't hurt exactly, but it did sting, though that dissipated quickly. It felt weird as hell, especially once the thickest part got past his entrance and the plug settled inside him.

"Okay, now I'm going to move it so you can feel what that's like."

The plug twisted back and forth inside him, easily thanks to the lube, but it felt weird as fuck. Worse, his dick stirred. Nick closed his eyes and tried to think about deboning a fish.

AVERY

"So, you and Nick are pretty serious now, huh?" Domi asked. "Is it too soon to start talking the L-word?"

"Of course it's not," Rae spoke up before Avery could respond, tossing her long braids over her shoulder. "He's getting plugged tonight for her. Even Meatloaf wouldn't do that."

"What?" The confusion on Iris' face was almost comical.

"That song—I'd do anything for love, but I won't do that—that's what she's talking about. Butt stuff."

"You don't know that for sure." Domi shook her head, though she was grinning.

Rae looked at Avery and Iris, mouthing, 'It totally is.' Avery giggled.

"I'm not sure that's love. It might be just the desire to put things in my butt," she pointed out. "There are plenty of Doms who go through that part of training without having a girlfriend, much less being in love with them. They just want to be allowed to do the butt stuff in the club."

"Yeah, but Nick also loves you."

"Agreed." Rae nodded along with Domi. Iris was nodding hers as well, even though she didn't actually say anything out loud. Avery looked at them all with bemusement.

"Does Nick get a vote?"

"Nah, we know he does." Domi waved her hand. "Deep down, you know he does, too."

"I think he might, but he hasn't said anything." Avery rubbed her hands together, then picked up another piece of pizza. She was almost full, but she could eat one more slice. It was amazing.

"You're in love with him, though, right?" Rae asked earnestly, leaning toward Avery as if she needed to know the answer.

"I mean..." It was scary saying it out loud, but Avery made herself tell the truth. "Yes."

"Don't mind her. Since she started writing romance, all she wants is happy endings for everyone." Domi smiled when Iris snickered. "Not that kind of happy ending. Well, that as well. She writes the sexy stuff."

"Damn right I do." Rae grinned. "That's the fun stuff. Domi's not wrong, but it's not the romance author thing. I just like to see my friends happy. Is that so wrong?" she teased, but there was a little edge to her voice, and Avery couldn't help but wonder if Rae was living vicariously through her friends.

One subject that had not come up tonight was Brian scening somewhat regularly with Morgan at Stronghold lately. Domi had invited Avery over before tonight and given her the heads up not to bring it up. She assumed Iris had been given the same warning.

"What about me?" Iris raised her hand, amusement dancing in her eyes. "When do I get a happy ending?"

"Well, first, we have to find the perfect guy for you," Rae said enthusiastically, lighting up from within. "Like Mitch was for Domi, and Nick is for Avery."

"To be fair, Nick wasn't completely perfect for me. I didn't want to date a guy I was working with."

"Yeah, but it turned out it was perfect," Domi said. "Just like I didn't want an actual relationship with Mitch, then it turned out he was perfect for me." She held up one finger. "Please note, I did not say he is perfect. I specifically said perfect for *me*. Please, for the love of God, never tell him I said he was perfect."

Rae snickered before turning back to Iris. "Okay, so what kind of guy does Iris need?"

"Someone fun," Iris said immediately. "With a sense of adventure."

"Don't forget loyal, honest, and bossy in the bedroom," Domi said, ticking the points off on her fingers. She tilted her head to the side, studying Iris. "At least, I'm assuming those are things you want?"

"Sounds good. Q is pretty cute, but since he's friends with Adam and Angel, I'm guessing he at least knows my brother, so I'm not sure I want to go there. Plus... sometimes, I get the feeling he's more switch-y than Dom-y. It also might be that he's new to everything. I think I'd like someone a little more experienced since I'm picking and choosing," Iris said, grinning.

Interesting. Avery hadn't thought to ask Iris about the others in the class, even though she'd been taking turns as their sub. That was a good point about Q being new to the scene, but Avery also trusted Iris' instincts. There were plenty of kinky people who could be a little switch-y.

"What about Connor?" Avery asked. The big guy was probably the quietest in the class, like a massive gentle giant, which made her even more curious. Despite his size, she didn't get the same aura of confidence from him she did from Nick or the other Doms. Though that also might come down to being new.

"He tries hard." Iris shrugged when the others laughed. "He does and does a decent job, but I'm not sure his heart is really into it. Sometimes, I think he's not actually all that kinky."

"Well, if he's not, this is a hell of a class to get through." Rae shook her head at the idea of someone putting themselves through the Doms course for no reason.

✢ 32 ✣

NICK

The inside of his ass was sore as hell. They'd gone through three different plugs, anal beads, a probe, and a lifelike dildo. It had been one hell of a primer. Granted, none of the toys had been used on them for long. Mistress Julie had pointed out when they used them on a submissive, it would be for longer periods with fewer changes between toys, but the overall impact gave them an idea of what those longer times would feel like.

Nick had a newfound respect for what the submissives went through, especially when it came to physical reactions that they couldn't control. He hadn't meant to get a hard-on while Master Law was inserting the probe, but his body had had other ideas.

On the other hand, it had opened his mind to what he might let Avery do to him. He'd heard a finger in conjunction with a blowjob could be pretty spectacular. That was something he hadn't been willing to try before that he might try now—at least, in a few weeks when he'd recovered from tonight.

The Doms had elected to stand through the last lecture in the class. Thankfully, Olivia had left the room as soon as the hands-on demonstration portion was over, so Nick didn't have to avoid her gaze. Looking at Mistress Julie was hard enough. He couldn't look Master Law in the eye right now, not after the man had become even more intimately acquainted with Nick's body than his own doctor.

"See you all next week for the final class!" Mistress Julie said cheerfully. "Don't forget to talk to me or Master Law if you want to sign up for individual sessions of any kind of edge play."

As interested as Nick was in fire play, he was going to pass. Doing the 'regular' kinky stuff would keep him busy for a while. Maybe when he felt more comfortable, he'd talk to Avery about doing the individual classes for some of the extra stuff.

Q and Connor seemed to feel the same. They all moved out of the room quickly, if a bit stiff-legged, into the lobby, which was thankfully empty. As if by some hidden signal, they all slowed. No one said they wanted to talk, but Nick knew they did. Tonight had made them feel more like a cohesive group since they'd all been through something together. He felt bad Sam hadn't been here but had to admit he wasn't sure it would have been the same if she had been.

She'd already been through it, whereas he was pretty sure it had been entirely new for Q and Connor, the same as it had been for him. Butt virgins no more.

"One more week." Q shook his head in disbelief. "And then we're Doms."

Connor made a noncommittal noise, but he wasn't a chatty guy, so Nick wasn't expecting much more from him.

"I've already been practicing with Avery at home. Do you two go to Stronghold?" He couldn't help but be curious. He hadn't seen either of them scening the night he'd been there with Avery, but he and Avery hadn't stayed much longer after Iris got into trouble. That had put a bit of a damper on the evening for their whole little group.

"So far, I haven't done more than visit and watch with some friends," Q confessed.

"Same." Connor's single-word reply was so like him, Nick had to smile. Besides, the conversation was distracting him from how his ass felt.

The door to Olivia's office opened, and all three of them tensed.

When Luke appeared in the doorway rather than his more intimidating counterpart, they relaxed. Connor and Q knew Luke was Olivia's sub, which meant he'd been through the same thing they had tonight—probably far more often.

Seriously, don't think too hard about that.

He was surprised Luke hadn't wanted to be there, considering Olivia had stepped in to teach. Other than an involuntary physical reaction, there hadn't been anything particularly sexual or sexy about tonight's class, which Luke probably knew. It was fascinating how kink could be incredibly sexy or completely platonic.

"Hey, Nick, got a minute?" Luke asked, striding toward their little group. Connor and Q quickly said their goodbyes, moving toward the stairs and leaving Nick with his brother. Not that he minded, even if it was a little awkward. "Just wanted to see how you and Avery are doing. Mom was asking me if you're going to bring her around for the holidays."

Holy shit, it was October. When had that happened?

"I have to talk to Avery," he said, knowing the excuse would only let him off the hook for so long, although it was true. He didn't know what her plans were for the holidays. They hadn't talked about it. Nick had never brought a girlfriend home for the holidays, but for the first time, he really wanted to.

Wow. He wanted to introduce Avery to the whole family. That was new and different, but it also told him how much he really loved her. You know, if tonight's class hadn't already confirmed that.

"It'd be great if you want to come by. Mom's torn between being interested in your new girlfriend and my and Olivia's reproductive schedule." Luke grinned when Nick groaned, his eyes dancing with amusement.

Ah, yes. The eternal quest for grandbabies. Maybe he shouldn't inflict that on Avery... On the other hand, since Luke and Olivia got together, they'd had his mom's complete focus. The brotherly thing to do would be to share the load, especially since Luke and Olivia were fairly ambivalent about having kids.

Did Avery want kids?

They hadn't talked about it. Ever. That was probably something they should do. Was it too soon? They'd already been together a few months.

"Hey, you okay? You look like you're about to have an aneurysm or something." Luke clapped his hands on Nick's shoulder, trying to peer into his eyes. Scoffing, Nick brushed him off and stepped away, wincing a little when his body reminded him it was sore in places where he wasn't used to being sore.

"Questioning whether I want to inflict Mom on Avery this soon in the relationship," he admitted.

"Hey, that's what we do to the women we love." Luke chuckled. "Besides, Olivia will help protect her."

"Ah, right." When Luke arched an eyebrow at him, Nick shrugged, shoving his hands in his pockets. "I, ah, haven't actually told Avery I love her yet."

"Oh..." Luke blinked, then laughed. "Well, definitely tell her before introducing her to Mom. That should help keep her from running."

"Is that what kept Olivia from running?"

"If Olivia felt fear, she'll never admit it."

AVERY

When Nick knocked on her door, Avery thought, not for the first time, she really needed to get him an extra key.

That or move in together.

Yeah, no. That was moving too fast. They hadn't been dating long enough, no matter how long they'd known each other before they started dating.

Right?

Answer the door, twit. Think about cohabitation later.

Right, right.

The look on Nick's face when she opened the door almost made her laugh out loud. As happy to see her as ever, there was an odd cast to his expression. He looked like she'd felt the first time she'd ever done anal play. The sensations lingered long after it was over, and the taboo of it had stuck in her mind.

"Hey, there," she said, smushing down her laughter as best she could, tipping her lips back for a kiss. His eyes narrowed suspiciously, but thankfully, he didn't call her on it.

"Hey," he said when he pulled away. "How are the ladies?"

"They're good." She shut the door behind him, admiring his ass in his jeans, then had to suppress more laughter when she saw his stiff gait. That was not his normal walk. If he was another submissive, she'd be giggling in fellow-feeling, knowing exactly how that felt, but she didn't think Nick would appreciate sympathetic laughter. He was more likely to think she was laughing *at* him, and she didn't want to make him feel like that.

"We spent most of the night building the perfect man for Iris."

That made Nick turn around, his brows furrowing. "What?"

Now, she could finally laugh, and it if was a little heartier than it might have been otherwise, he couldn't take offense.

"Apparently, she wants to be part of a happy couple, so we were talking about what would make the perfect guy for her." Avery grinned as Nick shook his head and turned around, heading for the kitchen. "What, you don't think there's a perfect guy for Iris?"

"If there is, he'd need the patience of a saint," Nick tossed over his shoulder.

Avery plopped on the couch, watching him with amusement as he moved around her kitchen as though he belonged there. She was the same way at his house. Maybe thoughts of moving in together weren't so far-fetched.

Maybe you should wait till you exchange the L-word before you go down that path so you don't scare him off.

"Iris is a brat, in the purest sense of the word."

"You're not wrong. She wants someone adventurous and fun."

Picking up a beer from the bottom shelf of the fridge, Nick made a face as he straightened. The hiss from the can opening punctuated his expression.

"She'd be better off with someone who could ground her a little."

"The way you ground me?" Avery teased.

Nick laughed, coming over to the couch, sitting gingerly next to her. Avery really felt she deserved a medal for the way she kept her face straight. Leaning in, he brushed his lips over hers for a brief, affectionate kiss. He'd taken a sip of his beer, so when he kissed her, he tasted like oranges and hops.

"No, the way you ground me." He winked at her. "I'm not fucking Gordon Ramsey after all."

"No, you're fucking me." She completed the joke, even though it made her want to groan. The big jerk chuckled, looking smug. He'd probably known she wouldn't be able to resist.

"So, what are your plans for the holidays?"

Avery nearly choked. It was a good thing she wasn't the one drinking beer, or she would have spat it out all over him. When she met his gaze, it was full of mischief, and he was grinning at her.

"Not what you were expecting me to say?"

"Well, there was no segue." She narrowed her eyes, a little miffed he'd amused himself at her expense while she'd been trying to be so good about not doing that to him, but she couldn't ignore the pounding of her heart. Was he asking what she thought he was asking? "I uh, hadn't really thought about it... but my mom asked if I might bring you home when I told her about you."

"Wow. Our mothers must be made from the same mold." He took another sip of his beer, but the amusement hadn't faded from his expression. If anything, it had increased. Shifting on the couch, he pulled her into his side, so she was nestled under his arm, head in the nook between his shoulder and chest. Her favorite spot. "I asked because Luke pulled me aside tonight. Apparently, our mom has been asking him if I'll be bringing you home for the holidays."

Nice to know she wasn't the only one with an importuning mom.

"Why doesn't she ask you?" she asked, curious.

"I've always been a bit of a contrarian. I'm pretty sure she worries if she asks me, I'll say no on principle. Luke was the good son who tried to make my parents happy. I was the one who would do the exact opposite of what they said."

"Why am I not surprised?" Avery shook her head, rolling her eyes.

"Be warned, if you meet her, she'll want to know if you want kids."

The casual tone of his voice threw her off as much as the actual conversation. As if this wasn't momentous, life-altering stuff they were talking about. Suddenly, she wished she could see his face, to see how serious he was, but she was kind of glad she couldn't. She wasn't sure what her expression looked like right now.

"Do you want kids?"

Act normal! Act normal! He's acting normal. You need to as well!

"Yeah, I always pictured myself with a couple of kids." She wondered if she was dreaming. The whole conversation felt a little surreal. "What about you?"

"Yeah. Luke was the one who was never sure if he wanted kids. I always wanted at least one, more like two."

"Two is a good number." She didn't lift her head from his shoulder, barely daring to breathe.

"Seriously, though, think about it. Your family is in Georgia, right? Maybe we could do one for Thanksgiving and the other for Christmas or something." He yawned as if he hadn't just knocked the breath out of her.

Yeah, she'd been having 'moving in' thoughts, but that had all been in her head. She hadn't said it aloud. Somehow, it had been easier to imagine moving in together than meeting each other's families.

"Want to watch some Great British Baking show?"

"Yeah, sure," she answered automatically, thankful for the reprieve from the conversation that had thrown her so badly.

Think about it.

She could hardly think about anything else that night, curled up in Nick's arms, eyes wide open while she thought about it. They hadn't said they loved each other, but sometimes, actions spoke louder than words.

He wanted her to meet his family. Wanted to meet hers. That was a big deal, right? Something people did when they imagined a future together. She loved him. He obviously felt something deep for her, even if he hadn't said it yet. Maybe that was enough for right now.

🙋 33 🙋

NICK

very was acting weird. They hadn't had much of a chance to talk this morning before leaving for work. Both of them had slept in pretty late.

Shit.

Had he really thrown her that much, asking about the holidays? He'd tried to keep it casual with his phrasing, alert for any indication she thought he was pushing things too fast. It didn't feel fast to him, though. It felt right. They'd known each other for a lot longer than they'd been dating, and they were good together. They fit together in every way, the way he hadn't with anyone else.

He could imagine spending the rest of his life with her. The thought didn't scare him at all.

"What'd you do?" George muttered under his breath to Nick, though his eyes were on Avery.

"I didn't think I did anything," he muttered back, passing a plate to George to garnish. They were shorthanded in the kitchen because he still hadn't found someone to replace Chad's, which meant occasionally, he and Avery had to step in for the fry station. They'd have someone soon. There had been a few promising interviews. "I told her my mom wants to meet her."

"And you think you didn't do anything." George snorted. "Meeting your ma is the scariest thing you could ask her to do."

Nick almost muttered that George didn't know what he asked Avery to do, but since he was pretty sure everyone had a fair idea of what they got up to at Marquis, it might not be entirely true. His ass still felt a bit odd today, although he was walking and sitting normally.

Besides, George had a point. Meeting the family was a big deal, which was probably why he'd instinctively tried to make it not a big deal when he'd mentioned it to Avery. Maybe he should have made a big deal out of it?

He was distracted from his thoughts when he noticed George had suddenly disappeared from his side. Turning around to look for him, he saw the man standing by a certain redheaded server he'd been pining after. Nick raised his eyebrows at their flirtatious stances. When Alanna hurried back into the dining room, she glanced back at George, who was grinning like a fool when he got back in his expo position.

"You and Alanna, huh?" Nick murmured, keeping his voice down. Not that they were discreet, but he didn't want to be the one to draw attention to them. "Kind of soon, isn't it? Aren't you worried about being a rebound?"

"It might be soon, but I'm the right guy." George grinned, brimming with confidence. "Alanna would be worth waiting for, but when you know it's right, why wait?"

When you know it's right, why wait?

"That's a very good point." Nick's eyes darted to Avery, who was still oblivious to everything happening behind her, her focus entirely on the food she was making.

AVERY

Nick was acting weird. Maybe because it was the final day of class, but more than that, he seemed almost jittery. Far more nervous than she would have thought the last day of class would make him feel.

All the submissives were standing by the side of the person they were working with that evening. Avery was with Nick, of course, and Freddy was standing beside Sam. Morgan had taken a place next to Connor and had a hand on his back as though she was encouraging him, which was a funny visual—she was tall, but next to Connor, she looked tiny. Iris and Q were standing beside each other, clearly friendly, but Avery didn't see a romantic spark between them or even the deeper friendship Morgan and Connor seemed to have formed.

Definitely not Iris' ideal man, but maybe she'd find someone when she was serving at Stronghold. That was a pretty devious maneuver on Master Patrick's part. Not only would he get free labor, but it would be a good way for Iris to meet a lot of the club members. For all her bravado and the many people she knew, Iris didn't go out of her way to meet anyone new. She was happy in her comfort zone.

Shifting by her side, Nick drew her attention back to him, where he was practically jigging in place. Normally, he had no problem standing still in one place, so his constant movement made her even more nervous. Did he know something that she didn't about tonight?

"Alright, everyone, now that you're all here... submissives, we have a surprise for you!" At Mistress Julie's words, it was Avery's turn to tense up. A surprise? That rarely boded well for subbies in a kink club. What didn't surprise her was Morgan and Iris tensed as well. Freddy didn't show any reaction, so either he was hiding it really well or already knew. She would bet on the latter.

Nick had finally calmed, which meant he probably knew what was coming and hadn't warned her. The big jerk.

"The Dominants arrived about an hour before you and have already completed their class." Mistress Julie grinned widely as Morgan made a confused noise. Avery's eyelashes fluttered in surprise, her brain working to catch up and figure out what was going on. "The rest of the evening will be yours with your Doms. They've each signed up for a private room at Marquis."

"All previously established hard limits will be observed," Master Law chimed in. "If you want to change any of them, you may talk to us beforehand, but otherwise, the same rules apply as usual, including sexual boundaries." He cast his gaze to Iris and Q, neither of whom seemed bothered. Iris had sex listed as a hard limit for the class, although she'd told Avery it wasn't one when she scened in the club.

Warm fingers wrapped around Avery's, and she snuck a peek at Nick. He was grinning, but she still thought he seemed a little nervous. Maybe because they were about to do a private scene in one of the clubs for the first time.

"Alright, off you go." Mistress Julie shooed them with her hands. "Congratulations, new Doms!"

Chuckling, Nick broke off first, tugging Avery by the hand. The others were right behind them, spilling into the hallway. Laughter bounced off the walls, and the Doms were grinning, jubilant. Avery glanced over her shoulder to where the submissives were, happy for them.

"Let's go," Nick said, tugging her along. "We're in the Dungeon."

She wasn't sure where the others ended up, except Morgan and Connor disappeared into the pink Littles' room. Nick was pulling her along too quickly for her to get a good look at where everyone else was going.

The Dungeon was exactly as advertised—decorated like a medieval Dungeon but filled with modern BDSM equipment. Pretty much everything that would be found in Stronghold's lower floor, but this was private, which she knew would make Nick a lot happier. It was like getting a do-over for their visit to Stronghold—she was even wearing the same latex dress she'd worn there—but now, they'd get to play.

In some ways, she still couldn't believe it. This was not how she saw her life going when she'd started working at Marquis. It was so much better.

Swinging her around, Nick pulled her into his arms, his hands sliding down over her back. His expression was tender as he stared down into her eyes, and a shiver went down Avery's spine. There was something in his eyes she hadn't seen before, and it stirred her emotions unexpectedly, as though he was looking at her as if she was the most amazing thing on the planet. Her heart beat faster.

"Avery, I wanted to say thank you—"

"Um, you're welcome?" she interrupted, partly because she was feeling oddly vulnerable with him looking at her like that. The intensity of his gaze was unnerving.

Nick grinned at her response but didn't stop. It felt like her blood was heating from the inside out.

"Thank you for introducing me to kink. I know I was a bit of a pain in the ass at first and didn't really understand it, but I feel as though I've connected with a part of myself that had never been acknowledged."

Relaxing slightly in his arms, Avery rubbed her hands against his chest hair. She knew exactly how that felt.

"I started out telling myself I was taking this class for you, but the truth is, it ended up being for me."

"I'm glad," she said softly, still rubbing his chest. Nick wasn't the most verbal of people. She could tell this was hard for him, so it meant the world to her that he was doing it, anyway.

"I'll admit, at first,"—his smile turned a little crooked—"I thought we'd be perfect together because you understood my love for the job, and we'd have plenty of time together because we worked together, but I've realized it's more than that. I love spending time with you, and I'm happy to make time for you, which is something I've never done in any of my past relationships. I know that working together isn't always great for relationships, but we make it work."

"Yeah, we do." She grinned back at him. It sounded as if he was working himself up to saying something. Her heart was beating faster and faster. She wasn't entirely sure where he was going—or maybe she was and was afraid to hope—but knew she wanted to hear all of it.

Nick took a deep breath.

"Anyway... what I'm trying to say is, I love you."

The poor, adorable man looked a little terrified as the words left his lips, his gaze boring into hers as if he was afraid she wouldn't say it back. Feeling his heart pounding under her hand, Avery had to laugh.

"I love you, too."

It was the kiss to end all kisses. Nick claimed her lips, conquering her mouth and devouring her with a desperation she matched. She felt giddy as if she could walk on water or dance on air. When he pulled away, his eyes were glinting.

"Let's celebrate."

"With a spanking?" she teased, still laughing.

"Eventually."

NICK

Was there anything better than a blow job celebration from the woman he loved?

Well, he could think of one thing, but they'd get to that soon enough.

Avery was on her knees before him, totally naked—peeling the dress off had been more work than he'd expected, but it had been fun —with pretty silver clamps on her nipples and her lips wrapped around his cock. The part he couldn't see was the plug in her bottom, which he'd inserted before putting her on her knees.

Wrapping her blonde hair around his hand, he used it to move her head up and down his cock, her pink lips sliding easily along the shaft. Every humming noise she made sent vibrations shuddering through him, and he groaned with pleasure.

"Fuck."

Dammit, he really needed a mirror. He'd love to see the back view with the base of the pink plug nestled between her cheeks. Of course, if he'd done that, he would have wanted to take the time to spank her, and he'd wanted to enjoy his blow job before they got to the really kinky stuff.

Right, because the clamps and plug aren't really kinky.

Not compared to some of the stuff he'd seen.

His barometer for kink had really changed.

🦂 34 🦂

Sliding her mouth up and down Nick's cock, Avery's buttocks squeezed together. It had been a long time since she'd had a plug inside her. She was pretty sure it wasn't the only thing that would be in her ass tonight and was aroused just thinking about it.

Talk about a graduation celebration.

Her nipples throbbed as they bounced, Nick's thrusts coming a little harder and faster as his breathing increased. Hand tight in her hair, he was staring down at her with half-lidded eyes. Avery looked up at him, sucking harder, sliding her lips to the base of his cock, so the head pushed into her throat. She gagged slightly, the muscles working around the intruder, and Nick's eyes rolled up into his head. Inner muscles clenching in pride and arousal, Avery pulled back and then slid down again.

"Fuck!"

Nick's guttural cry came only a moment before the hand in her hair pulled her forward, holding her in place as he throbbed against her tongue. As salty-sweet hot liquid splashed against the back of her tongue, her throat worked, swallowing convulsively.

Her buttocks clenched around the plug, pussy aching emptily. It didn't matter that her knees hurt or her nipples were throbbing painfully. It only added to the experience. She was fully submitting to a Dom again—to *her* Dom—and the feeling of fulfillment was overwhelming.

Not that the classes didn't count or the times she and Nick had played at home, but they hadn't been like this. Nick loomed over her, confident in himself and what he was doing. She was on her knees, aching and throbbing and squirming, pleasuring him and knowing there was more to come. Submitting to his desires and knowing he would lead her.

"Good girl." His hand cradled the back of her head as his dick softened in her mouth, leaving the taste of him on her tongue. Avery didn't stop sucking, and when he finally groaned and pulled away, he was still half-hard. Shaking his head in amusement, Nick chuckled, his dark eyes boring down into her. "Or maybe I should say, naughty girl. Let's get you up. I think you could do with a little flogging."

NICK

Securing Avery's wrists to the large square frame so they were spread wide, Nick grinned when she sucked in a breath when his chest brushed against her nipples. The tips sticking out from the clamps were dark red and ultra-sensitive. Her shoulders tried to roll forward to protect them, but with her arms bound the way they were, she couldn't protect them.

"Are these hurting?" he asked with false sympathy, tugging on the chain hanging between them.

Pain and arousal flared in her eyes as she sucked in another breath, this one far deeper than the one before, and squirmed in her bindings.

"Yes, Sir." There was a challenge in the way she said it.

A familiar tendril of guilt flickered, but he ignored it, leaning in as he tugged a little harder. She gasped, her pupils dilating.

"And you like it hurts, don't you, sweetheart?"

"Yes, Sir." Now the challenge had died down, and she admitted it with a whimper.

Letting go of the chain, Nick slid his fingers over her stomach. Avery closed her eyes, whimpering again, embarrassed by what he would find, and as expected, his fingers touched wetness as soon as they curved over her mound. Nick chuckled, stroking the tender folds and teasing the little nub of her clit.

"Oh, yes, you like it a lot, don't you?"

Avery didn't answer with words. Thrusting her hips forward, she rubbed herself on his fingers as if she might get herself off. Nick let her do it for a few long moments, enjoying the feel of her rubbing against his fingers, his cock slowly hardening again, before he took them away.

Her eyes popped open, meeting his with disappointment and anger. Meeting her gaze evenly, Nick held eye contact as he lifted his fingers to his lips and deliberately licked them. Avery's mouth dropped open. Nice to know he could still surprise her.

"Very sweet," he said, cleaning the last bit of her cream from his fingers. "But no orgasm until after your flogging, sweetheart."

Being denied turned her on even more, but it also sparked her temper—a lovely combination. Grinning, Nick moved to pick up the flogger. Out of all the whipping implements, this was the one he was the most comfortable with. His own ass still burned from where Master Law had demonstrated the whip and the cane earlier.

Nick wouldn't be using either of those tonight, though he might eventually work himself up to a whip. This flogger was right up his alley—soft falls of leather that could sting or caress, and none of the heavy knots or braids would do more damage. He felt comfortable with this one, especially for a lighter, celebratory scene.

Flogger in hand, he tilted his head as he examined her. Face flushed, eyes alight with anticipation, feet braced, hands wrapped around the chains attached to the cuffs on her wrists. He should take the nipple clamps off before he started. Her nipples were turning a dark red, and he didn't want to forget about them while he was flogging her.

Besides, this way, he'd be able to flog her front without worrying about catching the clamps and adding extra sensation to her already tormented buds.

⊗⊗⊗

AVERY

Naked and flogger in hand, cock half-erect, Nick looked every inch the Dom. She lifted her head in surprise when he stepped forward rather than walking behind her, then moaned when she realized his intention. Of course, if he waited to take off the clamps, it would hurt even more, but that was a problem for future Avery.

"Ow, ow, ow, ow," she chanted, going up on her toes as the first clamp came off, and a painful, tingling sensation rushed back into the crushed bud. *Fuck, that hurt.* Nick's lips came down, and his hot mouth enveloped the tiny nubbin, soothing it with his tongue, turning the pain into something hotter, more enjoyable. Her ass clenched around the plug, pussy throbbing.

He repeated the process with her other nipple, leaving her hotter and wetter, her breasts swollen and throbbing, leaving her panting. Letting her head drop back, she breathed through it as Nick circled behind her.

The first lash of the flogger against her ass made her moan, and she pushed her hips back. The sting was negligible compared to the pulsing pain in her nipples, but it felt so good. The leather came down, again and again, a hypnotic rhythm that had her dancing under its lash as her arousal curled around inside her.

"Yes, yes, yes, yes..." She was barely aware of chanting under her breath until she got a little louder, her own voice filling her ears and combining with Nick's increased breathing.

She didn't know how long he flogged her. The back of her shoulders and ass were heated, need pounding through her, then it stopped. Avery moaned, writhing against her bonds. She wanted Nick. Needed him. Needed to feel him.

As if he had heard her thoughts, he was behind her, cock nestling erect between her cheeks as his hands slid up and down her sides. The skin he'd flogged felt even hotter with him pressed against her. She moaned, arching her back and thrusting her ass toward him.

Cool air between them, she felt the plug being pulled from her. She moaned, quivering, waiting.

Nick returned, his cock, hard and hot, prodding at the entrance of her anus. Thicker than the plug but slick with lube, it pushed in. Avery gasped, doing her best to relax as her opening was stretched. The sting was delicious, the feeling of being filled decadently perverse.

It had been so long, it was almost like losing her anal virginity again. It felt right giving herself to him, taking the discomfort for him. This was something she could give him, do for him. Something she enjoyed as much for what it did to her head as what it did to her body.

"Oh fuck... Nick... please..." The thick shaft pushed deeper, filling her completely, his groin pressing against her heated skin. One hand moved to the front, between her legs. Avery cried out when she felt the buzzing hum of a vibrator against her clit. When had he gotten that?

Hard thrusts filled her, over and over, the vibrator rubbing over her sensitive lips and clit as she was rocked forward and back. Ecstasy swirled, crashing through her, claiming the sting and the pain, sending her soaring. Avery screamed Nick's name as she sobbed with the erotic torment of overwhelming rapture.

NICK

Fuck, fuck, fuck.

He'd known he wouldn't last long. This was his first experience with anal sex, the longtime taboo, and knowing Avery would do it for him, the shocking intimacy he felt with her guaranteed to make him cum faster than usual. That's why he'd done the celebratory blowjob, then grabbed the vibrator.

What he hadn't realized was Avery's reaction to the vibrator would have its own effect on him. Her muscles clenched, rippling, milking, and he was pulled into her orgasm.

Pressing into her, every inch of his cock was massaged as her orgasm went on and on. His own climax burst, jets of fluid filling her. Her clenching muscles pulled every last drop of pleasure from him, leaving him holding onto her until he could get his legs working again. Then he moved as quickly as he could, getting Avery down from the frame and carrying her into the other room.

One of the benefits of being the owner's brother, he had the room for the night, unlike the others. They'd be heading home, but he and Avery would be staying. Another surprise for her. He'd packed her overnight bag without her knowing and dropped it off earlier.

Snuggled up in the big hotel bed, he had almost fallen asleep when she finally stirred in his arms.

"Nick?" She sounded as sleepy as he felt.

"Relax, sweetheart." He stroked her hair. "We're spending the night. Surprise!"

"Are there any more surprises?" She giggled. "Not that I'm complaining." She rubbed her nose against his chest. "These have been the best surprises ever."

"Surely, it wasn't really a surprise that I love you?"

"No... I guess I knew, deep down, but I wasn't sure if you were going to say it. And stop calling me Shirley."

"Did you just quote Airplane to me?"

There was a pause.

Then a light snore.

She'd fallen asleep.

Chuckling, Nick gathered her closer. His sweet little subbie chef. He'd tired her out.

"I love you," he whispered into the darkness.

"Mmm." It wasn't an audible declaration of feelings, but he knew what she meant.

Feeling happier than he could have ever imagined, Nick closed his eyes, knowing he was exactly where he wanted to be—and for the first time in his life, it had nothing to do with the kitchen.

AVERY

Watching Nick, Avery pressed her lips together to hide her smile. He looked frazzled, pacing back and forth, running his hand through his hair. Coming to an abrupt halt, he rolled his eyes.

"Avery, are you listening to me?" Her mom's voice broke through her amusement, quelling it. It was hard to stay amused at Nick's reactions dealing with his mom when she had her own mom to deal with. Why had they agreed to call the parents at the same time? Oh, right. Misery loves company.

"Yes?" The word came out as a question, and her mom sighed.

"I asked why you can't come down for both holidays with him. We'll just move things around. Celebrate Thanksgiving on Saturday instead of Thursday."

Avery rubbed her forehead.

"Mom, you know how restaurant work means I only get either Thanksgiving or Christmas day off? Well, Marquis is really, really great and closes for both days, but they're still open the day before and the day after." Avery had been over all this with her, but her mom heard what her mom wanted to hear. Before her mom could respond, Avery plowed ahead. "One or the other of us has to be at work the day after the holiday. We're making an exception for one holiday this year, so we can come down to meet you. We cannot do that for both. It wouldn't be fair to everyone else in the kitchen."

There was a long silence, then her mother sighed.

"Sounds like you found someone just like you." Her tone was accusatory, and Avery had to laugh.

"In some ways," she admitted. "That's why we work so well together." In and out of the kitchen.

There was another moment.

"Fine. We'll take whichever holiday you can give us, but your father and I are going to come up and spend the week with you as soon as we get the opportunity. Spend some real time with your young man."

"That sounds great, Mom." To Avery's surprise, she realized she meant it. Normally, her parents didn't visit for more than a few days, which she preferred. She'd spend the entire time stressing over what they thought about her life, her job, her home... This time, she'd have Nick to lean on. Apparently, that made all the difference.

Turning, Nick caught her eye and mouthed, 'I love you.'

'Love you, too,' she mouthed back, grinning at him. Moving here had been the right decision. Giving Nick a chance had been an even better one. Her heart was so full and warm. When they finally managed to get off their phones with their respective parents, Nick opened his arms, and she walked into them for a kiss that curled her toes.

She was home.

EPILOGUE

IRIS

"Iris, do this, Iris, do that," Iris muttered under her breath. "No, no, it's fine. I totally wanted to have to take orders from my brother in a kink club."

Okay, so maybe she was being a little overdramatic since they were on the main floor of Stronghold rather than in the Dungeon. If she'd actually said that out loud to Andrew, he would have been horrified. He already wasn't thrilled having her here, especially since he had to give her orders and look at her all night.

Looking down at the corset she was wearing, which pushed her boobs up to a generous shelf nearly big enough to play Flip Cup on, Iris smirked. The hot, tiny shorts she was wearing hadn't made him happy, either, but she had to get her kicks where she could since she was basically grounded.

It wasn't her fault some people had kinks that got under her skin. She refused to use the word 'triggered,' which so many people overused. She wasn't the one who had been in an abusive relationship with an asshole who wouldn't shut up about her weight. Nope, that had been her friend Laura, who would have the right to say she'd been triggered if someone used fat insults during humiliation play, not Iris.

Iris had just been the friend who stood by, not knowing how to help or what to do. Laura had ended up in the hospital, looking like skin and bones and thinking she still wasn't thin enough. That had been long after she and Jason had broken up, but she'd kept trying to make herself skinnier for him.

Thankfully, Laura was okay now, but she'd moved clear across the country, and Iris didn't see her anymore. They kept in touch, but it wasn't the same. It had been especially rough since Iris didn't easily make new friends.

"Hey, Iris!" Ah, and there was one of her favorite exceptions to the rule. Domi was awesome—fun, friendly, and a fellow Latina. Iris had managed to make one friend, Avery, who had brought her two more.

She had a lot more fun hanging out with Avery, Domi, and Rae than she did with her other friends, but she also wasn't willing to let those friends go yet. They might not be as much fun or very good friends in some ways, but they had been the only people she could call friends for the past few years.

Seeing Andrew's encouraging look, she rolled her eyes. It was a good thing she'd gotten over her impulses to do the exact opposite of whatever big brother wanted her to do. He liked her kinky friends more than he liked her other friends, which was kinda funny when she thought about it. Though, since he was also kinky, it wasn't as if he had room to talk.

"Hey Domi," Iris said, sidling up to the table where Domi was standing with Mitch. Her heart was already a little lighter. If they were here, that meant the others were sure to follow, though since it was a Saturday, Avery and her boyfriend Nick would probably be working. Mitch had some fun friends who would be coming in. Iris particularly liked Kincaid and Zach and would have loved to scene with them—Andrew's head exploding in the aftermath would be a nice touch—but they hadn't been double-teaming anyone of late, unfortunately. They were still fun to flirt with, and Andrew's face got really red, even if he didn't actually blow up.

"Mitch. What can I get you?"

"Two Blue Moons, please," Mitch ordered for both of them, as he usually did at Stronghold. Domi didn't protest, giving Iris an amused look. He didn't do it when they were out, but in the clubs, he took his Dom role fairly seriously.

"Coming right up."

Iris headed to the counter where her brother was already waiting, lifting his head. She could understand why some of the subs had tried to befriend her in hopes of getting to him. He was a good-looking guy. Tall, dark, handsome, funny, and a wicked sadist... supposedly. She sure as hell never watched to find out, but she heard plenty. Unfortunately for them, he was also engaged, and Iris was a stone-cold bitch to anyone who thought they might be able to get between him and Kate. She fucking loved Kate, and Andrew was lucky as hell she'd given him a second chance.

"Two Blue Moons."

"Okay. Deliver these, then head downstairs for your homework."

Iris groaned. Andrew looked nearly as pleased saying the words as she was to hear them.

The worst part about her punishment for interfering with a scene was having to stand around and watch everyone else have kinky hot sex. She should have changed her limits for the Dom class graduation day. At least then, she could have had kinky hot sex with Q. So what if she wasn't that attracted to him?

Yeah, except you decided you were done with one-night encounters and wanted something more, remember?

She remembered, but she also wanted orgasms. Right now, orgasms sounded pretty appealing, even if they came without the relationship.

About the only good thing about her punishment was she got joy knowing her brother was tortured by her constant presence. Misery loving company, and all that, especially when it was a miserable sibling.

Feeling a little better, Iris smirked at him and took the drinks.

"Don't get in any more trouble," he called after her as she walked away.

She rolled her eyes, which was safe enough since her back was turned to him.

She was just going to watch. What kind of trouble did he think she could get into?

Master Law and Iris return in book 3 of Masters of Marquis - Law & Disorder!

ACKNOWLEDGMENTS

I have a lot of people to thank for helping me with this book.

My amazing beta readers, who are invaluable in helping me catch mistakes, doing the initial grammar and word checks, identifying continuity issues, and working through problems with me. Marie, Candida, Annie, Karen, Marta, and Katherine – you all make these books so much better!

Another extra special thank you to Katherine, who got me started down this career path and has been by my metaphorical side ever since.

My husband for his continued loved and support.

And, as always, a big thank you to all of you for buying and reading my work... if you love it, please leave a review!

ABOUT THE AUTHOR

Golden Angel is a *USA Today* best-selling author and self-described bibliophile with a "kinky" bent who loves to write stories for the characters in her head. If she didn't get them out, she's pretty sure she'd go just a little crazy.

She is happily married, old enough to know better but still too young to care, and a big fan of happily-ever-afters, strong heroes and heroines, and sizzling chemistry.

She believes the world is a better place when there's a little magic in it.

www.goldenangelromance.com

BB bookbub.com/authors/golden-angel

g goodreads.com/goldeniangel

f facebook.com/GoldenAngelAuthor

o instagram.com/goldeniangel

OTHER BOOKS BY GOLDEN ANGEL

CONTEMPORARY BDSM ROMANCE

Venus Rising Series (MFM Romance)

The Venus School

Venus Aspiring

Venus Desiring

Venus Transcendent

Venus Wedding

Venus Rising Box Set

Stronghold Doms Series

The Sassy Submissive

Taming the Tease

Mastering Lexie

Pieces of Stronghold

Breaking the Chain

Bound to the Past

Stripping the Sub

Tempting the Domme

Hardcore Vanilla

Steamy Stocking Stuffers

Entering Stronghold Box Set

Nights at Stronghold Box Set

Stronghold: Closing Time Box Set

Masters of Marquis Series

Bondage Buddies

Master Chef

Dungeons & Doms Series

Dungeon Master

Dungeon Daddy

Dungeon Showdown

Poker Loser Trilogy

Forced Bet

Back in the Game

Winning Hand

Poker Loser Trilogy Bundle (3 books in 1!)

Standalones - Daddy Doms

Chef Daddy

Little Villain

HISTORICAL SPANKING ROMANCE

Domestic Discipline Quartet

Birching His Bride

Dealing With Discipline

Punishing His Ward

Claiming His Wife

The Domestic Discipline Quartet Box Set

Bridal Discipline Series

Philip's Rules

Gabrielle's Discipline

Lydia's Penance

Benedict's Commands

Arabella's Taming

Pride and Punishment Box Set

Commands and Consequences Box Set

Deception and Discipline

A Season for Treason

A Season for Scandal

A Season for Smugglers

Bridgewater Brides

Their Harlot Bride

Standalone

Marriage Training

Rogue Booty

SCI-FI ROMANCE

Tsenturion Masters Series with Lee Savino

Alien Captive

Alien Tribute

Alien Abduction

Standalone

Mated on Hades

SHIFTER ROMANCE

Big Bad Bunnies Series

Chasing His Bunny

Chasing His Squirrel

Chasing His Puma

Chasing His Polar Bear

Chasing His Honey Badger

Chasing Her Lion

Night of the Wild Stags

Chasing Tail Box Set

Chasing Tail... Again Box Set

www.ingramcontent.com/pod-product-compliance
Lightning Source LLC
Chambersburg PA
CBHW070445200726
48293CB00007B/2120